ST. MARTIN'S

MINOTAUR

MYSTERIES

THE PATIENT'S EYES

THE DARK BEGINNINGS OF SHERLOCK HOLMES

DAVID PIRIE

St. Martin's Paperbacks

First published in Great Britain by Century, Random House Group Limited

THE PATIENT'S EYES

Copyright © 2001 by David Pirie.

Excerpt from *The Night Calls* © 2002 by David Pirie.

Cover art by Janet Holmes.

ISBN: 0-312-99098-7

Printed in the United States of America

St. Martin's Press hardcover edition / May 2002
St. Martin's Paperbacks edition / August 2003

St. Martin's Paperbacks are published by St. Martin's Press, 175 Fifth Avenue, New York, NY 10010.

10 9 8 7 6 5 4 3 2 1

For Joyce Pirie

AUTHOR'S NOTE

The most remarkable experiences in a man's life, in which he feels most, are precisely the ones upon which he is least disposed to talk.

Arthur Conan Doyle

This story makes no pretence to be based on some manuscript found in a tin trunk in Poulsons Bank in the Strand, or retrieved from the attic of a legal consultancy in Baker Street. Nor is it attributable to John Watson, M.D. But it can claim to be based in part on historical fact.

The arguments about Arthur Conan Doyle's early life continue to rage but two things are certain. Doyle's model for Sherlock Holmes, Joseph Bell, did investigate criminal cases. And Doyle suppressed so many facts and incidents of his personal history that his true relationship with the Doctor remains shrouded in mystery. Indeed, with Doyle's papers and letters still locked away from the world, the creator of Holmes remains, for all his great fame, among the most mysterious of Victorians.

More facts, however, are emerging every day, some of them startling. This story draws on them as well, of course, as Doyle's own writing. And in one respect at least the "Murder Rooms" cycle can indeed claim to be inspired by a mysterious manuscript. If it ever saw the light of day "Joseph Bell's Criminal Cases" by Arthur Doyle, a book rumoured to have been seen early in this century, would certainly mark the uncovering of one of world's greatest mysteries.

For we would finally have laid our hands on something once thought to be utterly impossible: *The True Stories of Sherlock Holmes . . .*

THE
PATIENT'S EYES

PROLOGUE

7:13 P.M., 12 OCTOBER 1898

And so finally I come to them. This moment, this bright autumn of 1898, when I have decided for better or worse that I will have to try to translate the cases with the Doctor into words.

They were always my secrets, sixteen in all, though I had knowledge of two others. And I can be sure only of one thing. If you are reading these words, I am dead.

Occasionally, of course, there were hints of them in my fiction. Some detail which had imprinted itself upon my memory—a weapon, an article of clothing, the furnishings of a room, a particularly strange object—would find its way into a story. "The Copper Beeches" in particular flirted with events that had actually happened. Fortunately for me, the Doctor did not see it until many years later. Naturally he did not care for it at all or any of these other hints. He would reproach me with one of the looks I knew so well: that withering straight-arrow glance that felt as if it could pierce a man's soul. You knew the terms, it seemed to say. Absolute confidentiality.

Not that there was any real need for his concern. How could there be when the cases themselves contained so much that was acutely painful to me? Matters of such

darkness and depravity could never be considered material
for fiction, let alone a history. Especially when any such
history would inevitably take me back through the years
to that awful afternoon on a beach near Dunbar where we
found Elsbȩth. Here was, I suppose, the true beginning of
our story when the Doctor stood by the waves and declared his fight against the future. The words may sound
foolish unless you know all that prompted them. For me
then, as we both recognised how profoundly we had failed
and all that must lie ahead in our own branch of interest,
it was the very least he could have said.

I was a young man then, only nineteen and in the second year of my medical degree at Edinburgh, where I had
met the Doctor about six months previously. It is true
there were problems in my family but even so I had everything to live for, before that moment on the beach all those
years ago seemed for a time to bring my life to an end.

Until now, that was the worst moment. So unbearable
that I have usually tried to avoid thinking of it. But in
general nobody could have such experiences as I had with
the Doctor in my younger years and not return to them.
They would come to me while I was sailing on the Arctic
whaler *Hope*, the first expedition I ever took. Or when I
stood alone in the evening air outside the Tennison Road
house in South Norwood, which I bought years later after
I abandoned medicine for good. I would reflect on each
extraordinary episode with Bell, considering what it told
me about my fellow humanity, and about the darkness
within my own sex.

No full accounts were ever compiled of our cases. But
the truth was I had not been entirely true to my pledge.
For each of them I still held boxes containing records of
a kind: a map worked and reworked, diagrams, objects,
odd hieroglyphs and puzzles and clues, which reflected
for me and no one else the intimate details of each ad-

venture. I came to think of these materials as my Murder Rooms. Although one box, containing all that led up to that beach and followed on from it, has remained at the back unopened.

Naturally I never attempted to explain these relics from years ago to anyone, not even Louise, my wife, when she was still in good health, though she often saw me studying some of the boxes and adding small details. The assumption, of course, was that I was planning a story, an assumption that now, in a way I never dreamed, almost comes true.

But before I write I must be clear about what has happened this autumn and why I am taking this step now. I will not pretend it has been a happy year, for despite my success there has been much inner turbulence in my life. But when two weeks ago I took Louise for a drive in the landau up on the heathland north of Hindhead, I had no idea of what was coming. Both of us share a love of this lonely and somewhat uncharacteristic stretch of wild country running above the home we built in the hope the air would improve her health. Since first setting eyes on it, the countryside here has reminded me of my native Scotland with its glens and valleys. But that day we did not travel far for, as we came on to the spur that is known locally as White Hill owing to its frosts, Louise began coughing.

It went on a few minutes only and, though she insisted we go on, I could see how glad she was when we turned for home. There I sat beside her bed for half an hour and was relieved at last to watch her sleep. I waited a little before coming down to my study, a room with broad windows offering a view of the woods behind the house. I sat down at my desk. And then I noticed the small brown-paper package.

It had been placed at the corner of my desk, as late

deliveries often are. I receive a great deal of post, but there was something different about this parcel, perhaps because it was done up very elaborately with yards of knotted string. It bore my typewritten address and the postmark was Bristol, a city I barely know. After observing these details I ignored it for an hour while I worked. But I think even then it gave me a tiny sense of unease. There was something so painstaking and excessive about those intricate lengths of string winding around it. As I worked I found myself reflecting that it was too thin to be a book, yet too broad and wide to be a personal item like my watch, which was soon due back from its annual clean.

Eventually, while I was drinking my late-morning tea, I took up the package. Cutting the string, I pulled the layers of brown paper back; all I could see were several pages torn from a periodical. I picked them up and stared at a familiar illustration of a woman removing her veil. This was an early story of mine, published in the *Strand Magazine* in the winter of 1892.

Naturally, I supposed it had been sent for my autograph, though it was the first time I had ever been asked to sign loose pages. I leafed through them and soon reached the last illustration, which shows the detective holding a candle aloft in front of the stricken villain. I could find no accompanying letter at all. There was nothing else here, absolutely no indication of who had sent this or why.

My first assumption was that there must be something in the pages themselves, which might explain the parcel: a typographic flaw, perhaps, or some other oddity that a reader had thought I would be interested to see myself. And so it was that I put my work aside and scanned the Sherlock Holmes adventure "The Speckled Band" for the first time in years.

What struck me most, reading it after so long, was its sheer wish-fulfilment. This may seem a strange expression to use of a story in which a sadistic stepfather attempts to murder his stepdaughter in the night by sending a poisonous swampadder down a bell rope into her room. But in my heart I know well enough that wish-fulfilment is indeed what gives it life. And anyone aware of the events I witnessed at Abbey Mill in Hampshire in 1882 after I had left Edinburgh and started out as a doctor, events which began with the eye condition of my patient Heather Grace, would see at once why I use the word.

Not that the connection is obvious in any banal way. I went to some trouble to change, soften and simplify those terrible events, and also to rework them into what I would have wished. The model for the stepfather, Dr. Grimesby Roylott, for example, was a landowner and natural historian called Charles Blythe, who was uncle and guardian to my patient, and who did indeed keep snakes and other poisonous creatures. But how often I have had occasion to wish that the truth about the whole affair had more closely resembled the fiction.

Having no desire to return to reflections of this kind, I turned the pages in front of me more rapidly. But they appeared to be from a perfectly ordinary edition of the magazine. There was nothing remarkable about them at all that I could see and I could think of absolutely no reason why they had been sent.

I was on the point of throwing them away when I saw the writing. I had missed it partly because I had not looked closely at the last page and partly because the tiny ink letters had been placed with such meticulous care. They were on the minuscule white line, marking the top of the stepfather's table in the very last illustration, where the man is found dead and seated bolt upright, the fearful snake clamped like a yellow band round his head. I took my magnifying glass to be sure but, once seen, I could read them anyway.

Herne House,
Alton Road,
Harrow

That meant nothing to me at all. It was an ordinary enough address in an area where I knew nobody. But I could hardly avoid reflecting that some care had gone into the placing and the execution of this lettering. Naturally, I now went through the whole text again, casting a detailed eye and a magnifying glass on all the illustrations. But I found nothing else. If this was a clue to the sending of the package, it was the only one.

That evening Louise did not feel well enough to get up for dinner and I read some of Wells's story *The Invisible Man* to her in her room. Later, downstairs, as I drank a glass of port, I cast my eye over the pages again, debating what to do with them. My curiosity was certainly aroused but I was also aware that the thing could easily have come from a half-crazed admirer of my work. If I visited the address and was greeted by some crackpot who saw himself as a detective or, worse, a master criminal and hoped to employ me in his self-publicising schemes, I would have only myself to blame. Yet something in the choice of story, and the care that had gone into that writing, made me doubt this explanation.

Eventually, I decided the best course was to enlist help. Three years ago, while I was writing "The Exploits of Brigadier Gerard," my editor at the *Strand*, Herbert Greenhough Smith, put me in touch with a useful member of his staff called Henry Walker, who was mainly concerned with proofing but was always happy to undertake bits of practical research. That night I wrote to Walker, telling him only that I had been passed some information and wished him to discover anything he could about the occupants at the Herne House address I had been given. Just to be safe, I added as an afterthought that the address might be fictitious.

Walker replied with admirable speed in little more than a day. But his answer puzzled me even more.

Dear Dr. Doyle,

I am not surprised by your interest in this tragic business though there has been very little in the press and you are clever to have sought it out. I had no knowledge of the matter until I received your enquiry, but it was not long before it led me to the details of the case.

I can confirm Herne House was indeed the address of Alice Macmillan. As I suspect you are aware, the lady was returning from a trip to New York on the steamship Oregon *which docked at Southampton the day before yesterday. Two days before disembarkation she was seen at breakfast but did not appear for lunch. One of her dining companions became worried when she found her cabin empty and a search of the boat was instituted without success.*

The weather was stormy and the lady was known to enjoy walking alone on deck so the Captain feared there had been some kind of accident, and this was reported by a few newspapers, though not in any great detail. His fears proved justified, it seems, for a fishing vessel has brought ashore the body of a woman at Gravesend. From the description of her clothes alone it seems clear this is indeed Alice Macmillan. Barring any further developments,

the inquest seems likely to share the Captain's con-
clusion.

As to the personal situation of Alice Macmillan,
the shipping company, who provided me with most
of my information, confirm she was a woman of
means, aged around forty who was not married.
And I understand the heir to the property is an aged
aunt, for this poor lady had not been alerted and
came quite unknowingly to meet the boat. I have not
actually been to the house, which I believe is quite
grand though there are only servants living there at
present.

I rather fear, sir, this may well be providing you
only with facts you already have and little more is
expected in the way of news on the matter, but I am
more than happy to go on searching if you wish.
Mr. Greenhough Smith wanted you to know he
thought it could well have potential as a story, and
might even involve the man himself from the time
before the matter in Switzerland, though as I told
him that, of course, is entirely your affair. I would
only conclude by thanking you for enabling me to
be of some small service. And we all join here in
our fervent hope that Mrs. Doyle is gaining some
benefit from the country air.

    Yours truly,
    Henry Walker

What on earth could this mean? I was so baffled by this
intelligence that I did not even feel much irritation with
Greenhough Smith and his ceaseless badgering for more
of my detective (or "the man himself" as he has persisted
in calling him ever since I forbade him to mention the
name).

I had never heard of Alice Macmillan and knew nothing of the matter at all. Nor could I see what this sad but entirely unremarkable story (for all Greenhough Smith's humbug about its "potential") might possibly have to do with me. Of course, it occurred to me to wonder if my correspondent could have some involvement in her death. But pushing someone off an ocean liner is not the easiest or subtlest of murders and any lingering doubts were dispelled by a study of the dates. The boat had docked two days before, on 30 September. My package was postmarked 29 September from Bristol. The sender could not possibly have been on board the ship but must have read the news story about the disappearance.

It was, I supposed, just possible to conjure up a criminal conspiracy and someone on board communicating with the sender by telegram. Yet, even supposing such an improbability, surely they would have contrived a less risky method of murder, far less advertise their whole scheme to me? And on top of everything else, an aged aunt was the sole beneficiary, hardly the most likely accomplice of such people. No, this appeared to be an accident, of a kind that was not so unusual in bad weather, but what it had to do with me I was at a loss to understand.

The time had come for me to dismiss the package as the work of an imaginative joker. I wrote back a highly appreciative letter to Walker, for he deserved it, telling him his help had been invaluable to me and he was among the reasons why I felt so much loyalty to the *Strand*. I hoped Greenhough Smith would read that, and added for his benefit I was not for the moment planning a detective story around the incident, especially since my detective was not in the land of the living.

While writing this, I had quite made up my mind to tear up the pages and be done with the whole business. But that night, as on every other night since I had received the thing, I found myself staring at the drawing of Dr. Grimesby Roylott and the tiny writing inscribed on his desk in the final illustration of the story. Why was it there and nowhere else? Was it possible that someone had made a link through Roylott and his snakes, which was in effect the only real clue, to the actual events of 1882, events which began with my patient Heather Grace? It could hardly be anyone involved, that much seemed sure. Indeed, there seemed to be only one other option and I refused to think of it. But something had been at the back of my mind ever since I had seen the string on the package. Something that took me back to the beach and worse. I would not go down that road.

I did not wish to involve Walker further but I had to set my mind at rest and, after a series of telegrams, it proved surprisingly easy to arrange a meeting with the police in Gravesend. The body was still in a mortuary, awaiting an inquest, though nobody seemed to doubt the death was accidental.

It was three days ago that I travelled there and met the policeman responsible for the case, a straightforward ex-army man with lank hair and a sweating brow called Hector Murray. In his cramped office filled with smoke from a spluttering fire, I capitalised on my credentials as a doctor and scientist, explaining I was making a study of the properties of bodies that had been exposed at length to salt water. Fortunately there was no reason for him to doubt me, in fact, he did not even indulge in humorous speculation that I might be returning to detective fiction. But he was kind enough to offer me a rough draft of some details of the case he had compiled for the coroner.

And so, finally, I was escorted to the mortuary and there an old attendant, who smelt of tobacco and peppermint, led me to the slab to see the body of Alice Macmillan. I remember that I felt little expectation or excitement. I was sure I would satisfy my curiosity, prove finally and for ever this was all a false trail and throw that foolish parcel away for good.

The sheet came away rather slowly. I saw a pale shoulder, a ravaged face. And then I saw the eyes.

I staggered back, my hand went to my mouth. My heart was racing and I felt I was about to be sick. The attendant had moved away to deposit the sheet, but the noise made him turn to look at me. I forced myself to bend forward as if studying some detail of the corpse's arm. In fact, though he could not see it from where he stood, my eyes were closed.

Somehow I kept my head down and managed to stay still. When he had at last decided that I was after all closely absorbed in study, I heard him move away to another slab, which needed his attention. This gave me more time to steady my heart and take a breath. At last I was able to look again.

Her eyes still stared at me. Their beauty had survived intact even while the ravages of water and death had contorted and defiled her other features. The dark hair hung in long tendrils, and on her face and shoulders were the abrasions that occur where tide and current has battered a body against rocks and other flotsam. The skin was stretched and emaciated. The mouth seemed shrunken, possibly because the lips were so pale as to be invisible. But the eyes still held you. And in 1882 I had stared at them for so many hours, while treating the condition, which led me inexorably into the whole Abbey Mill affair. The body on the slab was my former patient Heather Grace.

Now my immediate physical shock had subsided and I was intensely aware of her form so near and yet further away than she had ever been. Tears sprang into my eyes, but I knew I could not possibly let them be seen. If there was the slightest suspicion I had come here for personal rather than scientific reasons, there would be serious questions and who knew where they would lead? I forced my tears back, and turned away to bend over the corpse's side, for I felt I was strongest when I could not see her eyes. After a long time I compelled myself to look at the face again and I whispered a prayer, though to my shame, I suspect it was less for her than for me.

I do not know how long I stayed in that mortuary. I was certainly not prolonging my visit out of choice for I had done all I needed to do, noting almost incidentally that there was nothing unusual about the body itself, given it had been in the sea so long. But at all costs I had to present the appearance of scientific investigation and try to regain some composure.

Eventually the attendant shuffled out of the room. He was only away a few minutes but by his return I was seated at a bench on the other side from him, writing some words in my notebook. I have no idea what they were. Medical gibberish, I would think, combined with some half-remembered chemistry and bits of Latin. I was merely trying to present a decent appearance and gain time.

At last I summoned up all my courage, got heavily to my feet and thanked him. He looked at me slightly curiously but I was sure he merely thought me eccentric. On the way out I met Murray and shook hands with him rather peremptorily. He probably saw me as stiff and ungracious. Like many others, it is a manner I have sometimes used to disguise emotion and I think it was a small price to pay in the circumstances.

On the train home I tried not to think about the events of the day or what they signified. I did not even glance at the papers Murray had given me. Instead, I stared out at the fields and telegraph poles, recognising how insecure a grip we hold on the certainties of our lives.

That evening I put aside all my work. Since then, I have spent much of my time trying to make sense of what has happened. The police notes on the case turned out to be a testament to my researcher's skill for they contained little more than I knew already except for the question of her changed name. But with the help of an otherwise meagre obituary that Walker has sent, acknowledging that one error in his earlier letter, I have arrived at a fuller picture.

The Christian name Alice was merely a middle name she had taken to using, though I had never known it. As to the other, it appeared that Heather Alice Grace had in the past few years undertaken occasional charitable work as a hospital visitor in and around London. This was not so unusual in a wealthy woman of means and, according to the obituary, her contribution was thoughtful and valued. During the course of these visits she had become friendly with an ailing hospital patient called Andrew Macmillan, a poor but evidently sweet-natured man who was bedridden and dying of a tumour at St. Mark's Hospital on City Road. With only a few months to live, this man had conceived a fixed notion that he must be married before he died. And he had a huge affection for his visitor, Miss Grace. Eventually he had found the courage to ask her if she would do him this honour and although there was no question of the marriage being consummated, or indeed her even staying beside him, she had agreed. Macmillan died a few months later, a happier man.

I do not know what to make of this story, but I have had many more things to think about in the three days since that afternoon in Gravesend. Over and over again I revisit my memories from all those years ago. I think of how much I tried to protect her and how greatly I failed, never anticipating the horrors that surrounded her. And then I think of this sad end, which I still must believe to be accidental.

But there have been other matters to consider, matters even more immediate in their implications for me. Perhaps, as I explore again the matter of Abbey Mill, I may find someone involved who could have sent this. That is hardly a pleasant thought but God knows I prefer it to the alternative. For there is another possibility. It has been haunting me and I have refused to go down that road, but I know the pattern well enough, I have known it ever since the beach in Scotland.

I never dreamed that there could be another Room. This new one, wherever it leads, can only be the last. But the Doctor is older now and such news will weigh very heavily on him. So I have reached the decision on my own. I can no longer be sure of what will happen but because it may be very bad, I am bound to put aside my promise and leave some word of all that has led up to this.

I shall outline what has been long suppressed, namely the full story of how the Doctor and I met. And then move to the boxes I can see from my desk now, placed so discreetly on a low shelf towards the back of the room: an evidently insignificant collection of disparate material with that one unopened box pushed behind. Already the Abbey Mill box, describing the events surrounding Heather Grace, sits at my elbow. And as I open it I see first a telegram and a music box.

I know some of what follows will seem shocking to many. There can be no time for refinement and I am breaking the Doctor's trust, exposing material that could perhaps disturb and corrupt. We live in an age where such things are not often discussed. But in view of what I believe is coming, I can no longer let them rest.

And so I take up my pen and return to a dark Edinburgh evening long ago and a walk along a corridor. The way into the past and all of these adventures certainly leads down that corridor . . .

THE RED CORRIDOR

Its dark crimson, an unnerving colour, was matched by a brown carpet, which led to an oak door on the second floor of our home in George Square in Edinburgh.

The year was 1878 and, as I have said, I was in the second year of my medical studies. It was, I remember, a damp, foul night with gusts of that typically squally Edinburgh wind which sometimes blows before it patches of rain and sometimes just cold air and mist. But it was not the wind that summoned me. I was brought up to that corridor by a scream.

I stood at the far end, staring along it at the door. I do not think I am a coward, but I can tell you it took every ounce of courage I possessed to walk on. Even now, the sound that came from that room, a great howl of pent-up rage and terror, echoes down the years after me. Could there ever, I wonder, be anything so utterly destructive of a home and of the familial relationships within it than such a sound? No matter how often I heard it, I never grew used to it. But on this night in particular the scream was so horrible that it prompted a crucial decision.

Looking back, I feel as if I stood there for hours, watching and fearful. There was no other sound. But in the end I walked slowly down the corridor. I intended to face the occupant of that room. Before I had reached the door with its scratched woodwork around the handle, my mother appeared. Whether she too had heard the scream and was intending to enter I do not know. But, once she saw me, her small figure interposed itself between me and the door. I was determined to go on, but she would not let me.

Later we talked in hushed voices downstairs, for my sisters were already asleep and we did our best to keep them and Innes, then hardly more than a baby, clear of this. I have said my mother was small, but when you looked into her face you forgot that at once. It was a strong, fine-boned face, as formidable in its way as the Doctor's, though its strength depended on a deep emotion. And it was awful to see how distracted that face was now. I barely remember what was said that night. I know we went and prayed down by the fireplace, and that we both knew what we were praying for, only with no idea what form our deliverance could take. I composed myself as best I could to the prayers, but I was impatient with all of it and she knew that.

"Arthur, you must keep finding strength," she said quietly at last as she returned to the jacket she was carefully mending. I barely replied. Rage and despair were so close to the surface, I knew they could erupt. But in my mind I had decided something. My studies were proving quite barren and it seemed suddenly mad for me to stay at the university. In view of all we faced at home, I must at all costs give up my degree and find some kind of employment. My mother would fight against it, but she could not force me to continue.

Later I went out, sensing that the streets were a better place to work off these feelings. I turned out of George Square down the wynd and soon I was in one of the coarsest thoroughfares of the old town, a place that often worked on my spirit as a relief at that time.

I passed two brightly dressed women in a doorway; one of them came out and did a curious little mock-curtsey that made me smile. I knew, of course, how she earned her money but she was not remotely destitute. Her face was impishly pretty and she wore a bright-green scarf. She asked where I was going and, when I said I was out for a walk, she roared with laughter. "You liar, sir, you are for Madame Rose's."

She pointed along the street but I had never heard of the place and said so. She stared at me. Then, seeing I was telling the truth, her smile became deliciously mischievous. She put her face close to me, and I could feel her soft breath on my cheek.

"Why, then you had better come up with me. Here is a reward for being so sweet." And she kissed me. After a moment I pulled away awkwardly, feeling a confusion of flushed embarrassment and desire.

It was an affecting little meeting and it stays with me for good reason. Less than a year later I saw the same woman lying in a hideously over-furnished room. There was a fire that had spilled out of the grate, burning an old newspaper, there was a bed and some splashed wine and shadows. She was bleeding from shallow cuts that had only just missed her vein and there was a figure crouched over her . . .

But no, I will not come to that yet. I want to be sure the reader understands my world, before its darkest and most miserable corners are revealed. It will be hard enough to expose all of them even then.

On the night I describe I returned home, knowing it was fruitless to tell my mother of my decision to quit the university. First I must make it official and so the following morning, with the frost still thick on Meadow Walk,

I made my way to the university to say my farewell to
the students, who had become friends. There were not
more than two or three of those and, as for the staff, they
cared little who came or went. But I knew my mother's
determination and, before telling her, I must make it official. Then there could be no going back.

I came through the arch into the small square of irreg-
ular ramshackle buildings known as Surgeon's Square,
where a crowd of medical men were gathered outside one
of the lecture halls. A few of the women stood to one
side, looking a little apprehensive but for once nobody
was troubling them. Colin Stark, a cheerful student from
Dundee, waved at me. They were waiting to enter a clinical surgery class.

It was then, and only then, that I remembered. I had
stumped up an advance of two guineas to attend that class
just the previous week. I had not formally enrolled, for a
friend handed over my money, but it made no difference.
The rules on such matters were typically mean: once fees
had been paid, they were never in any circumstances returned. I knew it was hopeless but in view of our strait-
ened circumstances at home I felt I must at least try to
get the money back. And so it was that I walked over to
the rear of the hall in search of the enrolment office of
clinical surgery.

With its dark stone corridors and vault-like rooms,
much of the building was quite a labyrinth, and I was
totally unfamiliar with the warren of doors and passage-
ways behind this lecture hall. I wandered somewhat aimlessly, my footsteps echoing on the grey flagstones. There
was nobody to ask and at last I came to a large room with
an open door, which I assumed was the office of clinical
surgery.

The mistake was obvious as soon as I entered. Indeed,
as my eyes grew accustomed to the darkness, it was like

no other room I had seen in the university. The door
opened on to a kind of tunnel between huge shelves of
various compounds and chemicals. The tunnel ended at
an enormous tank, which ran halfway to the ceiling. In its
watery depths a very grisly exhibit was on display. A
blood-splattered shirt and vest covered a human torso that
appeared to have been severed from the rest of the body.
Much later I learned some bloodstained clothes had been
draped around a wax impression to give the bulk of a
body. But to me then it looked fearful.

Staring around, all I saw were chemical and anatomical
and surgical instruments, many of a highly unfamiliar
kind. A huge shelf of books towered to my left and,
though the room extended well beyond that, the volumes
blocked my view. Ahead of me was a door and I walked
to it quickly, not wishing to be accused of loitering in this
place. Here I assumed was the office at last and I turned
the handle eagerly. It did not open.

"That door is always locked."

The voice seemed to come from nowhere. It was dis-
tinctive, firm but also a little languid.

To find its owner I peered round the bookcase obscur-
ing my view. A tall, wiry man with silver hair, in a filthy
lab coat, stood in a shadowy corner of the room. He had
a raised stick in his hand and was consulting a watch.

This was obviously one of the many lab assistants, who
prowled around the medical buildings. Quite often, they
were of an eccentric nature and a few had given up better
jobs to follow their whims.

"I'm sorry. I was looking for Dr. Bell's office to enrol . . ." But my words tailed away as he brought the stick
down hard on something before him with a great *crack*.

He hit it again. And again. Though advanced in years,
his movement was lithe and the force he used was considerable. You would almost have thought the man was

fighting some deadly creature. I moved closer to see what exactly it was he was hitting so violently. And started in shock and disgust. For below him was the grey and pathetic cadaver of a middle-aged man.

"In heaven's name, what are you doing?" I said and he did not even turn.

Was I dealing with a madman? But as he moved eagerly to inspect the corpse, I realised there must be some method in this madness.

"He is dead?"

The man looked up quite jovially. His face was sharp-featured and intelligent. "Oh, yes, he died about fourteen hours ago. Of a burst blood vessel. He was a soldier, I believe. But see how little trace is made. Not a bruise, not the slightest mark."

"But why in the world would it matter to a soul? This man is past curing anyway."

The lab man gave me a quick look as he moved past me. "In one sense," he replied. "Now, I would ask you to step to one side." And he pointed something at the corpse.

There was a sharp report, which made me jump as, to my astonishment, a bullet from a revolver slammed into the sternum. I sprang back, bewildered. "My God, you take a risk! The bullet could easily ricochet." I was starting to wonder if I would have to report this man before there was a serious injury.

"Oh, I am a great believer in risk," he said calmly, his eyes gleaming with anticipation as he moved forward to study the result of his shot. "Especially if care is taken over the angle of entry."

I had been aghast. Now, as I marked the loving care with which he observed the result of his actions, I became slightly amused. There was no real danger. He was merely the most eccentric lab man I had yet encountered. But he might prove useful.

"Tell me," I said, "do you work for Dr. Bell?"

The man shook his head, as he put his finger over the bullet wound and produced an instrument of some kind to measure its diameter.

"Then I can speak freely. Should I bother to take his class? I am aware he has a reputation, but to my cost I have begun to find that means little here."

The lab man studied the wound. "Little to show," he mused. "But I want to try another angle . . ." Then he seemed to register my question. "The standard is rather low, I agree. So you are not impressed?"

I was quite glad of a chance to unburden myself. "I hoped I would be enlightened," I said. "And I am being bored to death. To tell you the truth, sir, I am on the point of giving up. I have nothing else to follow and it will cause a lot of grief to my people, but if I am truly honest, why I never dreamed there could be such . . . imbeciles."

I normally reserved such harsh comments about our teachers for my friends, but I had a feeling they would not trouble my new acquaintance and I was right.

"Medicine attracts them, I find," he replied, as he shook out some bullets to prepare his revolver for another round. "It is one of the problems of the profession."

"Yes," I said, warming to him now. "And this Dr. Bell seems quite as ridiculous as the rest. I am only here because I paid my fees and cannot get them back. Have you read his twaddle? I saw one article where the man claims to be able to distinguish personality and occupation by someone's fingernails and boots! What a charlatan! I'd like to set him down in a third-class carriage and make him try to list the trades of his fellow travellers."

"Perhaps you should suggest it," he said with just the hint of a twinkle. "He's probably arrogant enough to accept."

I laughed. I was beginning to enjoy this strange new

acquaintance, but before I could continue berating my teachers, something that I did frequently enough, he seemed to lose interest and cut me short. "Well, let me show you where to go to enrol. If you paid, it would be folly not to see at least one of his lectures now you are here, even if it is only for the fun of it."

And he marched off with a long stride that left me running to catch up. Once out of the place, he pointed down the corridor to a door at the end and then disappeared back into the room with the merest nod of goodbye.

A few minutes later I was conversing with a lugubrious clerk, who confirmed my fees were strictly non-returnable but he was quite happy to enrol me. As usual, his tone made it perfectly clear that neither he nor anyone else cared a jot whether I actually attended.

And so, after a few minutes, I walked gloomily back to Surgeon's Square, reflecting that the lab man was the first person in the whole university, other than a few fellow students, who had shown the slightest interest in what I felt.

Twenty minutes later I sat high up in the Cairns lecture hall, amidst a growing throng of chattering students, feeling slightly cheated. I had intended to make a grand gesture and now, here I was, awaiting yet another dull lecture.

My friends Colin Stark and James Cullingworth were on either side of me, both equally oblivious of the fact that I had come to say goodbye to them. Stark was a solid, twinkling character from Dundee who managed to enjoy himself despite everything and was always generous-spirited. Cullingworth, the tall and wiry son of a Borders doctor, possessed a very high intelligence and an even higher opinion of himself. While we were talking Neill, a dark good-looking man from the colonies, sat down behind us. He was in some ways my closest companion for we shared a love of stories, especially Poe.

"It is all fixed," Cullingworth was announcing with his usual sweep of the arms. "We are going to dress a tailor's dummy tomorrow and wheel it out before Dr. Peterson. The man's half blind, Croom is taking bets on the diagnosis."

"Arthritis," said Neill from behind. "Two years ago they put a waxwork into the class of the oldest surgeon here. He described it as having an arthritic condition."

"Then perhaps a corpse would be better if we dressed it," said Cullingworth, vexed. The hubbub began to fade and he turned to me. "Your first time? Well, prepare yourself. He's quite a performer."

I looked down as a solemn man of nearly sixty with a monocle, entered carrying a medical bag. The sight made me groan aloud, though I will admit some of my mood had lifted. I felt more cheerful. I turned to my friends. "He looks like just another pompous ass."

"No, that's Dr. Carmichael," said Cullingworth. "Bell has quite a retinue. Here."

Now there was a real hush. A majestic figure swept forward through the doorway on to the platform and turned to face the audience. I can recall my shock at the sight of him to this day.

For there, in front of my eyes, transformed and resplendent in a dark suit and tie, every inch of him exuding authority, was my lab man.

Having been so caught up in my own thoughts, I had failed to see what should have been obvious. No assistant would ever have been granted such liberties. I shrank back in my seat. Indeed, I would have bolted for the door if I could. But no such action was possible. I was pinned in the middle of a row and Bell was now scanning every one of these rows like an eagle.

Soon enough he had seen me. He took a step forward. "Ah," he said. "Mr. Doyle. I am glad you have condescended to come and say good morning to us." My friends turned in amazement. "Gentlemen," he continued, "Mr. Doyle here is a little concerned he may be in the presence of yet another Edinburgh charlatan."

He spoke the last two words with soft relish. There was a great roar of laughter. Faces were turned eagerly in my direction. "But I have something rather serious to tell you, Mr. Doyle." He paused. A ripple ran through the audience. Was I to be ejected, solving my problem at one stroke?

"Be careful. From the astrologer came the astronomer. From the alchemist, the chemist. From the mesmerist, the psychologist. The charlatan is always the pioneer. The quack of yesterday is the professor of tomorrow. Who knows what strangeness the future brings? And now . . ."

A cadaver was being wheeled behind him and one of his retinue pulled back the sheet to reveal the corpse of a woman. "The knife . . ." Bell grinned at his audience as he raised his gleaming scalpel, preparing to begin his dissection. "Or . . . is it a wand?" And with the same agility I had witnessed earlier, he plunged the blade home.

When the lecture was over there was much mockery from my fellow students, yet I had changed my mind about leaving. It was not that I was impressed by Bell or his teaching. He struck me as just another plausible but bogus egotist with a fancy line in oratory. That kind of spiel might well impress elderly Morningside ladies and naive students, but I was not about to be fooled.

No, I felt as if a challenge had been made to me. Who, exactly, was this man to tell me what a wonder he was? And to mock all my misgivings, when in private he had virtually agreed with them? I would see his course through, since I had paid for it, and find out if it amounted to more than claptrap. I had my doubts on the subject.

THE FAERIES OF DEATH

As I look back, I must admit (for I am trying to be as honest I can) that even now after all these years a part of me wonders, perhaps even with a small tug of regret, whether I was right to stay. Suppose I had followed up my original resolution and gone out to work? Perhaps I might even have pursued my own boyhood dreams and enlisted, for I was brought up to heroic tales of my mother's great-uncle who led the Scottish brigade at Waterloo. I would have missed the greatest experiences of my life, but equally the worst. And I would never have faced all that now compels me to write this down.

Yet even to think this is to do Elsbeth and myself no honour. All of us have battles that must be fought. For me to wish I had not gone is like my illustrious ancestor abandoning the great fight against Napoleon and retiring to his farm in Perthshire. Despite all that happened, I have to thank God for my many blessings including the fact that I knew her.

I never breathed a word to my mother that I had intended to leave the varsity. I continued with Bell's lectures, though my opinion of him hardly improved. At home we struggled, as ever, to keep our miserable secret, for my mother would have died rather than let anyone know what we endured.

But it was becoming increasingly difficult. And I knew we were beyond hope the night I heard another sound from that corridor. Not a scream this time, more like the crash of something falling. I went down there. But this time no one appeared to stop me. I walked down the corridor and entered the room at the end.

How easy it is to write that, how difficult to do and how hard to face the memory of what happened next. For this is something I have never wished to describe. I remember that for a moment, as I entered, the room seemed empty. I glimpsed only his chair and the embers of the fire, and an open desk and the broad couch with rugs and a fur where he slept. Drawings, as always, were everywhere, the one nearest the door showing a frog with a pixie in its mouth.

Yet his chair was empty and for a wild moment of hope, I thought perhaps he had gone downstairs to talk and have a bowl of soup like some ordinary father. But of course I knew he was there. For I smelt him. And soon I saw him. He was on the floor not far from the fireplace. Crawling on all fours.

At first I thought he was crawling into the fire itself. But then his head turned towards me, peering. I saw his matted black hair and straggly beard, and his flushed, mottled skin. His face, once good-looking, was almost contorted by excess. He tried to make a sound. At first I could hear only rasping breath. And then there were words. "I wish you would take the ashes out of my mouth," he whispered. "They hurt my teeth." I moved forward to him. "And see what I have found down here," he went on. "There was a nest of them in the pot."

He half rose up, clutching something.

I came forward to look. My mother always tried to

keep new flowers in his room; it was as if she were determined to have something fresh and living in there. And now he was holding a bunch of scarlet rose petals. I opened my mouth to say as much but he threw them in my face, crying out, "The faeries of death." Then he dissolved into tears.

I do not know if the reader has ever seen a loved father drunk and humiliated and on his knees. I was, I suppose, comparatively familiar with the spectacle. But at that moment I felt such a sense of his anguish that my eyes filled with tears. I swear on my last breath these were not, or not only, tears of self-pity. This man had so much to give; his drawings had once electrified me. Yet here he was, caught every day and every night in this morass of nightmares.

Would I have taken him in my arms in that moment? Or is it just the fact he has been dead for six years, and shut away for a decade before that, which makes me think so? No. The anguish I felt for him then *was* genuine and I believe I would have acted on it. But here, as always, the cursed constraint of our household arrangements meant I never made the gesture I longed to make. For we were interrupted by the opening of the door.

We both turned and our lodger Charles Waller's smooth, good-looking features stared down at us. His dress and coiffure were, as always, immaculate: the dark jacket and silk tie; the exquisitely combed hair. I felt my father noticeably snap to attention in a way that almost made me jealous for he never did so with me. Here, even to a drunken madman, was Authority.

Waller, who was no ordinary lodger, ignored him completely and addressed me in his soft, cultured voice: "He has been drinking all day. I tried to examine him and he flew into a rage. I will try again if you will leave us."

There was surely a hint of superciliousness in the little

smile he gave me and I hesitated. The ritual of Waller's nightly "examination" of my father was, for me at that time, one of the most brutal and degrading aspects of our whole household. Indeed, I suspected it was little more than an excuse for Waller to exercise his power and perhaps even indulge in calculated cruelty. So, as he stood there before me, the truth is I would have liked nothing more than to plunge my fist into his soft face. Waller was a powerful man, but his power was all in his mind and little in his body. So that often when I boxed or swam or rowed, I delighted only in the thought: Waller could never do this, never.

But now I saw my mother behind Waller and I quickly put a hand on my father's shoulder. For once, here was a gesture of support that really came from the heart! Then I left him.

A few moments later I was pouring out my indignation to my mother in the small drawing room downstairs. "But why should he examine him? He is only our lodger!"

"He is also a doctor, as you well know."

She was right. For it was Waller over the past three years who had kept us out of penury and the workhouse, and paid many of the bills we could not pay, including more often than not our entire rent. The man was in more gainful employment than any other member of the household. But I hated this arrangement almost as much as I hated my father's drunken madness and I was in no mood to accept it. Indeed, in those days I could never understand quite how my mother tolerated the man, or how we had ever allowed ourselves to get into this situation. "Just because he pays our rent," I said, "is he to be given rights over everyone here?"

My mother effectively ignored this, for they were old arguments. "That is not fair," she said, "but we will not go back over it now. I have something I want you to see."

She had gone to her bureau and opened a drawer, which I know she reserved for its most precious treasures. Out of it she took an object that had been wrapped very elaborately in oilskin. She unwound the cloth with great care and took out something that gleamed in the light of the lamp on the desk.

I stared at it. It was a beautiful pocket watch of an old and grand style. I had not seen it for years but it had a particular poignancy for me; indeed, it even had a childhood name, which was Ibo. For when he was younger and happier and I was small, my father would often sit me on his knee and ask me to breathe on Ibo and bring it back to life. As I blew he would release the catch and the lid would fly open to reveal the watch face. Of course, I thought it was great magic and I would laugh with joy and he would laugh too, and the memories of Ibo were among the happiest I had of him.

My mother saw my reaction and it seemed to please her. "I want you to have this," she said, holding it out. "It is the most valuable thing your father owns and when he was well he always said it was for you, so you must take it now and keep it safely. Otherwise he will pawn it or even break it. Last week, in one of his moods, he almost smashed it against the wall and I brought it here. But he comes to this desk, looking for things to sell."

I stared at it, unsure whether I wanted the responsibility. It held such happy memories and now it was another focus of our pain. But at last I took it and pressed the catch: the lid sprang open just as it had when my father took me on his knee. It was a pretty enough sight but it only made me mourn for my lost power to breathe life into things.

Dr. Joseph Bell stood bolt upright at the podium in his black four-button frock coat and white silk shirt, his eyes fixed on the serried ranks of students before him. Two assistants were busily escorting a well-dressed woman patient to a chair. From her fixed stare and groping arms we could see that she was quite blind.

By now I had attended enough of Bell's classes to confirm all my prejudices against the man. No doubt a part of me still smarted from my earlier mistake, but I had been disgusted to observe how easily and shamelessly he transformed the teaching of medicine into a theatrical spectacle. And now, as he stood there in front of the woman, enjoying the hushed expectancy of his packed audience, I could tell we were to be treated to some new piece of drama.

Bell turned back to the patient. "Mrs. Harrison, you have recently suffered sudden blindness in both eyes, is that correct?"

"Yes," she replied. "It has been three days now."

He stared down at her. "And you can see nothing?"

"Nothing whatsoever."

After a moment he picked up a lamp and moved it in front of her eyes; his gaze fixed carefully on her. At last he put it down, turning back to us with a hushed admonition that we should watch closely. Then he reached round for something. It was hard, at first, to see what he was doing, yet I could see his hands holding what looked like a long, glinting stick.

There was a sudden cry of horror from his audience as quite abruptly and with all his strength he swung the object, which we now saw was his heavy silver-topped cane, right at the woman's head.

She screamed and jerked away to one side, while the cane itself missed her by inches. Bell's hand was strong and his judgement keen, but even so there was something so reckless in the action that some of the audience jumped to their feet.

Quick as a flash he had dropped the cane and his hands were on the patient's shoulder, comforting her. "Do not fear. You are ill but you are not blind." He turned to face us. "Gentlemen, I do not doubt Mrs. Harrison's honesty or her suffering. She endures what she thinks is blindness. But once again close observation, in this case of the eye's reflexes, tells us that, although genuinely ill, her condition is of the mind and not the body."

It was, as ever, a very pretty display. He had enlisted his audience's emotions to great effect and in a way that underlined his diagnosis. Such tricks amused and pleased the undergraduates, and greatly boosted the numbers who attended these lectures. But in my view this was hardly a justification for them. Why should medicine and its logic be turned into a kind of theatrical show? We were supposed, surely, to be seekers of truth not vaudeville entertainers?

As the blind woman was led away, I could not contain my derision and turned to Stark, scribbling some notes beside me. "The man is just a show-off. They should offer him a tent on the common and let us get on with the practice of medicine."

Meanwhile another patient—a big bald man with a limp wearing an olive-green jacket—was being escorted to Bell, who greeted him and turned in our direction. "Now, before I address the next patient, may I ask you to look at him carefully, remembering the methods I have taught you. How every tiny detail, every button, every gesture, every hair, is of use and value to us. I would like you to tell me what you can observe from his appearance." His eye flicked across our row and came to rest on my companion. "Mr. Stark?"

All eyes turned on my friend. I could see him struggling to come up with something. "That he has a limp, perhaps a sprain of some kind?"

"Not very much, in other words," said Bell curtly. "You see but you do not observe. Can no one observe? Mr. Doyle! Using your eyes, your ears, your brain, your boundless perception, what do you see?"

Perhaps I was unduly sensitive but the scorn in his voice seemed an uncanny echo of the superior tone of our arrogant medical lodger, Bryan Charles Waller. Was this not just the way Waller talked to my father as he subjected him to the nightly humiliation of the "examination?" I found myself hating the superciliousness of it all. Why did Bell need to chide us in such a way? We were supposed to be his collaborators, not little children. But, as I reflected on this, Bell was becoming impatient: "Come on, man, can you tell nothing from this man's appearance here today?"

My words slipped out before I could stop myself. "Of course. I can tell he is in need of medical attention. Why not ask him and see?"

There was a gasp, then the hall erupted with laughter. They had never heard anyone challenge Bell's notions in this way. I regretted it, fearing he would take the reply and the laughter badly. But to his credit Bell seemed to accept the bald logic of my answer.

"I admit that he has few distinguishing features," he said with a smile. And he paused for effect. "All I can observe for sure from looking at him is that he comes from Liberton, that he drives two horses, one grey, one bay, and that he has recently been discharged from the army."

The audience's applause was thunderous, and the patient himself looked astonished. "It's true," he exclaimed. "But how in the world did you know that, sir?"

Bell went over to him, smiling. "I am tempted to keep you all wondering. It is always so much more effective.

But I will explain. There is Liberton clay on his toecaps. The colour is quite unmistakable. His boots are new and undoubtedly ammunition boots of the kind offered to any soldier on his discharge from the army. He has white equine hairs on one sleeve and bay on the other. Two horses."

There was more applause. I was intrigued by this list of facile clues but it merely served to reinforce my own scepticism. Bell went on about his "method" as if it were something new. But when you actually analysed it, you could see at once it was merely a series of simple tricks, generally aided by bits of good luck like the clay and the horsehair. If this man's jacket had been given a good brush and he had slipped off his boots before he entered, Bell would have been able to produce nothing at all.

I started to outline my feelings about this to Stark, pointing out that a clean jacket would have stopped the Doctor in his tracks. "When you boil it all down," I said, "it is little more than a conjuring trick."

I was speaking loudly but I had forgotten Bell's sheer command of his audience and did not see him raise his hand for silence so he could continue his diagnosis. The students obeyed instantly. As a result, my last sentence was audible to everyone in the hall.

Bell stopped what he was doing and turned all his attention on me at once, his eyes gleaming, his profile slanted like some eagle about to descend on its prey. "Mr. Doyle"—his voice was lightly threatening—"you were saying?"

There was no escape. I knew I was cornered, but I was still determined not to show fear to this amazing egotist. "I am sorry, Dr. Bell. I did not mean to interrupt. But I was merely doubting the practical application of such tricks."

He stared at me a moment. "Oh, really, were you now?" he said very quietly. "Well, such doubts may well have a practical application to your career at this university! I will see you afterwards."

My friends stared at me in horror. But their anxiety was nothing beside mine. My mother had made great sacrifices for me to come to the university. I had found it hard enough to tell her when I was considering giving up my studies voluntarily. Imagine returning home with news that I had been thrown out altogether for rudeness to one of its most eminent medical teachers.

I recall nothing more of that afternoon until I stood waiting for Bell in the labyrinth of his book-lined room, staring into the stygian depths of his tank. I almost felt as if I would be better plunging into it and drowning. Then I heard him enter behind me. I turned.

He stood there, looking at me. "So"—he was very still—"you believe my method has no practical use?"

In my misery I had toyed with the notion of an abject apology. But now, as he stared at me in that queer way of his, I felt sure that a recantation, especially if it were untruthful, would be the worst move of all. "I do not mean to give offence," I said, trying to choose my words very carefully, "but the truth is I have yet to see one."

He stood there for a moment, weighing this in the balance. "Come with me." His tone was not rude, exactly, but it hardly left room for dissent.

I followed him round the shelves, wondering if he was going to escort me to some office and strike my name out of the student register there and then. But when we reached his desk I realised he merely wanted to put down the folder he was carrying and collect his things.

He turned back to me. "You know that I could have you thrown out of this university for impertinence?"

I said nothing for there was no denying it.

"However"—his tone changed—"when someone has so much to learn, it is better that he be taught a lesson."

This did not sound promising. I stood there looking down at the strange collection of objects on his desk. A funnel that seemed to be made of leather, I remember, a plastering trowel and a discoloured bronze ring. I had no conceivable notion of their purpose. The silence continued, then Dr. Bell sighed and put on his hat. His next words were utterly unexpected.

"I would like you to become my clerk."

THE IRRITATION OF THE CLERK

To this day I am still not sure why he chose me to be clerk. It was an honorary position, paying no wage, but he had, after all, the pick of far better minds, all of whom were his slavish admirers. I can only suppose, looking back, that in some small way I represented a challenge. And, as I now know, the Doctor was never a man to turn a challenge down.

My friends were amazed, and even a little jealous at my sudden elevation, for in that mass of dull and lazy teachers the Doctor was something of a hero. At home I naturally tried as hard as I could to inflate the importance of my new role. But Waller pointed out at once that most of my tasks would be little more than manual labour and he was quite right. Even my friends ceased to be jealous when they saw me with a bucket and mop, cleaning the floor after a messy dissection or sweeping the flagstones outside Bell's study.

In fact, I saw little enough of Bell himself in those early days. I was too busy preparing the lecture hall, helping to dress and escort the patients, sorting through his papers and mounting an endless series of specimens. My most glorious moments were the occasional afternoons when I assisted at operations. But even here I was allowed to do little more than wipe the perspiration from Bell's face with a towel as he worked. At that time speed was the most vital attribute to a surgeon; it was the difference between success and abject failure, between getting your patient back to bed alive and having them die from shock in front of you on the table. My sole task in the operations was therefore to facilitate Bell's speed.

In this respect, and others, the Doctor was a taskmaster but he was a fair one. And yet, despite my promotion and these small privileges, I have to report that my harsh opinion of the man barely changed. I was now prepared to admit that Bell was dedicated and hard-working. He had made no attempt at all to charm or impress me, so the man could evidently leave vaudeville behind when he wanted to. But on his beloved "method," the major issue at stake, I simply would not relent. My friends and I often debated the matter, and I was more cynical about it than ever. What meaning could it possibly have, I would declare, to the poor wretches who nearly died on our operating table? What did they care whether Bell deduced one was a tea drinker from the stains on his jacket and the other rode a chestnut horse? All that mattered to them was that he got them off the table alive.

And then, on a cold morning in early November, something happened.

It was one of those rare occasions when Bell actually spent a few minutes with his humble clerk. He was planning a series of lectures that would involve several anatomical samples and he was anxious to make a selection from a department of anatomy outbuilding, which was then situated outside Surgeon's Square in a quiet street of buildings, some of which were residential. He had asked me to accompany him so that in due course I could make the necessary arrangements for boxing and transporting the samples.

We crossed the road amidst busy traffic and, not for the first time, I witnessed the Doctor's extraordinary physical dexterity as he weaved through the vehicles with expert judgement. He carried his silver-topped cane as always and, having seen its accuracy with the woman patient, I feared for the fate of a cyclist who swerved rudely past him with some oath. An inch nearer and I am convinced the Doctor would have brought the cane down full on the man's hands and probably broken them. As it was, Bell contented himself with a warning feint, which streaked past the cyclist's handlebars and had the desired result. The man was forced to swerve away, and I saw him blanch at this near miss and pedal off furiously without looking back. Bell seemed utterly unperturbed by the dozen narrow brushes with horses and wheels during his crossing. He stepped on to the pavement as if he had just strode from one room to another, turned into a narrow street leading to his destination and stopped dead.

I was a little behind, for the man walked at such a clip that it was often hard to keep pace with him. And now I assumed he was about to talk to someone. But the street was empty apart from a black carriage which stood at its far end. Two men were seated within it and, as they saw us, a white-gloved hand reached up and snapped the carriage blind down as if in some kind of signal.

At this Bell's whole manner changed. "Ah, it seems I will have to leave you now. We will undertake the samples another time. If you could proceed with the task of cataloguing the surgery papers?" Then he walked on towards the carriage.

I could hardly stand staring, so I turned back the way I had come. But later, as I was nearly at Surgeon's Square I saw that same black vehicle on the main road, heading at speed into the centre of the city. And from what I could make out, there was now an additional passenger.

Over the next few days I thought of every possible explanation for that carriage and could find none that seemed to fit. Then, a few days later as I was filing into a lecture, I looked out of a grimy window and saw it again, with Dr. Bell emerging from it, looking extremely tired and worn. I was just resolving in my mind that I would find out what lay behind this when my thoughts were interrupted.

"Ah, look, Doyle," Cullingworth was at my right shoulder and had followed my gaze. "There is your mysterious Dr. Bell. What does it mean, do you think? Does the man have a mistress?"

In fact, such a notion had already occurred to me but I had discarded it almost as soon as it did. Not only was it unlikely in itself, but what man attends his mistress in a black carriage with two officials?

"Oh, no," Stark was saying as he came to join us. "But I think he is up to something. We should investigate."

"There is no point," I said almost too quickly. "It is just charitable work. I have known for weeks he takes an interest in such things."

Few people enjoy spying on the charity of others so my comments had the desired effect: my friends lost interest and fell to discussing the prospects for Saturday's rugby match against the veterinary college. Nor was the lie entirely implausible for Bell did publicly contribute his time and money to three poor hospitals. But I was suddenly aware of how much I disliked the idea of anyone else involving themselves in what I now felt was my mystery. If there was some secret to Bell then, as his sternest critic, I wanted to be the one to discover what it was.

The Doctor had recently engaged me to sort out his surgery papers, and the work meant that I was constantly in his laboratory and office, often at odd times. Perhaps because my curiosity was aroused, I began to realise that his comings and goings were a great deal odder than either I or my friends had ever appreciated. Moreover, it seemed to me they were intimately connected with the locked room that I had mistaken for an office when I first met him.

Once, early in the morning, he made me jump as he came through that locked door wearing his coat and looking as if he had not slept a wink all night. On another occasion, quite late in the evening, he emerged from the same doorway dressed as if for an excursion. He saw me and made no remark, but gathered some things including his cane and went back through the door, locking it behind him as always. I stayed for another two hours but he did not re-emerge.

From this it slowly became obvious to me there must be another exit from the room behind the locked door, yet not at all obvious in that labyrinth of corridors where such an exit could be. I had already drawn a map of the Doctor's workroom itself without finding it very illuminating. Now I spent days working on a new map of the layout of rooms and corridors around it in the hope that it might throw light on the riddle of the inner room.

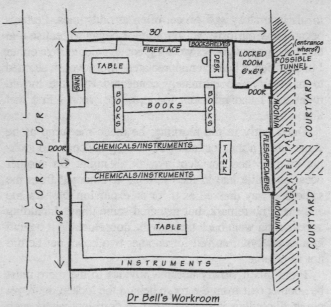

Dr Bell's Workroom

There was certainly no sign of a door connecting that locked room to the main corridor or anywhere else, and a quick examination of the layout of corridors and rooms on that floor showed me at once that the locked room's dimensions must be extraordinarily small. I used to have fantasies, as my map shows, of a tunnel leading from the Doctor's locked room to the outside grounds, but even that seemed absurd. The university floors were of solid stone and I was sure there was no basement. In any case, I reasoned, if there was an exit, why did the Doctor keep his coat and stick and bag in the large study and laboratory where I worked? It is true, sometimes he would disappear through the locked door with them and I was sure he was going out. But also on occasions they would sit behind his desk, not far from where I was working, while he vanished through the same door for hours and hours. What could he possibly be doing in there? From its dimensions the room could hardly accommodate a chair, let alone a desk. The more I observed his routine at close quarters, the more puzzles seemed to multiply around the room and the man.

In desperation I decided to apply the Doctor's own principles to the problem. I still stuck to my view that most of his claims for his so-called "method" were bogus, but here it might serve some small purpose. Thinking it over, I decided that if the Doctor had some hobby or activity that took him out and consumed so much of his free time, then certainly the nature of that hobby would be reflected in the extensive library which, as his clerk, I dusted every morning.

And so, during one of the weeks when his absences were prolonged, I made as complete a study of the titles as I could. From wall to wall and ceiling to floor, I analysed the precise range of books and subjects, the exact number of books in each category, and the overall distribution and arrangement of each volume in a concerted attempt to examine the intellectual and personal slant of the whole collection. I pulled out the more obscure tomes to see what exactly they were and even (congratulating myself on my canniness) took special note of those titles, that appeared to be the most thumbed.

After completing this work, however, I found to my fury that all I had done was add yet another mystery to all the others. For when you stepped back and analysed the titles, it emerged at once that, while the whole collection was strange and eccentric in the extreme, its overall purpose was quite baffling. It was not as if that strange assortment of books even properly mirrored the subject of medicine. Certainly there were treatises on surgery and anatomy, and they stood at the front of the nearest shelf, but only as if they were planted to deceive. For, upon close inspection, this subject range terminated relatively quickly. Indeed, I soon realised that the only medical subjects adequately and exhaustively covered in the entire collection were pathology and chemistry.

That was my first discovery, but the range of other subjects was just as peculiar. I had until this point been naively wondering whether Bell was engaged in some great debating society, a forum, perhaps, where the thinkers of the town, which had given the world David Hume and Adam Smith, were busily contemplating the leading subjects of our age. A study of the books showed at once that any such idea was quite ridiculous. You would have looked in vain throughout the entire library, for a single volume that told you anything at all about the great intellectual debates of our day. It contained no philosophy, no astronomy, no economic theory, no politics and virtually no history. The classics were thinly represented, as were languages, while the mathematics on display were mainly obscure treatises on numerical cryptography.

And what, exactly, was included? Well, besides the pathology and the chemistry, geology was well represented and so was botany. There was typography, too. The subject of law was accorded so many books that I almost wondered if the Doctor had begun as a student and teacher on the subject, but I knew quite well he had studied medicine and at this very university. There was also a well-stocked shelf on the history of weaponry. All of these subjects appeared to be frequently consulted, as did some quite new volumes concerning abnormal psychology. Then, last of all on the furthest and lowest shelf, came a wholly weird surprise from which I could infer nothing whatsoever: namely an extensive collection of sensational popular literature.

At first I was taken aback to see this collection of

Penny Dreadfuls with their lurid covers, howling of horrors and bloodstained deeds. Then I decided it must be some aberration or indulgence. And so at last I set about compiling my list. Carefully I scribbled down the subjects to see if I could detect a pattern:

> Anatomy/General Medicine/Pathology (Poisons)
> Geology
> Botany
> Typography
> Abnormal psychology
> Cryptography
> Weaponry
> Mathematics—some obscure
> Anatomy
> Law
> Popular literature

I sat there staring at this list for many minutes, determined to see what it meant. For a wild moment it crossed my mind that the weaponry might indicate some military interests but then I realised there was not a scrap about the military in the rest of the collection. Finally I recall giving it up and deciding that all this showed me was what I already knew: namely that the Doctor was an eccentric, whimsical and infuriating individualist who followed his own tastes regardless of anyone else. I tore the thing up and threw it away in disgust. But in my heart I knew I had failed.

And it was the knowledge of that failure which spurred me to more extreme action. The idea came to me as I was crossing the square a few days after the business with the books. Why in the world, I thought, should I have bothered with the Doctor's so-called "method," a process which I knew to be flawed and based on luck and bluff, when there was a far simpler and more direct means of pursuing the matter?

That very night events played into my hands. All day the weather had been unsettled and by the evening it was foul; a great wind roared around the square, blowing gusts of rain against its walls and windows. The Doctor was, to say the least, unsettled. Twice he came through that locked door and twice returned inside it. Finally, as I sat there alone, one of the janitors handed in a telegram for him. I was about to go and knock on the door, but as so often Bell was ahead of me and came out before I could reach it, taking the telegram, which he had obviously been expecting, and turning back into the locked room. However, he reappeared almost at once, locking the door behind him. He had put on his coat and was clearly in a hurry, for he collected his cane and exited the room without even addressing me. Here was my chance.

Outside, the rain was now coming in gusts, but despite the weather no black carriage appeared for him on this occasion. The Doctor buttoned up his coat and moved quickly, but I could be fast too when I wanted and soon I was suitably placed fifty yards or so behind him as he hurried past the shops and taverns of the Cowgate. Fortunately, despite the threatening weather, there were still people about and I was able to keep them between me and him. Once I had to duck into the opening by a butcher's shop when he stopped for a moment to adjust his coat, but then he hurried on, turned into a side street and entered a large grey building.

I waited a few moments and then I entered it too. It appeared to be a public office of some kind. Halfway up the stairs ahead of me a lamp with a badly trimmed wick gave out a flickering and unpleasant light. I looked down a grey stone corridor, which seemed empty apart from a black bucket. The only door Bell could have gone through was directly opposite me and had not been properly closed. Outside, the rain had started to lash down in earnest. Hugging the wall and keeping deadly quiet, I applied my eye to the crack.

At first I could see nothing, for the room beyond was even more grim and shadowy than the hall. Then I made out the figure of the Doctor, looking down at something and talking softly to another man who was professional in appearance. All I could see before them was a blur and then Bell moved slightly and I caught a glimpse of pale skin and ghostly white hair. It was the body of a woman. I was in a mortuary.

I felt slightly disappointed. Had I gone to all this trouble, merely to find the Doctor was engaged in more medical work? But then I reflected that in his normal duties Bell would rarely have reason or need to attend a mortuary. He was an indefatigable researcher but if there was research to be done, as I had seen when I first met him, the corpse would generally be brought to him. Moreover, there appeared to be nothing very medical about the conversation I could hear, which seemed highly confidential and rather urgent.

"But who exactly was in the house?" Bell's eyes were fixed on the corpse. "Is nobody to question them?"

The other man said something I did not catch. But I caught Bell's reply, which was angry: "I do not care. Beecher is wrong, as he has been wrong before."

I had never heard of any doctor called Beecher, but the name did sound familiar.

The other man turned back to the body. "But there is not a mark on her! Surely, you must be satisfied now?"

"I will be satisfied," said the Doctor grimly, "only when I know the whole truth. I would like you to tell Walton to prepare for a full post-mortem. At once. Time is crucial."

The man made ready to leave, but I lingered, for after all he did not know me and I could pretend to be on some errand if he saw me in the hall. I was intrigued by what I had learned. If the Doctor was ordering a post-mortem, it showed me he was involved in some kind of forensic work, even though I was sure that was neither his speciality nor his official vocation.

His next words, however, turned my legs to jelly. "Oh, Summers," he said. "Could you send my clerk in on your way out? You will find him on the other side of that door."

THE MURDERS OF MR. CARSTAIRS

I stepped back, but it was far too late. Escape was now useless even if it had been possible. I had to stand there like an idiot while the man came out. "Are you his clerk?" he asked with a smile. "Well you'd better go in."

"A word of advice," said Dr. Bell as I hung back in the doorway, not knowing whether to go over to the slab where he stood or stay where I was. "When you are following someone, keep well away from lighted windows." I reddened, feeling very foolish. "Did you enjoy scrutinising my library last week? What did it tell you?"

I said nothing, amazed. "Oh," he continued. "I have followed your enquiries with interest. In fact, I will admit you have shown more application than any other clerk. Therefore I propose to make you an exception." And he beckoned me over.

I moved forward until I stood across the body from him. "Forensic work?" I asked.

He nodded. "Yes, initially it was forensic advice I was asked for in confidence by the city's constabulary. It was many years ago. Summers, the forensic pathologist whom you just saw, was away and they wanted urgently to know how a man had died. That was the beginning. But everything I have seen since, Doyle, confirms me in my most cherished belief that there is so much beyond forensics. We have only scratched the surface of the thing. I am utterly sure now that crimes can be diagnosed in the same fashion as we diagnose a disease."

"So it is the 'method' again?" I still felt sceptical.

"Yes and there, right in front of you, is its practical application. Her name is Mrs. Canning."

I had been so intent on the Doctor, that it was only now I looked closely at the corpse. I was a medical student. I had seen plenty of dead bodies. Yet something about this one was deeply distressing. On the slab lay a woman of around forty covered up to the waist by a pale sheet. You could see that once she had been very beautiful. A mane of long silver hair was brushed back over her shoulders. Her features were pale and rather fine. But there was an expression on her face I still recall to this day.

Dead she was, but the emotion in that face was living. Her eyes started from their sockets, the teeth were set, the mouth contorted. She had bitten a lip at the edge for the mark of the tooth was visible. In spite of its immobility that face still screamed at you.

Seeing this, I looked down, expecting to see the marks on her body of some fearful accident or attack that had caused such anguish. There were none. The body seemed quite untouched, the skin unbroken. From what I could see, there was not the slightest evidence of any violence.

Bell's voice broke through my thoughts. "From this point I will need an undertaking of absolute confidentiality." He was staring at me, my answer was clearly important to him.

"You have it," I said, making the promise I had kept faithfully until now.

He seemed satisfied and proceeded to pull back the rest

of the sheet carefully, almost tenderly. The lower body showed nothing unusual and he glanced from it to me. "So what is your opinion?"

I turned back to him. "She is quite unmarked. Do you believe she was murdered?"

"Yes, I do, but they fall back on heart failure." He waited a moment, then he took a pace back and turned away, evidently frustrated. "Soon after I took up this work, Doyle, I discovered one of its great problems, namely that the authorities investigate as little as they can and only when they are absolutely sure of obtaining a conviction. The result is, of course, that most of the murders they detect are so stupid they are hardly worth the name. A traveller is bludgeoned to death over a game of cards. A man steals a horse after slitting its owner's throat. A woman sets out to poison her husband and uses so much arsenic she is half dead herself. That is the type of murder the authorities prefer. It gives comfort to the ignorant while enabling the worst kinds of crime to continue unremarked."

He broke off, as a man in dark overalls entered the room, accompanied by a young tousle-haired assistant who carried an array of grisly saws and knives, and cleared his throat.

The Doctor was evidently pleased to see them. "Ah, Walton." He put his hands together. "Good, you are starting . . ."

Later, the Doctor and I moved down South Bridge in a hansom cab, which Walton had instructed to wait for us, and just as well, for the storm had truly begun and there was not a soul out. I was doubly excited not only that I had discovered the truth but that I was being allowed to witness an investigation. What I could not know then was

the particular urgency of the affair. Ever since the Chantrelle case, which I will describe in due course, Bell had
endured a very fallow period in his work as an investigator. It was only recently that the police had, somewhat
grudgingly, consulted him again. He was, therefore, risk-
ing a great deal by his insistence on further enquiries into
Mrs. Canning's death and neither he nor anyone else
could possibly be sure of the outcome. Cases like this one
rarely occurred, and even more rarely came to such a
quick and dramatic conclusion.

Eventually the cab deposited us at a large but slightly
forbidding town house on the edge of the new town. On
that street, at that hour, it was one of the only houses
where lights were still burning. A policeman opened the
door and nodded respectfully at Bell. I had just taken to
wearing my father's pocket watch, which had been newly
cleaned and, as we entered and passed the policeman, I
remember the pride with which I removed it from my
breast pocket and consulted it, noting that it was already
nearly ten o'clock.

Ahead of us were a staircase and a corridor. I followed
Bell up the stairs past some fine portraits of steamships
to the second floor where my feet sank into one of the
thickest hall carpets I had ever seen as I walked behind
him through a door ahead of us.

We had entered a very ornate and luxurious lady's bedroom with rich hangings, brocaded wallpaper and a large
bed. Two men were standing by the window and they
turned as we came in. One of them was Summers, the
pathologist, whom I had seen earlier.

The other was a large and impressive-looking figure,
with thick dark hair and an official manner. "Ah, Bell."
He turned. "At last you are here; we have hung on long
enough. Have your autopsy by all means and then I think
we can close the matter and let the poor woman rest."

Bell ignored this and introduced me to them as his clerk. The larger man was Beecher and I remembered where I had heard the name: he was a senior detective of the city's constabulary and often mentioned in the newspapers.

Beecher looked at me for a moment. "In confidence, I take it?" I nodded but I could sense his irritation. "Well, I doubt you will learn anything tonight for I wish to conclude the matter as soon as possible. There are some unusual features, but the fact remains she was locked in here, with her maid outside. There is no evidence of any crime and no living person could have got near her."

Bell had been examining the area around the bed, but now he looked up. "No living person! Perhaps I agree."

"She was locked in!" I said. "Why?"

"Oh, the woman was an hysteric," said Summers. His words were so brutal and dismissive that they made me almost indignant, for I remembered the expression on the corpse's face. I was suddenly conscious of the pain and suffering this room had seen, and I found myself staring at the bed where she had died.

Beecher was keeping his eyes on Bell. "It is fortunate for us in a way that she was. Her maid tasted all her food and drink in the presence of other servants. That is confirmed by the whole house, so I feel sure we can rule out poison."

Partly to get away from the bed, I walked over to the window, looking for signs that someone had broken in. Since the Doctor had been generous enough to include me in this expedition, I wanted to try to defend his cause. "Have you considered suffocation?" I asked. "It would not necessarily leave marks."

"Except you will find no possible way in there or anywhere else except the door," said Beecher scathingly. "The walls are solid. And there is no hiding place."

I felt very foolish now for I saw he was right. The window was nailed down from the inside and from the look of the wood had not been opened for many weeks. Beecher clearly enjoyed my embarrassment. "Oh, yes, apart from Bell here we are all quite certain this death was natural."

"Tell me," asked Bell from where he was studying the carpet at the end of the bed, "did you follow up the matter of the husband?"

"It is just as he told us," said Beecher. "He was away that night until long after her death, playing in his club's annual bridge competition, which lasted throughout the entire night. There are innumerable witnesses. You wish to meet him?"

"In time," said Bell. "First I want to talk to the maid."

A few minutes later we were seated in a neat servant's sitting room in the basement of the house. Mary, a tearful, dark-haired Irish maid, sat opposite us, twisting a hand-kerchief in her lap, which she used occasionally to dab at her eyes . . . "Myself and the cook and the other maid, we all took turns to stand watch outside the mistress's door all night, sir, as she asked," she was saying in answer to Bell's first question. "It reassured her. But I heard and saw nothing."

"Why was it you guarded her in this way?" said the Doctor who had utterly cast aside the imperious manner of the lecture room and spoke with every appearance of genuine kindness. "I understand the door was in any case locked and bolted from the inside, so you could not have entered."

"That is true, sir, but she was still frightened. She said she feared she would be attacked."

"By whom?" Bell spoke gently but I could see how interesting he found this.

"Someone invisible. That's all she would say about it.

She talked of an invisible thing that would come and murder her." She bit her lip but could not stop a fresh flood of tears.

"And do you think, Mary," enquired the Doctor looking concerned, "that anyone *was* trying to hurt her?"

"I cannot see why," spoke the girl fiercely through her tears. "For a nicer, sweeter person never lived. But she had been all nerves for some time. And she was not helped by the loss of her poor cat. I did not mention that before, sir. But it ran off some days ago."

"While she was away?" Bell asked quickly.

"Why, yes, sir," she answered in surprise. "But how did you know that for as I say, I have mentioned it to nobody. It was while she was staying with her sister."

Bell seemed thoughtful as we left the room after this talk, though it was hard to see how he could have learned much from it. I asked how he had deduced that the woman was away when her cat had gone missing, but he gave me a glance which indicated that such questions were highly unwelcome.

Perhaps I should have known better, for the longer we stayed in that house the more clearly I began to observe a change in the Doctor. He was demonstrating all the signs of a man who has begun to immerse himself in a favourite, even a sacred, activity. Not only was he more intent, focused and involved than I had yet known him, even his movements became more precise. He would fall into long silences then equally sudden bursts of urgent conversation. Once he asked me to comment on an arrangement of flowers in the drawing room, which was clearly nothing to do with the case but momentarily preoccupied him. I felt the quickening of his whole being.

In due course I would come to recognise this rush of energy, but here was the very first time I ever saw it. In the midst of a criminal investigation it was as if he came at last on to his native ground, at one with himself and the work he loved.

Outside, the wind had now become almost a tempest and the rain was lashing against the windows. For a time the Doctor moved lithely around the house in thought, throwing out an occasional observation, which it was clear required no answer. Then, quite late in the night, he suddenly asked if we might be introduced to Mr. Canning.

We met in Canning's study along the corridor from his wife's bedroom. He was a stocky and good-looking man, who certainly seemed tortured by his loss. I recall how he stood with his back to us, staring out of the window with tears in his eyes.

"What a night," he said with a shudder of horror. "I understand you are performing an autopsy at last. Well, I only pray it will tell us the answer. Please God, there is some answer. It is bad enough that she had these fears but now . . ."

While Canning talked I noticed the Doctor was continuing his manic activity and taking a great interest in this study. He lingered around the fireplace, looking at the mantelpiece and even ran his hand along the wall on the panelling to one side of it almost as if he were checking for dust.

He also scrutinised the books on the shelf with far more interest than I thought they warranted, for there was nothing remarkable about them. There were some annuals, dictionaries and novels, and a shelf of architectural studies, which was Canning's trade. Bell even removed several books from the shelves and glanced at them, yet he was still listening to Canning by the window.

"Indeed I wanted to ask you about your wife's fears," said Bell leaving the books at last and again I noted his respectful tone. "Can you tell me exactly what she was frightened of?"

The question seemed highly disturbing to Canning, but

he controlled himself after a moment. "You do not know?" he replied. "Very well . . . I admit that I hate even speaking the name. It was Nicholas Carstairs."

Bell started. "You have heard of him, I see," Canning was almost whispering. "The man was hanged at Cawdon Square not far away from here."

"Did he live here?" I asked.

"No," said Canning, his voice still low. "But it was the scene of one of his crimes. A whole family! My wife heard about it shortly after we came. A silly gossiping friend told her. Her nerves were never very strong, but from then on . . . Oh, how I just curse myself now for moving here at all." He was crying now and there, in that room, with the wind and rain outside, I felt sorry for him. I did not wonder he felt guilty about bringing her to the house for the whole place reeked of fear.

"And tell me," demanded Bell, "did she say she saw Carstairs?"

"No," said Canning, wiping his eyes and making an effort to compose himself. "But she felt his presence. She felt it here in the house at night. She thought he would come for her and now . . . it is as if it has all happened just as she feared." He turned back to the window but it was only an attempt to hide more crying. Bell motioned me out and we left him. It would have been too cruel to continue.

We walked back along the corridor to the dead woman's bedroom and I had a question I was burning to ask. "This man Carstairs? How did he murder his victims?"

His reply was flat: "He strangled them."

The thought that Carstairs had strangled people in this place added a new and horrible aspect to the house and I began to wish fervently for morning. But the Doctor gave no indication of leaving. Indeed, his mood had become even more introspective as we waited alone in that grim bedroom with the wind howling outside.

I expected the Doctor to make further investigations. But slowly it became clear to me that he had already gathered all the data available to him. For a while he sat down on the end of that awful bed and was completely still. The energy I had seen earlier had gone. In fact, I could tell he was far from happy.

Bell stood in the same position for a long while. I took up a place by the window and there we stayed until quite suddenly he was back on his feet, moving from one place to the next as if impatient.

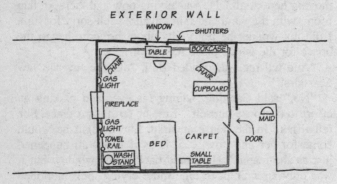

Canning's Sealed Bedroom

Finally he stopped at the wall furthest from the door and drummed his fingers on the mantelpiece. From here he turned and paced back and forth within the room. I watched his face closely. It was clear that he was turning something over and over in his mind and the bed-chamber itself fascinated him almost as if it contained the mystery within it. A little later that night, during a lull in our vigil, I made a sketch map of the room in my notebook and, though I did not know it at the time, it contains exactly the details that Bell was examining and re-examining throughout the night in order to reach a conclusion.

Again he moved back to the bed and I realised he was surveying the room as if from the perspective of the woman who had died in it. By now I was completely absorbed in the Doctor's thought processes and longed to know the nature of the internal debate that raged within him. Finally, unable to bear it any longer, I opened my mouth to ask a question.

I should have known better. He raised a fierce hand, indicating he would tolerate no disturbance, and subsided into reflection. After that the silence continued for the best part of two hours. I say "silence," though in fact the night outside was so foul that all I could hear was the wind roaring around the window and chimney.

It must have been between three and four o'clock when the Doctor's curious trance was finally broken. There was no knock at the door. Instead, it opened slowly and silently, and a policeman entered. He evidently knew the Doctor of old for he said nothing at all, but walked over to him and respectfully handed him a piece of paper before withdrawing.

Bell took the paper and looked at it for a while. Then at last he broke his silence and I could see the strain on his face. "Well, they have done the autopsy. There is not a trace of poison or anything else in her. And as you saw, no marks of any kind. They are still making tests but despite the lack of any marks, there is some evidence that her lungs were deprived of air as if . . ." He broke off and turned to me. "Yes, as if . . . she had been strangled."

"Good God," I said. For I remembered the expression on her face, and now it was almost as if I could see the impression of Mrs. Canning's body still on the bed beside us and feel the agony of those last moments.

But Bell merely crumpled the paper in his hand with evident irritation and turned away to the window, looking quite crestfallen.

"Well," I said quietly, "it must be as they thought. She worked herself up into a terror, inspired by what once happened here, and her heart gave way."

Bell leant on the window, completely still. I was beginning to feel annoyed with him. Very well, he had got nowhere, but what was that beside the suffering that had taken place just a few feet away from where he stood? Outside, the wind was louder than ever.

"And after all." I raised my voice. "We cannot bring her back. To think of that poor woman lying here in that state with the wind howling in the chimney like this. It is horrible."

I could hardly believe the impact my words had. The Doctor suddenly sprang round and came towards me.

At first I thought he was angry at my interruption, but

his tone was pleased and excited. "What? What did you say?" But he did not wait for an answer; indeed, he did not truly seem to see me—he was effectively talking to himself: "Yes! Yes, of course. You have cleared up the very matter that has been bedevilling me." And he moved rapidly to the door.

I was glad enough to get out of that room. "So you agree with me?" I asked as we came out into the corridor.

He looked at me and at last seemed properly to register my presence. "My dear fellow, I am sorry. When I have a case to work through it is important to me to have the mental space to resolve it. You have shown admirable patience and I am sure you are hungry."

I am not sure how hungry I really felt, but a few moments later we were raiding the servants' large but empty kitchen where the Doctor was able to avail himself of a joint of lamb and some bread and butter that had been prepared for the master of the house that evening but had gone uneaten. I will never forget the relish with which he cut thin slices of lamb and wolfed down the bread and butter.

I drank some water, feeling quite proud that he had come round to my way of thinking. "Then it is your conclusion that she died of terror because of those unfounded fears?"

"Unfounded?" he queried, looking up from his energetic meal. "No, they were very well founded. The woman died just exactly as she feared." He removed a few last crumbs with his napkin. "She was deliberately choked to death."

"But by whom?" I was beginning to feel all my old incredulity.

"Both the maid and her husband told us quite clearly. Did you not hear them?"

"What are you talking about?" I was beginning to feel

real irritation. "They spoke of the invisible ghost of a dead man."

At this point the door opened and Beecher entered. He had evidently been up all night too, but he was smiling now and in his hand was a copy of the results of the autopsy. "Well, there you are, Bell," he said. "Her breathing was constricted but there was nothing blocking her throat or her lungs. It *must* have been her heart."

"No, it was not her heart," the Doctor replied. "It was as she feared, Beecher. An invisible thing entered Mrs. Canning's room and squeezed the life out of her."

I had had enough. "I cannot believe you would indulge in such unprovable claims," I said. "Claims which must clearly be nonsense."

I suppose I was vehement partly because I was tired and had been cooped up in that awful room all night. As yet, it must be remembered, I had little experience of Bell's skills. I could see only that he was making fantastic claims and enjoying their theatrical effect. Indeed, here was more proof of what I had suspected all along. The Doctor was a charlatan; and, what was worse, the kind who believes his own twaddle.

Beecher looked delighted with my outburst. "Good for you, young man. This is too much even for you, Bell. A ghost! It is childish nonsense."

But the Doctor did not look at all put out. He was taking great interest in the roster of work that was laid out in that kitchen for the servants. Such things were not so uncommon in the larger town houses and they set out the precise times and duties of each maid and servant during the day with particular attention to household chores. The chart in front of us was as detailed as any I had seen, evidently the house was run on very meticulous lines. "Yes, it is childish," said Bell absently as he studied it.

"Even you admit it," said Beecher.

Bell had found what he wanted and looked up. "You misunderstand me, Beecher. I mean it is childishly simple. And if this chart is strictly observed, as I am sure it must be, then we can see it all for ourselves now."

The door opened and Mary, the Irish maid we had talked to hours earlier, appeared, dressed for her duties for the day. She was a bit taken aback to see us in the servants' kitchen, but Bell rose to the occasion:

"Ah, Mary, I am sorry. We have helped ourselves. And now we believe you may be able to help us."

"I will help you in any way I can, sir," said the girl with astonishment.

"Well, fortunately"—Bell was now very much master of the occasion—"we need not interrupt your duties while you do so. For if I am not mistaken, one of your first tasks is in your master's study. Is that right? We will follow you."

So our little party trooped up the stairs behind the surprised maid to the study where we had talked to Canning earlier. The room was fairly dark, its gaslights turned down, but Canning, who was still dressed and had clearly not slept, heard us and came along the corridor to see what we were doing.

"Ah, Mr. Canning," said Bell. "I have come to the conclusion that your belief in a lethal but unseen presence in this house is entirely justified. But in order to prove it to these sceptics here, I need the assistance of your maid."

"Of course," agreed the man, his eyes still red from crying, "Mary, give the Doctor any assistance he requires. I am eager to hear it."

And now came one of those bizarre moments which the Doctor always seemed to relish. For all of us—myself, Beecher, Canning and the uniformed policeman, who had brought the autopsy report—sat down in that still-darkened study and watched, somewhat stupefied, as Bell gave orders to the maid.

"I want you, Mary," he began, "merely to proceed with your duties in this room."

"My duties, sir. Why, of course!" said Mary.

"Just do as you would do when you come down here so early in the morning."

Not surprisingly, Mary seemed rather flustered. "What I do, sir? Well, I would enter the room and do the fire."

"Ah, yes." Bell sounded rather absent-minded, a trait I was beginning to see was entirely deceptive. "Now, just to be clear, this fire adjoins the one next door in your mistress's bedroom, is that correct?"

"It is, sir."

"So would you be so kind as to show us what you did here yesterday morning, some hours before your mistress was found dead."

"What I did, sir? Why, I got down and . . ."

"In the dark?" asked Bell.

"Why, no, sir," replied the girl. "I always turn up the gas."

Bell indicated she should do so. She moved to the gas lamps and turned up the flame. The room grew brighter around us. "Excellent," Bell said. "And then?"

"Why, sir, I go to the fire and open the flue."

The Doctor seemed particularly interested in this operation and, seeing this, the girl got down on her knees and pulled at the metal rod. Bell was behind her, watching like a hawk. "A wee bit stiff, is it not?" he asked softly.

"Yes, yes, it is," she said, struggling. "I do not know why that should be, but it has been stiff for a few days. There! It is open."

"Very good, Mary." The Doctor straightened up. "That is all I require of you, thank you."

"I can go?" she asked, rather surprised.

"By all means recommence your other duties in the kitchen, though I think you will find it an unusual day."

She bobbed to us rather sweetly and went out, while Bell turned to his audience who were none the wiser for this display and becoming slightly restless. I did notice, however, that Canning himself was staring at the bookcase, just as Bell had done much earlier that night.

"Ah, Canning," said Bell in a very friendly tone. "Yes, I must ask another favour of you. I wonder if I might borrow this. It was lying behind the books." He held up a narrow length of pink rubber tubing about three or four feet long. It was an innocent enough object on its own, but even then there seemed something very unpleasant about it.

Bell moved deftly over to the fireplace. Again he returned to that space of panelling beside it and ran his hand over it as he had before. But his next movement told me why. For he proceeded to insert one end of the tube through a small hole in the panelling, while he attached the other to a gas spigot he had opened above the lamp. Now, he lowered the flame of the gas lamps, causing the whole room to darken and turned to us with a smile of pride.

"*There*, gentlemen, is your invisible agent, moving into the bedroom next door through this tube. Quite capable of asphyxiating the occupant of an adjoining room with absolutely no ventilation."

We could see at once he was right. For now the flame was turned down in the study, it left far more pressure of gas for the spigot and tube. In fact, I could hear a gentle hiss as the gas was pumped lethally into the next-door room, where we had spent most of that fearful night.

Beecher was aghast, as were we all. "But why," he asked, "did they not smell gas when they got in?"

"That," said Bell, "was exactly what I could not

fathom. I kept returning to it all night. The window was sealed shut. The thing seemed quite impossible. Until young Doyle came to my rescue. You see, the gas would disperse within an hour or two if the room were ventilated and the pressure were down. And you, Doyle, mentioned the wind howling in the chimney."

"What of it?" I said.

"There was the means of ventilation! And Canning's alibi remained intact. It was the maid, as you have just seen, who acted as his accomplice." The word took me aback but he anticipated the objection. "Oh, quite innocently as she demonstrated for us," he said. "She entered and turned up the gas to light the room, lowering the pressure on the system. Little gas was now escaping into the room next door. Next she went to the fire and found the flue stiff. Why? Because if you look . . ." He bent down and pulled at the lever, thrusting his arm into the aperture. *"It had been connected by a wire to the flue in the fireplace of the adjoining bedroom. Opening this one, she opens that one as well."*

Now, of course, we all saw the full extraordinary ingenuity of this scheme and our eyes turned with Bell to Canning. He still sat in his armchair, as if engrossed in the account, but he was unnaturally still.

"Yes," said Bell, addressing him directly. "You realised it would be hours before her body was discovered. That left plenty of time for the gas to escape and for you to remove the tube, which was not very noticeable in any event. There was no time to dispose of it, but concealment in your library must have seemed safe enough. I must admit I combed the house before I found it here."

Bell's eyes locked with Canning's. The man got up. I do not know whether he was contemplating flight but it would have been useless in any event. The uniformed policeman was right at his elbow. "Congratulations," he said to Bell after a moment's pause. "A fine piece of work. But I rather wish you had been in the room with her."

After Canning had been taken out, Beecher went to the gas spigot and examined the hole and tube in great detail. He affected an air of nonchalance, but I could see it was only to conceal a fair degree of amazement.

"Very well, Bell," he pronounced at last. "I have to acknowledge your success. But how in heaven's name could the man know for sure his scheme would work?"

"Because," said Bell, "like any good scientist, he had tested it all to his satisfaction while she was away. One of the first things I noticed here was the new gas fittings. And the lady's cat, you will recall, was missing."

It was almost dawn before the Doctor and I returned to his workroom. Without hesitation, he led me straight to his locked door. "After tonight," he told me, "I think I can justify your admission here." And he turned the key.

As soon as it was open I saw my folly. For it did not lead to a room at all but to a staircase. Finally the dimensions of my puzzling map made sense.

He climbed the stairs ahead of me and soon we arrived at another locked door at the top. There were, it seemed, even more warrens to his labyrinth than I had suspected and I felt sure that somewhere near here was another way out. Now at last I understood the secret behind the Doctor's sudden appearances and his ability to come and go without being seen.

He unlocked this last door and we entered a large room, which looked at first like a comfortable study. A fire was burning in the grate, so evidently someone cleaned and serviced these quarters, though to this day I do not know who. The shelves all around me contained a strange assortment of objects, besides photographs and pamphlets and books.

I moved to examine these and the first object I saw was so odd that I could not begin to think what it was. The thing consisted of a strap attached to a large hollow shape like a cucumber. I was picking it up when the Doctor stopped me.

"Careful," he said. He took it cautiously, applying pressure to the top of the shape. As he did so, a horrible-looking blade with a serrated edge sprang out and up.

"But what is its use?" I asked.

He looked at me. "I will tell you if you want to know, but first I think I should explain something to you. The motives for murder are usually commonplace. The mechanisms, however, are confined only by human ingenuity and the limits of the imagination. There is nothing decent about the subject and this apparatus is about as indecent as you can imagine. Even when it was discovered, it was never written about."

"I would still like to know."

"Very well. It was the device of a fanatically jealous husband, who wanted his wife to die during the act of love in the most painful way he could devise." He put it down carefully.

"Here? And did he use it?" I could hardly believe anything so horrible, yet I will admit I was fascinated.

"No to both, I am glad to say. The thing came from Belgium and he was arrested for another crime. But I fear it is not unique. Think of it, Doyle, and it has probably happened . . ."

I continued, now, to examine the room's collection of items and case histories. It was vast and I realised that the shelf of sensational literature downstairs was merely a minor offshoot of what was here. The books and pamphlets and illustrated material all related to crime, mostly murder.

"You may like to try writing up some notes of the case we saw tonight. They will be destroyed, of course," he said, as he unpacked his bag, containing the various tools of his work. "It is a condition of all my Crown work that it remains completely confidential and will never be revealed, but it might aid your understanding."

I was greatly flattered and readily agreed. "How long have you been studying crime in this way?" I asked.

"Oh, a few years ago something happened which made me unsure how to go on. And then, like a miracle, this work, my work, began."

It was clear he would say no more so I did not ask, but I could be sure he was referring to the death of his wife.

I walked home at dawn, pondering this and so many other things. Fortunately the house was not yet astir and I slipped straight upstairs. There was no hope of sleep. I felt like a traveller who has entered a new and strange land. It was obvious I would never look at things in quite the same way again.

DR. BELL'S METHOD

Here, then, was the start in earnest of my working relationship with the Doctor. Now that I was taken into his confidence, the reader might well assume our dealings with each other became easier and more relaxed, and that I settled down to be a disciple of the man and his method.

The assumption is understandable but it could hardly be more wrong. The honest truth is my relations with the Doctor never precisely mirrored the smooth cordiality between the two detectives in my fiction. Even there, I occasionally allowed a touch of asperity to show itself and this was but the tiniest hint of the true state of affairs: namely that for many years I could not easily reconcile myself to my mentor.

In part this might be seen as merely a matter of age and temperament. I had my pride, he had his and, though he could be magnificent company, I would not describe him as a particularly easy man to befriend. When I first encountered him I was having to come to terms with my own family problem and, not much later, with the urgent need to make a living. All this made our collaboration uneasy. But in my heart I know there is much more to it.

Put bluntly, the Canning affair proved far less troubling

to me than the two awful cases that followed. It may be asked how I can write in this way about a man who deliberately scared his wife till she was in abject terror and then killed her. But it is a plain fact. What came later was more violent, more disturbing and, as I will show, unexpected. The Canning murder was deeply unpleasant, but the man was in his way a traditionalist and the case could usefully stand as a model for some of my later fiction. If the Doctor and I had confronted only his kind, our relationship would have proved less volatile. But the Edinburgh case that followed Canning took us into uncharted territory, as did the matter of Miss Grace's eyes. Here was material that could scarcely be considered fit for public consumption and would test our relationship to the limit. But before I come to Miss Grace, I must recount a much smaller incident, which vividly illustrates the clash of temperaments between myself and Bell, even though it did not involve any crime at all.

It happened in his room on a dull afternoon in early February, some time after I met him. I was still at least a year away from graduation and spent many more months as a medical student. But, as I look back, a trick of memory makes me almost feel as if this incident marked my final afternoon at the university. In my mind it is as though I went home after it, packed my bags and left the town. No doubt this is partly because there is much I wish to forget in the spring and summer that followed. But it is also true that the events in his upstairs study that day do, after a fashion, sum up my early relationship with the Doctor.

The incident occurred after I came in to tell him that I had prepared the lecture theatre. We had half an hour to spare and Bell, who was sitting by the fire, invited me to take the chair opposite while he read my notes on the Canning case.

"I know there is cruelty in the world," I was saying as I sat down, "but for a man to frighten his wife till she is in such a turmoil of horror, and then take her life in the way she most feared. It just seems utterly barbarous."

"Agreed," he said without much interest as he languidly turned over my pages. Then, without looking up or saying anything further at all, he finished reading the composition I had struggled for hours to write and threw it on to his fire. I watched the pages burn with some amazement and not a little irritation. Of course, the Doctor had warned me that any written record would be destroyed. The Eugene Chantrelle case had occurred some time before I knew the Doctor but he constantly referred to it and it had left him with an obsession almost amounting to paranoia about keeping all his activities as an investigator confidential. Chantrelle, a Frenchman, had killed his wife in Edinburgh and was eventually brought to justice. The amount of official bungling during the investigation had been almost comical. Vital clues were destroyed. Others blindly missed, but Bell had solved it, on the assumption that his part would be kept confidential. In this instance it was particularly important, for there had been much hurt pride and any publicity could only make matters worse. The Doctor made sure his name was kept out of the trial and all seemed well. But unfortunately he had fatally underestimated his man.

For Chantrelle had observed not only Bell's role in his prosecution but also the Doctor's craving for anonymity. Now the murderer saw a magnificent way of taking his revenge. On the day of his execution he appeared at the gallows, dressed in his best suit and smoking a cigar, and asked to have a last word. Whereupon he addressed some remarks to the official forensic pathologist, Henry Littlejohn, airily asking him to convey his compliments and congratulations to the absent Dr. Bell for bringing him to justice.

Chantrelle hanged, but this last shot proved devilishly effective, humiliating Littlejohn and compromising Bell's dealings with the authorities in Edinburgh for months to come. There was jealousy and controversy from the police, complaints and questions from the university, even some ribald interest from the populace. When I met him, Bell was still struggling to repair the damage. Indeed, his secretiveness and that locked room were a direct result of the Chantrelle affair.

I knew most of this as I sat in his room that afternoon but it still seemed to me that sometimes he took his secrecy too far. I was annoyed to see those notes burn for I had taken time and trouble over them, and his subsequent remark did nothing to improve my mood. "But what of the method, Doyle?" he murmured after a few minutes' contemplation of the fire. "Those notes revealed nothing of it. Yet it is where you should have concentrated all your attention."

I found myself inflamed by the sheer egotism of the man. It was as if he cared nothing at all for the woman who had been murdered. As if her brutal death was only of any significance for the light it shed on *his* blasted "method."

"But is it, finally, a new method?" I asked with more composure than I felt. "You cite Canning as a demonstration and I grant you were far ahead of everyone else, but it did not really take much for someone of your experience. Very well, you guessed that coal gas might be a cause. That is reasonable. Carbon monoxide would have shown in her blood eventually anyway, making even that leap redundant. All you needed then was the trick of ventilation and by luck you came upon it. Far from a new method, I would argue the Canning case proves only that everyone's box of tricks is the same. It is merely that some are quicker than others in their use of it."

His face visibly fell and I actually wondered if I had gone too far. "But I swear I did not guess," he said, never for a moment suspecting I was being deliberately provocative. "It is an appalling practice, which betrays the chain of reason and reduces it merely to a series of leaps in the dark. In the end, guessing can actually, I believe, destroy the proper mental faculties. For it encourages fatalism and laziness. I promise you there is all the difference in the world between applying logical observation of the kind I am trying to pioneer and guessing."

"Possibly," I said and to my discredit I was enjoying his discomfort. "But without seeing it systematically applied and subject to a properly observed series of tests and demonstrations, you must grant your method will forever remain unproven."

"Yes," he admitted with much less resistance than I had anticipated, "just so. Anyone can follow the reasoning afterwards and talk of what would later be discovered. I only wish there were a way I could illustrate it better for you."

"Perhaps there is," I said. He stared at me gloomily, an eyebrow raised. "You have written in one of your essays that it is difficult for a man to keep any object in daily use without leaving his personality about it. That is an example of your method in its purest form, is it not?"

"Certainly," he agreed.

"Well, then." I took out my father's watch as I spoke. "If you make something useful of this watch, you may convince me."

The watch, with its chain and gold facia, gleamed in the light of the fire. "Months can go by without a single case. I would rejoice in a challenge . . ." he said and the watch was duly handed over.

I still remember Bell's expression as he studied it. His face was a perfect picture of disappointment. In fact, I could hardly keep from laughing. "But there are hardly any data," he said miserably. "This has recently been cleaned."

"Yes, I know," I said. "I oversaw its cleaning myself. So you see, Doctor, I rather feel this illustrates the limitations of your so-called method."

The Doctor could certainly be arrogant, but he was never a bad loser and I expected him now to return the watch to me with a shrug of defeat. But he did no such thing. He held on to it, and turned it round and round under the light, opening its back and studying the works. Then he took out a powerful concave lens to examine it and at last, still a little crestfallen, he handed it back to me.

He sat in his chair, eyes half closed. "Yes," he mused. "Perhaps you are right. But my investigation was not entirely barren. The watch is about fifty years old. Its owner is a man of untidy habits—very untidy and careless. He was left with good prospects but threw away his chances. He has lived some time in relative poverty with a few short intervals of prosperity. After that he took to drink and his mind went. That is all I can honestly tell you."

I jumped to my feet in anguish. I felt in that moment as if he had casually ripped my soul apart. Here was the awful downward spiral of my father's life, a downward spiral that we lived through day after day, a secret torture to me and all my family, being recounted like some casual smoking-room anecdote.

"This is unworthy of you, Dr. Bell," I said. "I could not believe you would descend to it."

He looked at me in amazement. "I do not follow."

"This is the watch of my father. You have somehow got wind of our family history and now you pretend to deduce this knowledge in some fanciful way! To parade a painful family secret in such a fashion is not merely unkind, it . . . is pure malice."

The Doctor looked quite concerned. "My dear Doyle," he said with some feeling, "viewing the matter purely as an abstract problem, I had not considered your personal reaction. But I can assure you I am quite unaware of your family situation. You could have been an orphan for all I know."

His tone was so genuine that slowly some of my rage ebbed away. "Then in heaven's name," I asked, "how?"

He came to me, then, took the watch and looked at me with a directness I had rarely seen before. "The same as always," he said quietly. "Observe the small facts on which larger inferences depend. Careless? Well, the lower part of the watch is dented and cut and marked from the habit of keeping other hard objects such as coins or keys in the same pocket. To treat a fifty-guinea watch like that marks a careless man."

Now he opened the watch and continued in the same soft, mesmerising tone, determined to let me see the process he had followed: "Through the lens I can see many pawnbroker's marks—hence the hard times. But clearly sometimes he had money to redeem his pledge. Finally— look at the scratches round the keyhole—mark where the key has slipped! What sober man's keys could have scored those grooves? And then you will observe here how they become seriously disturbed and destructive, well beyond mere drunkenness."

We looked at each other. So he had indeed stumbled through his deductions upon our darkest family secret, a secret my mother, my sisters and I were at such pains to conceal. I was impressed, but in that moment my humiliation was so intense I could only nod.

"So have I shown you something at last?" His voice was still very gentle, as was his expression.

"Yes, you have," I told him. But my heart felt it would break. And shortly afterwards I left him.

THE PATIENT'S EYES

I still have my father's watch. Indeed, it is on the desk before me as I write this, having just returned from its annual clean. Looking down at it, even now all these years later, I still feel some of the pain and humiliation of that afternoon.

I see also, of course, how much of it was chance. If the Doctor's demonstration of his method, a demonstration I so recklessly invited, had only concerned a more neutral object then it could not possibly have had the same effect. But it had felt like torture to me to see the glittering Ibo, the plaything of my childhood, so brutally transformed into a forensic record of my father's decline into drunken insanity. Little wonder that, while I accepted its creator's brilliance, the method continued to arouse doubts in me, doubts which were only fuelled when later it failed us.

Therefore the episode still stands in my mind as a reason I pushed him away after I left the town. Though by then he had witnessed my innermost anguish and grief in far more harrowing circumstances, and to a degree that hardly seems fair, especially since I was barely grown up.

I told myself, I think, after I passed my medical exams

and left Edinburgh, that I no longer needed him. We corresponded occasionally but there was in some respects little to say, in others far too much and, as is the way with such things, soon we were not in communication at all. The silence between us continued into 1882 when I returned from a short and unsuccessful trip to Africa and began my first proper medical job. And so it was that one late October afternoon I came to be sitting opposite a patient in a South Coast consulting room without the slightest notion of how soon I would need the Doctor's help.

My patient's face was perfect, I thought as I looked across at her. Not the dull, cherubic face of an angel, nor the bland, rosy face of a doll, but the deep, soulful face of a saint. The eyes, in particular, were so filled with pure emotion that I found it hard not to stare at them. Bell had, of course, drummed into me the notion that a doctor may observe more from seeing than conversing so, while she talked, I tried to study her hands and clothes, and her general demeanour. But still I found myself oddly fearful that, once I stared into her eyes, I would be unable to look away again.

Miss Heather Grace was only the third patient who had sat across my desk since I accepted my first medical position, a very junior role in that South Coast practice. Perhaps one reason why she made such an impression was that, since Edinburgh, I had been avoiding the company of women. Also, I was still getting used to the idea of being a doctor as I sat opposite her, forcing myself to look at her directly.

"It is like a blurring," she was saying. And, so distracted had I been, it was only now I fully understood that the problem she was describing was not some stomach malady or a fever, but a condition of her eyes.

"How often do these symptoms occur?" I asked,

quickly starting to make notes, hoping this would give me a more professional air.

"Oh, it goes away, but it always comes back, especially at this season. I admit I feel stupid about it. I did not wish to bother Dr. Cullingworth, my usual doctor. But . . ." here she hesitated, "I have been a little troubled by it."

There was something about the way she said the word "troubled" that would have melted a harder heart than mine. Miss Grace had a happy enough demeanour, but I sensed some deeper problem was concerning her.

"Tell me," I asked. "Do you live with your family?"

She looked up at me. "I live with my uncle and aunt. My parents died. But it was some years ago."

"I am aware years make little difference," I said gently. She looked at me closely. "But is there something else troubling you now?"

"It is stupid." She gave a sad little smile. "But I will tell you if you do not laugh. A road. A road has given me bad dreams."

It was about the last thing I expected her to say. "A road?" I replied.

"Or a part of it, at least, which runs by a wood. I always hated the place. But I cycle it every day, for it leads to the rectory where my aunt and uncle live." She fingered a little locket that hung round her neck.

"And have you seen something on this road?"

She hesitated. "At first just . . . a shape in the trees. I put it down to imagination. My uncle says I have far too much of it. But the truth is that now, yes, I see . . . a figure . . . a cyclist. It follows me, doctor."

"And you have seen the figure close?"

"Never. Though from a distance . . ." she struggled. "I know this will seem foolish, but it is as if . . . as if it has no eyes." It was pitiful to see the fear in her now. I kept quiet, wanting her to continue. "If I stop, it does not appear. Once I turned and the figure turned back, and again it was gone. If I am accompanied, it never comes."

"I see," I said. "And this has been some weeks." It was a pitiful response and it got the answer it deserved.

"I know how it sounds." And she put out her hands for her gloves.

"No," I said more forcefully. "I am glad you told me. I am a doctor and I will of course look into your symptoms. But if this other matter troubles you there is an easy way forward. I would consider it a privilege if you would let me at least investigate your small puzzle. I merely need, after all, to observe your daily journey on the road. I once knew someone who took an interest in such matters. I would do my best to help."

"I would be so relieved." She leant forward towards me, her eyes shining with gratitude, "All I want is someone with a little common sense to shed some light."

"Then," said I, "all I want is the loan of a bicycle."

And so it was that I found myself on a dull November afternoon crouched in a ditch by a lonely stretch of moorland road. Looking around me, it was certainly hard not to sympathise with Miss Grace's feelings about this place.

A few hundred yards to my right along the road stood a gibbet where, it was said, highwaymen were once hanged. Behind was the moor itself, dank and forbidding. But worst of all was the dark, oppressive wood in front, which crowded in on that road like a black, swirling fog. When I had started out from town it had seemed a reasonably warm day, but now the dank undergrowth in that ditch made me feel as if I were crouched in cold water and I was shivering.

We had agreed that I would be in position by four o'clock and about fifteen minutes later a figure on a bicycle appeared in the distance. The shadows were lengthening and I could not see it clearly at first, but as it came closer I was able to make out the elegant figure of Miss Grace. I had not told her precisely where I would hide and she was cycling along, keeping her face firmly forward. But her clenched jaw and fixed expression as she passed showed what an ordeal this journey had become. Soon she was receding and I waited hopefully, my eyes fixed on the road.

All was still, apart from a pigeon fluttering into a tree opposite. I kept watching but saw nothing. There was not the slightest sign of anyone else at all. Indeed, now she was out of sight, the road could hardly have been more deserted. I stayed there twenty minutes longer, then, with a slightly heavy heart, I got out my bicycle and cycled after her.

She was waiting for me expectantly by the gate to a pleasant ivy-clad rectory. I dismounted beside her. "Did you see him?" she asked, as she looked up at me, pushing back a lock of hair that had fallen in front of her ear. Her eyes were wide with hope.

"I fear I saw nobody at all," I said.

It was heart-rending to see her face fall, but there was still defiance in it. "So what do you think of me now, Doctor? Either I must be a liar or I am going mad."

"No," I said with more firmness than I felt. "All I can tell you is I did not see him. Did you?"

She looked at me very directly. "What if I say he was beside me the whole time?" If she meant it, I would have to pass her to another doctor for she would be well beyond my help. So I waited. "The truth," she said, breaking the silence, "is that I did not look back."

My relief must have been obvious. "Then we cannot be sure of anything yet, not even if this has anything to do with your eyes. It may simply be that he saw me."

"Yes, I thought of that and I am grateful to you." She came forward a little. "I want nothing but to be believed."

I was about to say something when suddenly a window was thrown open behind us and there came a great shout. I think her name was called, though the tone was so fierce that I could not be sure.

Her expression changed at once. "Thank you for your help, even if it came to nothing. I will not forget it. I would . . ."

But I was not destined to know what she was about to say, because the front door opened and she turned to move away.

A moment later, as I was riding down the drive, I did look back at the house. Heather Grace had already reached its porticoed entrance and there I saw the owner of the voice, an elderly man with a large, muscular face. I do not know if he saw me, but I could understand now why she hurried.

THE STRANGE PRACTICE

As I cycled back to the town, I found myself wishing that I could confide this odd little adventure to my employer. Nothing could or should have been more natural. But it will soon be clear enough why such a course of action was utterly impossible.

Until he offered me employment, I had only seen Cullingworth, who was older than me, once since he left Edinburgh. At the time I was in my last year at university and he was struggling with a difficult practice and risked bankruptcy. Debts had piled up and, though deeply ashamed, he had dragooned me into a month's locum work as a favour. I did not resent this for I felt I was helping a friend. Yet after that I never heard another thing from him until I had graduated and was actively seeking work, having just returned from overseas. It was then I received his telegram:

COME BY NEXT TRAIN IF POSSIBLE STOP STARTED HERE LAST JUNE STOP COLOSSAL SUCCESS STOP FORTUNES TO BE MADE AND THE ONLY MEDICAL COMPETITION ARE FOOLS STOP NO MORE DEBTS
CULLINGWORTH

Perhaps, if it had not been so welcome, the tone of this message should have alerted me to the change in the man. At university, when I first met him, James Heriot Turnavine Cullingworth was reckless and arrogant. But he was loyal and he was spirited, and his passionate outbursts could be a pleasant counterweight to the conceit of our teachers. Certainly the moment I got off the train in that south-coast town, his exuberance and recklessness were fully in evidence. He was entertaining three ladies he had evidently just met, regaling them with his heroic exploits as a doctor, but they were dismissed in an instant.

"Wonderful to see you, laddie," he said with a great roar. "Why, it seems an age since university." He set off at a great pace, leaving me struggling with my shabby portmanteau to keep up. "You know why we're going to clean this town out?" He flung the question over his shoulder as he strode through the station's entrance hall.

"No," I answered, struggling to keep up, "but I think you are going to tell me."

"Because," he continued as he walked, "we both know that etiquette is merely a dodge for keeping the business in the hands of older men. But my father was a doctor, so I was born inside the machine and know all the wires. I have cast etiquette to the devil and you will see the result. Already the doctors in this place find it hard to get butter to their bread and when we work together they'll have to eat it dry. But that is not all. I propose we start a newspaper."

"I am open to all suggestions," I said as we turned up the street. He had moderated his pace and I had recovered my breath. "But you are a doctor, not a journalist."

"I am anything I want to be," he replied, looking at me in a rather strange way. It was my first indication of how easily he took offence.

We were now close to a rather large town house with

a small courtyard and outbuildings. Even from far away I could see a great crowd of people swarming around the entrance. We stopped in front of his imposing brass plaque:

DR. J. CULLINGWORTH

I was astonished by the throng and Cullingworth watched my emotion with great pleasure as his locum, a somewhat harassed-looking young man with fair hair, came scurrying up.

"Ah," said Cullingworth, "here is Baynes, who spends far too much time at the gaming table. Baynes, this is Dr. Doyle come to join us. Waiting rooms full?"

"A hundred and forty, sir," said Baynes pointing a delicate hand, "and the stable's full too. There's just some room in the coach house."

Cullingworth turned to me. "I'm sorry we haven't got a crowded day for you, Doyle."

"So is there a shortage of doctors?" I asked in amazement as we entered the crowded hallway.

"A shortage," cried Cullingworth. "By the devil, the streets are blocked with them. You couldn't fall out of a window in this town without killing a doctor."

All around us patients were milling frantically, though many of them looked so poor and wretched I wondered how they could ever afford a doctor. There was a ragged queue pressed against the wall, where a large sign read:

FREE CONSULTATIONS BUT PAY FOR YOUR MEDICINE

Here, it seemed was the attraction of the practice, for people were pointing to it and chattering, while one man, who had evidently waited for a glimpse of the doctor, shouted, "You promise to give free consultation, Doctor?"

Cullingworth ignored him and everyone else, pushing his way down a large, overcrowded corridor. "Pooh," he said taking out his handkerchief, "what an atmosphere. Can you not open the windows? I never saw such folk. Not one with the sense to open the window to save himself from suffocation."

"But there's a screw through the sash, sir," protested a lanky individual with a bushy beard and torn trousers.

"Ah, laddie," said Cullingworth striding over to it, "but you'll never get on in the world if you can't open a window without raising a sash. Look!" And he grabbed a man's umbrella and smashed it through two panes of glass. "There," he went on. "Baynes, talk to someone about taking the screw out. Now, Doyle, let's get to work."

He led me to a consulting room which was smaller than his own. "Sorry to give you the smaller, laddie, but it will do for now. You have surgery, which is not, I fear, of great importance and you won't see many patients. I prescribe, which is where our fortune is made. You have a lot to learn." He went to the window and looked out happily at the throng of patients in his courtyard. Then he turned back and fixed his eye on me. "Two rules on patients. Never let them see you want them and don't be polite. Break them in early and keep them to heel. Here!"

With that he sprang to the door and bellowed out into the house, "*Stop all this confounded jabbering down there*! I might as well be living in a poultry house. Form an orderly line and I will begin my consultations shortly."

"But do you not offend them?" I asked in astonishment.

"Of course I do and offence, laddie, is the finest advertisement in the world. Put a high price on yourself and they assume genius. I tell you, when I go to Harley Street

I shall see patients from midnight to two in the morning and charge bald-headed people double."

Now, at last, I began to grasp the true reason for his telegram. What should have given the game away was the phrase "No more debts." Cullingworth did not really need my assistance at all. There were plenty of men like Baynes to assist him for a paltry sum if he needed them. But he was still deeply ashamed that I had once encountered him when he was in debt and wanted to trumpet his success to me. I had been summoned here purely to feed the man's vanity.

It was not, indeed, long before I concluded that all Cullingworth's negative qualities, so familiar from our student days, had been magnified a hundredfold, while the only tolerable one, loyalty, had all but gone. He had, in short, turned into the most conceited, inquisitive, domineering, competitive, boastful and generally infuriating individual I had ever encountered. And as for his highly lucrative practice, of which I was now a part, it was run like a weird combination of brothel and circus.

Cullingworth had, as he said, appointed me as the surgeon, which in fact meant I had very little to do, for surgery was the last thing his clientele demanded. All the money was made from prescriptions, which were handed out from the neat little dispensary at the end of the corridor by his pretty assistant Hettie. My first impression of this space was a mass of glasses and jars. But then I saw the piles of gleaming coins and knew I had reached the heart of this little goldmine.

Once they were lured by the promise of a free consultation, even his poorest patients could evidently be persuaded to buy the medicines he prescribed. And, of course, Cullingworth's own patent medicines came top of the list. Tonics were the speciality of his house. There were tonics for excessive tea drinking, tonics for poor

circulation, tonics for choleric disposition, tonics for stiff-
ness of the joints; nerve tonic, bowel tonic, iron tonic,
every kind of tonic. I could have endured this, I suppose,
if his patients had been rich, but it was obvious they were
not. And so, predictably enough, it was Cullingworth's
zeal for tonic that caused the first quarrel between us, one
which had a bearing on all that followed.

The incident occurred late on my very first day, when I
had very little to do and was standing at the door to my
room. The queue of patients outside Cullingworth's door
was thinning because it was late. Inside, I could hear him
talking earnestly to an old woman. "The way is to drink
less tea," he was saying. "You suffer from tea poisoning
and here are two prescriptions for my own patents. A
shilling each, but it is what you need."

At that moment I became aware of a commotion down
at the end of the corridor. Someone was shouting and a
woman screamed. I rushed along to find that a man of
about forty with crutches and a wide, livid scar on his
neck, had fainted dead away.

"He has been in the campaigns, sir," said a stout man
as I loosened the poor fellow's collar. "Had a bayonet in
his neck from the look of it."

That winter, the streets were full of soldiers who been
maimed in the terrible war against the Boers in Africa and
this man's wounds were as bad as any I had seen. I managed to prop his head up a little and checked his pulse,
finding that it was steady if a little weak. Then his eyes
opened and he looked at me. "When did you last eat?" I
asked.

"I had nothing today or yesterday, sir. I was saving for
the doctor's prescription. For the tonic."

I had already heard enough about tonic to last me a

lifetime and the thought of this poor old soldier depriving himself of food in order to purchase it made my blood boil.

"Use your money to buy soup, bread and a bit of meat," I said. "You need it more than any tonic. If your war pension leaves anything spare at the end of the week, then return but never put it ahead of food. One of these people must help you home."

The man was walked out and I went back down the corridor to find Cullingworth himself blocking my way.

"What in heaven's name are you doing, laddie?" he said. "If you have nothing better to do than turn away my patients, we part company now. I told you how we make our money here. The prescriptions are the bedrock of the practice." A furious row followed, and a little later he angrily insisted on marching me through the town streets, carrying a great bag of coins that his patients had delivered and jingling it loudly as he passed the other doctors' houses.

I do not, however, want to give the impression that Cullingworth and I were estranged from the first. Being lonely and poor I was, initially, in no position to take the moral high ground, and was grateful enough for his company and the employment he offered. I had noticed, too, that in his treatment of patients, despite the endless prescribing, he sometimes showed great perspicacity and I still believe he had amazing intuition. On these early evenings, after our work was finished, we would drink brandy by his ample fireside, talking about every subject under the sun including even detection, though of course I never revealed my own experience.

I recall he also took a particular interest in the book I happened to be reading, which was Mary Godwin's *Frankenstein or the Modern Prometheus*. "That story," he observed, "is an astonishing achievement." He went on to a bombastic lecture about its qualities.

I admired the book, but a part of me wanted to take air out of his balloon. "Still," I replied, "in places its science is palpably absurd. The narrator talks of anatomy, yet there is hardly any here. The only hint of it is his collection of bones from charnel houses to build a being of gigantic stature. He claims this will make his task easier. But *why* in the world would it be *easier* to create a giant than an ordinary man? I am utterly baffled how the thing could stand on its skeletal legs at all, let alone walk or breathe!"

Cullingworth leapt to his feet in excitement as he saw the point. "You mean it would collapse under its own weight?"

"Certainly." I warmed to my theme. "And there is worse to follow. This man reaches the end of his labour, succeeds in his experiment and, just at the pinnacle of success, *while his creation is being born*, what does he do? I will tell you. He has second thoughts, abandons his experiment and takes to his bed! No scientist who ever lived could or would do such a thing." I slapped the book down, feeling pleased with my analysis, which I could see had made my host rather uncomfortable for he hated to be outdone at anything.

He paced up and down, frowning. "But even so," he came back at last. "The idea of creating something that has a life of its own, even after you have finished with it, which takes on its own shape and form. What he calls 'the workshop of filthy creation.' That is power, Doyle. One day, I tell you, I will write such a novel that when they read the first chapter the folk will start a riot until the second comes out. Soon they will be in rows around my door fighting the patients in their hope of hearing what is coming."

And, happy to have regained the initiative, if only with more boasts, he proceeded to lecture me on his intention to create his own form of drama. I gathered this would embrace people from life rather than actors, but the details were hard to follow and I found myself staring round at his study's bizarre furnishings. Beyond the furniture was a large space, which seemed to contain a bewildering mass of billiard cues, packing cases, pistols, rifles and cartridges, as well as what looked like an electric battery and a large magnet. The walls at this end were pocked with bullet marks.

With his usual acumen, Cullingworth saw my interest. "You wish to know what it is?" he demanded. "Then I will show you. You are looking at my magnetic ship protector."

I assumed he must be joking. Of course, I should have known better. "I will demonstrate it," he said as Hettie appeared through the door with some fresh brandy and water. "I am taking the thing up with the admiralty in a week or two." And he sprang to his feet and went over to the magnet. I followed him.

"Hettie, come here," he called. "You will help me to show Dr. Doyle?"

"Why, yes, sir, of course," she said, smiling prettily.

He picked up the magnet and, to my amazement, pulled Hettie's head towards him and started fiddling with her bonnet and hair. "What I will do," he said, with more excitement than I liked, "is to put this in Hettie's hair here. And fire six rounds straight into her face. How's that for a test? You wouldn't mind, Hettie, eh?"

The girl went a little pale, but she smiled and nodded submissively.

Quickly I snatched it away. "No," I said. "I will be the guinea pig."

Cullingworth looked a little peeved, but he could hardly insist. "Oh, very well," he said. "But it's perfectly safe with steel bullets. I'll use the pistol. Hettie, you may go."

Hettie left us, looking relieved. I held that magnet as far away from me as I possibly could and he aimed the pistol. "See," he said. "I aim at your finger and you will find I do not hit it. The magnet will take the dart. When the ships are protected with my apparatus, why nobody will be able to hit them for a farthing! See?"

He fired and the magnet went flying "There!" he shouted triumphantly. "Plumb in the middle, eh?"

"On the contrary," I said. "You never hit it at all."

"Never hit it? I must have hit it."

"You did not."

"So where's the dart?"

I held up my bleeding forefinger with the dart still in it. "Here."

"My dear chap," said Cullingworth, "I must have moved. Quickly." He rushed me to the basin and used his forceps to remove the thing, bandaging me up with great care and solicitude. "My profuse apologies, Doyle. Tomorrow we will study the trajectory on the target. I must be out somewhere on my calculations." But fortunately we never did study it further. For, by the next day, Cullingworth had moved on to plans for his newspaper and a new political party.

It was a part of the odd routine of Cullingworth's strange practice that every Wednesday he abandoned his noisy flock, changed his working methods and offered *paying* consultations.

The object here was to attract a better class of patient and certainly none of the usual rabble put a nose inside the practice on that day, though it could hardly be said we saw enough people to make up for their absence. It had been on a Wednesday, while Cullingworth was away pursuing some scheme for patenting bulletproof steel, that I encountered Miss Heather Grace and a few days later that I made the visit to the road by her house. In the weeks that followed I found myself constantly hoping she would return. But for two Wednesdays running there was no sign of her.

Instead, as I waited listlessly in the corridor with little to do, I was introduced by Baynes to Cullingworth's proudest Wednesday catch, a large and evidently wealthy Spaniard with gold rings on his fingers, called Garcia. Señor Garcia grinned at me and shook my hand, and had so much trouble saying "Good morning" in English that I was surprised Cullingworth could converse with him at all. But his suit was resplendent, a velvet and lace affair with silver buttons like tiny mirrors. The man also had an odd mannerism of touching his ear lobe as he talked, though it was hard to understand much of what he said.

"The man is stuffed with money and I have made quite a friend of him," Baynes said to me after he had shown Garcia into Cullingworth's consulting room. "He keeps several hundred in a chest in his house just for eventuality. Why, if we lured him into a game of cards, perhaps I could come by some of it and we could turn our backs on this place for good."

After that, we went on to talk gloomily about our respective futures. Baynes, who as always was juggling a pair of gaming dice in his agile, delicate hands, told me he would have to go back to Barts and finish his training, while I saw little hope of easily obtaining another job until I had something behind me. I would have to continue here until I had saved some money.

By this time I was in truth heartily sick of life in Southsea with Cullingworth. Our night-time drinking was already a thing of the past and much of his friendliness had vanished. The quarrel over the tonic was never overtly renewed but the memory clearly rankled and he would make sly remarks about my "pauper's sense of honour." I could ignore this and I could avoid him, but I had begun to ask myself what exactly I was doing with my life. It was not as if I seemed to be making much of my medical degree. I had struggled to find a position, yet my patients were few and far between, and in the one case where I might have done some good I had behaved like an inept Don Quixote, leaving my patient more confused and demoralised than before. Little wonder she had not returned.

What was worse, a part of me felt more than ever concerned that Miss Grace did need some kind of help. I was haunted by the memory of that road and the rectory, and the fierce figure I had seen at its door. There was a sense of fear about the place. Yet, if anything, I had only added to her unhappiness.

The fact that I had so little to do made things worse, for it gave me time to indulge myself in such introspection. Looking back, I was indeed very lonely. And I could not even write home to Edinburgh, for in the sense I had once known it there was no home. My father was in an asylum and had been for some years. My mother had abandoned Edinburgh for Waller's estate in Masongill on the Yorkshire borders. She had her own cottage there, from which she wrote, but Waller ruled the whole place as his fiefdom. It was very hard to think of it as home.

And so it was that my thoughts turned back to Joseph Bell. As I have said, our meagre correspondence had faded out completely, we were estranged. Yet I often thought of him, and since leaving Edinburgh I had rarely been so much in need of a friendly letter and his advice. Moreover, I reflected, he might be interested to hear I was working with another of his old pupils. Once I had thought of it, the idea took hold. I would write to the Doctor . . .

Inevitably, perhaps, in the circumstances, the letter grew. I wrote of my lack of success abroad, I wrote of Cullingworth's practice, I wrote of various features of my current life and, of course, because I felt it would interest him, I wrote in confidence of my patient, Miss Grace, and her persistent cyclist. Also, knowing that Bell quite often came south on various matters of business, I expressed a hope that we might meet at some future date.

I sent the letter off full of anticipation and was severely disheartened when a week went by without even an acknowledgement. The doctor was a meticulous correspondent, so I wondered if he thought it better to end our acquaintance. Given my silence and our past disagreements, it would in some ways be understandable.

One afternoon, at the end of a day when once again I had seen no patients, I was seated in my consulting room deep in such gloomy thoughts, when slowly I became aware of raised voices outside in the surgery corridor. At first I thought one of the patients had had a seizure, except I knew the practice was almost empty. Then the door of my consulting room flew open and Cullingworth burst in. His face was flushed red and he had a letter in his hand.

"Not only do I regard it as a breach of etiquette," he was shouting. "It is a breach of hospitality! And worse, of friendship!"

"What breach?" I stood in surprise.

He brandished the thing in front of me. "I bring you in, Doyle. I entrust you with my practice, my household and even show you my magnetic ship protector. In return you whine on about ethics to anyone who will listen, run your work like a charity and now you steal my patients."

"Steal?" I asked, baffled.

He was so angry it was hard to follow him, but his

next outpouring at least gave me the writer of the letter. "What the deuce is this about you helping Miss Grace with her mad problems? Is this more of the detective babble you spoke of one night? Why, you would no more make a detective than an egg-laying hen."

"But I merely helped her in a small matter . . ." Of course I knew Cullingworth's whims, but I was still at a loss to understand this outburst.

He was shaking the letter in his fury. "And now she says she wishes you to have exclusive claim as her practitioner. She was always a liar and a trull! Why, she was once in an asylum!"

I understood at once, now, and my pleasure in the contents of the letter was matched by my anger at such vicious insults. "I know, Cullingworth," I said, my fury making me speak slowly and distinctly, "that this practice is run on exploitation and greed. But I scarcely realised it also attacked and dishonoured its patients."

His face became even redder. "Now you question my honour!" He dived for a cupboard where some sporting equipment had been stored and grasped two pairs of boxing gloves. "Then I will fight three rounds with you here and now."

"No. This is tomfoolery." He seemed to have taken leave of his senses.

But he pulled the gloves on himself and squared up to me. "Come on."

I would have none of it. Cullingworth taunted me, however. He moved round me, whirling his arms, still roaring, and landed a punch on my shoulder, then one much harder on my solar plexus.

"It is absurd," I said, putting up my hands to calm him. But this only goaded him to further fury.

He swung savagely at my head, landing a blow that knocked me back on my feet. I saw the idiocy of it all, but I was past caring now myself and another punch almost cut my eye. That was enough. I was not going to let him use me as a punchbag, so I pulled on the gloves, squaring up to him.

He smiled at this, but not for long. I feinted with my left, landed one hard on his head and then jabbed another squarely under his chin, which sent him reeling back; indeed, he almost fell to the ground.

As fate would have it, this was just the moment that Baynes looked in and grinned broadly to see his employer nearly on the ropes. Cullingworth ran over to the door in a fury and slammed it in his face. Then he turned back to me and, seeing I was fully prepared to dish out more, he changed tack.

"No, you refuse, you will not fight? Well, so be it, but I will not stand by while you let this practice go to the devil. We part company here and now, laddie. And if you think yourself so high-minded a doctor, then you may take your chances on your own."

"Once you pay me for my services, I will certainly try," I replied.

"I will give you more than I owe," he said. "Only in rent."

"In rent?" I was not sure what he meant and, rather ominously, I noticed his good humour was returning.

"Yes," he continued. "I already have a town house earmarked for the expansion of my practice. I will pay your rent for a year, which is more than I owe you. The sale room will give you credit for a desk and a couch, and the chemist for drugs. You may box foul, but let us see who does best as a doctor. We will discover how you fare with your milk-and-water tactics soon enough, laddie."

With that he clapped me on the back, for all the world as if we were the best of friends again, and summoned me for a brandy that would seal the end of our association.

Of course, his sudden generosity could not be taken at face value. He had an agenda of his own. But over the years I have come to believe there was more to it than that. I think, thanks perhaps to his odd intuition, he sensed something of what lay ahead for me and it gave him pleasure.

THE SOLITARY CYCLIST

And so it was that a few days later I stood somewhat aghast in the hall of a large town house that now counted as my own. Everywhere was silent and deserted. I was the occupier of a property in a pleasant road and yet there was not a stick of furniture in the whole place. After a night on a bare bedroom floor, I spent hours renting the meagre furniture I could afford and the best of it had to go into making a credible consulting room. I struggled to pull in a desk, two chairs, a table and a cabinet. Soon it was the only properly furnished room in the whole place, though I tried to make two bedrooms habitable for I reasoned I would be of little use to patients without sleep. Some hours later, in the dead of night, I mounted my plaque outside the wall.

Next day, a Tuesday, I arranged my credit with the druggist, asking him to put word around and optimistically awaited my first patient. After a time I stood nervously at an upstairs window, counting the few pence I had left in the world and watched the street. A few passers-by saw the plaque but seemed to make nothing of it. Soon it was past one and my pride began to drain away. I was wondering what I had let myself in for.

On Wednesday and Thursday I spent my time watching from the window or walking through the town in the vain hope of seeing some kind of accident. By Friday I was beginning to realise that, while my old employer had not succeeded in beating me at boxing, he had certainly set me up for a fall. It was not as if I could even have upped sticks and gone back to Edinburgh. For now I owed money, which I did not have, to the chemist and the sale room.

But at least one matter diverted me. On the first evening after I left Cullingworth I wrote to Miss Grace, explaining that although my circumstances had changed I would be more than grateful to attend her as my patient in my own premises. There was no reply by the Friday but even so I had decided to occupy the useless time I had at my disposal that weekend by a further attempt to help her and perhaps solve her puzzle.

With no prospect of borrowing Cullingworth's bicycle on this occasion I had to walk and so I did, for thirteen miles that bright Saturday. Fortunately I knew Miss Grace was likely to cycle the road for she had given me a full account of her weekly journeys. Her uncle was very particular about his Sunday fare and various fresh items were always collected from a nearby farm late on a Saturday. So, unlike before, this would enable me to watch her outward journey on the road as well as her return home.

I had also made up my mind that she would only learn about my weekend expedition when I had something concrete to report. If she was suffering from some form of hysteria, I had no intention of aggravating her condition by announcing another failure. So I took up my position early on that Saturday afternoon with some care. I reached the start of the lonely stretch of moorland road some time after two, and arranged myself behind a broad bank that was covered in grass and bracken. With a long wait ahead of me, I whiled away the time by trying to recall Bell's precepts for the task ahead. The Doctor had Four Stages of Detection he would always intone: Investigation, Observation, Deduction, Conclusion. Of course, a part of me feared there might be nothing at all to observe on this occasion, but I was still resolved to follow the precepts as carefully as I could.

Far away to my right I could just see the gibbet and, as I stared, I almost fancied I saw a grey shape swaying in the breeze below it, but I knew perfectly well it must only be a branch. Then I became aware of some movement beyond the shape. Only a blurred outline, but it was growing in size and soon I could quite distinctly make out Miss Grace cycling furiously towards me along the road.

I watched her intently but could observe absolutely no sign of anyone else. This made it all the more vital she did not see me, so I crouched down very low to be sure I was invisible. Now I could only watch the road directly ahead of me and within a few moments she came into view, looking straight ahead, pedalling fiercely. Her appearance shocked me. She was pale and frightened, utterly rigid in the saddle, all her features tense. She seemed determined to keep going at all costs and I found the spectacle thoroughly unnerving. There was nobody else on the road. She was obviously fleeing from some phantom of her mind. How was I to tell her this?

After she flashed past, I lay there with a heavy heart. But just as I started to get up in order to watch her disappear round the bend of the road, there came a noise like rasping breath. A shape loomed up directly in front of me. It was on a bicycle and crouched very low as it rode, but it was travelling fast, so fast, indeed, that the head seemed a mere blur, yet there was a horrible intensity about its posture. It reminded me of some quivering insect closing on its prey. Then it was gone.

I had no scruples about showing myself now and leapt to my feet. Miss Grace had turned the corner but the figure was still visible and I ran into the road after it with a shout, cursing the fact that I had no bicycle of my own.

I do not know if I was heard, but it seemed to ride faster. I always had speed on the rugby pitch and now I set a pace as fast as I could. Not fast enough, for the shape reached the corner of the road. I was there a few moments later and turned. Stopping in amazement, gasping for air, my heart pounding. Far ahead of me in the distance I could see Miss Grace and the outline of the farm that was her destination. But that was all. The mysterious pursuer had vanished. There was not a sign of it anywhere.

Naturally, I examined the ground for tyre marks and hunted all around the edge of the wood. But it would have been hard and slow (and noisy) work to push the machine through these thickets and surely impossible to avoid a broad trail. I searched every inch of ground the cyclist could possibly have reached. Eventually I had to accept it was quite gone. Worse, there was not the slightest evidence that it had been here at all.

After a time I abandoned these futile endeavours and took up my position to watch Miss Grace's return journey. I waited patiently, crouched low in the same spot. But this time, though I waited and looked, there was nobody behind her and she seemed to know it, for she was no longer rigid but more relaxed. I watched as she reached the rectory drive quite safely. Then I turned to walk back to the town, feeling that I had fulfilled at least one small objective in my new practice.

Naturally I hoped for some letter from Miss Grace on the Monday, but none came. This saddened me because I longed to communicate what I had seen and did not think the subject was suited to a letter. If the figure I had observed never approached her, I could not suppose she was in any immediate danger but the affair was still very curious. If necessary I could visit her but it would be infinitely preferable to discuss it in private and so I decided to wait, contenting myself with another letter to Bell, though I was now sure he had given up on me. Perhaps, I thought, gloomily reflecting on my current unpopularity, Miss Grace had decided to reappoint Cullingworth as her doctor, for he would certainly have done everything in his power to ensure it, including blackening my name. If she chose not to follow me to the new practice or have any further dealings with me I would never see her again and there was nothing whatsoever I could do about it.

On Monday and Tuesday of the following week I sat staring out of my upstairs window again, willing a single patient to ring my bell. Nobody did. My funds were running extremely low, indeed I was living largely on a stale loaf I had purchased when I moved in and a few ounces of bacon cooked over my gas lamp. But at last, when I had reached Wednesday and thought I would go mad if nothing happened, the postman called. For the most part he carried bills, but there was another letter among them. I was to have one patient at least and it was the one I wanted.

At first she sat opposite me in my consulting room, rather gravely discussing her eye condition. She was wearing an olive-grey woollen dress with a purple velvet ribbon at its neckline and, as she talked more intensely, she would put up a hand to lift her hair from the nape of her neck in a way that was very affecting, for there was something so gentle and unknowing about the action. But once I told her of my discovery and what I had seen on the road behind her, the transformation was quite startling. She smiled, a wondrous smile, and pressed me for more and more details. "It is a miracle," she said. "You saw it too! You know what I feared?"

I had been longing for this moment and was eager to offer reassurance. "You need fear it no more for I swear you are not imagining things and it certainly has nothing to do with your eye trouble. He was there exactly as you described. Hard to make out but the man is perfectly human."

She leant forward and her eyes reminded me of a child with the longed-for present on Christmas morning. "It is just such a relief to know I am not mad. Believe me, Dr. Doyle, I consider myself to be a modern woman. And it is awful to doubt yourself. But who could he be?"

"I have hopes we will discover. I am glad you say he does not come after you if you stop, but even so I will do my best to find out more. You are sure you do not recognise him?"

"No," she said with such speed that I was taken aback and some of her merriment left her. There was a long pause. "But it is certainly true he makes me think of someone."

"Someone you know?"

I could see her visibly tense at the question. "Someone dead. I don't wish to talk of it. I am sorry. I suppose we all have things we do not care to remember."

"And cannot forget." My words had slipped out almost unintentionally. She looked at me sharply. "Yes, certainly," I went on, hoping to smooth over the moment, "it is common enough to all of us. You said you had bad dreams?"

"Yes, though I rarely talk of it. The truth is I have not spoken of these matters to anyone. I suppose I should be able to tell Mr. Greenwell. He knows I have seen someone following, though not more."

"Mr. Greenwell?"

"He is a local schoolteacher who has asked me to marry him."

"And you accepted?"

"No. I have told him that I wished to consider. You see," she said with a slight hesitation, "I was engaged before to someone who asked to be released from his obligation. And so I am cautious."

I could only nod, any comment would have seemed superfluous. But her tone changed. "Dr. Doyle," she said. "When we first met, we discussed my loss. And you seemed to be talking—forgive me if this is forward—as if from experience. Are your parents living?"

Her tone was so sweet and brave that I felt compelled to offer some answer. "Yes, they are," I said. "But someone . . . like you I never speak of it. Someone I cared for a great deal died."

"How?" she asked.

"It was a crime." I had no intention of saying any more.

"It is why I feel I can talk to you," she said and we left the subject.

Later I established she had not in fact seen the cyclist for a few days, so it was even possible he had been scared away by my intervention. As our interview came to a close, I told her I would hire a retinoscope to try to discover what lay at the root of her eye condition. I was just reflecting rather guiltily that little of our conversation had been in any strict sense medical at all when she demanded that I send her a bill for the consultation.

"You are generous, Miss Grace," I came back rather

quickly, "but I cannot possibly accept a fee for merely conversing. You will have your bill only when I have procured the retinoscope and made an eye examination."

She looked at me with concern. "I am grateful," she replied at last. "But you must be aware of one thing. Without connections of some kind, this town is not open-minded. Dr. Cullingworth is not to be relied on. I very much hope and pray you have the resources to carry on for some months until you are accepted."

How could I tell her the truth? That I doubted my ability to last another fortnight. By then bills would be due and I had nothing whatsoever left over with which to pay them. However, I merely thanked her with what I hoped was a confident smile and ushered her from the room.

THE LOCUM'S SECRET

I woke abruptly the following morning from a dream in which I chased a figure like Miss Grace's cyclist along a dank path covered in undergrowth.

Something was standing over my mattress.

I started; for one moment I could have sworn it was the creature of my dream. It spoke my name and gradually I made out Baynes, the young locum from Cullingworth's practice. He looked fearful. Dishevelled and pale, and visibly trembling.

"Baynes?" I said, sitting up in alarm. "What is the matter? How did you get in?"

"I am sorry to disturb you." He said, twisting his long-fingered hands in agitation. "There was a window open and I climbed through. I am in terrible trouble and I recall Cullingworth saying you talked to him of detection. I need your help."

I was fully awake now. Had he been robbed? But he shook his head and said I must come with him at once.

Reflecting that I could probably be more help to Baynes than to my non-existent patients, I agreed. But he still refused to tell me what had happened, saying it would be better to show me.

After I got dressed, he would still say nothing but indicated we had to do some walking. Outside, as we left the house, the prospect was not at all cheerful. There was a thin drizzle and the streets were only just getting light. I tried to ask more questions but he moved ahead of me, saying nothing. We turned north and walked through a good many streets where people were starting to go about their business until we reached the outskirts of the town. Baynes's steps were becoming faster and more urgent as we climbed a steep hill. At the top he stopped.

In front of us was a large and rather forbidding modern house in its own grounds. It had an ugly turret and was exactly the kind of building favoured by those who make their money quickly and wish to flaunt it.

I turned to Baynes, who stood staring at the house as if it held some unknown terror for him. "Who lives here?" I asked.

"It belongs to Señor Garcia, that wealthy patient," said Baynes. "He asked me here three days ago for dinner and cards."

"So what of it? Is he the cause of your problems?" I was curious but also irritated with his reticence, for I was well aware I had enough worries of my own without taking on his.

"I do not know," he said bleakly. "Oh, I do not know, Doyle, but if you come with me I will show you."

We walked up the gravel drive. The place looked quiet. Baynes rang the bell. "Will he tell us what has happened?" I asked.

"Oh," said Baynes distractedly, "if he answers the door, all my worries are over *but he will not answer it*!"

His tone disconcerted me and indeed, nobody came in answer to the bell. Baynes looked at me, then pushed open the door. It was not locked. I was becoming impatient, but I followed him into the hallway. "We will be had up for trespassing," I said, "and I still cannot fathom your problem. You came here for dinner and from what you say you had dinner. What is there in that?"

Baynes turned to me, evidently unnerved by the eerie stillness of the place. "Firstly he has not been seen since. He broke an appointment with Dr. Cullingworth yesterday."

"Good. He has probably found a better doctor."

"But it is not merely that. His manner was odd throughout the evening and he invited me to stay the night, but when I woke up he had gone."

"You say his manner was odd? In what way?"

"He was behaving strangely, agitated. He was not very sociable. He ate little dinner though there was plenty and kept leaving the table. He would not even play; he said he felt discomposed. I told him there was no need for me to stay the night but he insisted."

"And you last saw him in the morning?"

"No," said Baynes. "We said goodnight normally enough. I was shown to a comfortable room. But I woke up at daylight with a terrible feeling that something was wrong. I rang the bell by my bed, nobody appeared. I got up. And the house was just like it is now. There was nobody here at all. No servants, nobody. All the bedrooms were empty. Come in here, it is where we dined."

I had not been very impressed by Baynes's rambling story. But now he led me into a large room off the hall and my mood changed. For the place was a remarkable sight. We were in a grand formal dining room with dark-blue flock wallpaper and long, still-curtained windows. The house was ill-ventilated and the last few days had been mild, so the atmosphere was warm and very stuffy. The table appeared to have been set for a sumptuous and lavish meal, but it showed every sign of having been suddenly abandoned. Everywhere were plates of mouldy food, the candles were gutted and right in the middle a huge side of mutton was adorned by buzzing insects. It looked as if the whole room had been left untouched since Baynes was here three days earlier.

Until we entered this place, I had assumed the matter worrying Baynes must be trivial. Perhaps he had been accused of cheating at cards and would be admonished by his wealthy host. Or there had been some kind of drunken quarrel. But now I sensed a real mystery.

"You see, Doyle?" said Baynes, observing my reaction. "Nobody has been back here. We left this table suddenly and I went to bed, for my host said he had urgent business. In the morning I came down here and it was just as now."

I examined the food, which was beginning to smell foul. "Well, perhaps there was a telegram," I suggested. "He was called away urgently."

"And the servants? Where are they? None of the beds had even been slept in. The whole house was deserted."

"What about the kitchen?"

Baynes indicated a door, and I went through it and down a short corridor. We entered a shadowy room, which was messy and somewhat disgusting with many unwashed pots and dishes. Here again it was warm and insects had gathered on rotting food. I stared down at a plate of mouldy curds and another of what I took to be leftover jam omelette.

My eye fell on a zinc pail beside the table that was half open. I went over and removed the lid. There was a congealed crimson mush in the pail and I knew its sickly smell at once.

"But this is blood!" I said.

Then I saw that there were more stains on the floor. It was as if someone had used the pail for washing. I looked back at Baynes who was cowering away by the door. Until this moment I had trusted him. Now the first terrible doubts emerged.

"Baynes, I am sorry but I have to ask you." I moved over to him, avoiding getting the blood on my shoes. "You spoke once about cheating or robbing this man. They say you have gambling debts. Have you carried out your plan?"

Baynes kept looking over at the blood; he could not keep his eyes off it. "I swear I did not, Doyle. I am telling the truth. You must believe me."

His expression was pitiable yet I was hardly satisfied. "But this was three days ago. Why did you wait and what brought you to my house today?"

"I was worried." He forced himself to look at me. "But I tried to put it out of my mind. I hoped Garcia would arrive yesterday for his appointment and explain. But he did not appear and then I became more agitated, for I was sure I was being followed. I hardly slept last night and this morning decided I had to get help from someone. I had no hope of Cullingworth. You were the only one I could . . ."

He would have gone on but I put up a hand to stop him. For heard a noise in the corridor and then footsteps. There was hardly time to move away from the door before it was flung open and a tall man with a long face and a military bearing stood there and stared at us.

"You are John Baynes?" said the man with his eyes fixed on my companion. Behind him I could now see a uniformed policeman.

Baynes was so nervous it was all he could do to nod.

"Detective Inspector Warner." I would ask you both to come with me," said the man gravely. He led us to a small room near the front door. It was evidently a study but in the middle of it on the floor was a large black metal strongbox, whose lid had been forced. Baynes looked at this in horror.

Warner watched him. "Three nights ago a neighbour heard voices raised in this house," he said. "We did not take it seriously at the time, but we have had more reports since, so yesterday morning we made an investigation. This box had been pushed into a cupboard but it evidently contained money. We also found a note of Mr. Baynes's name and address, which referred to a dinner engagement three nights ago. Rather than question you, I decided it might be preferable to watch your movements for a day and I think I am proved right."

"My friend here was merely a dinner guest," I protested. "He is a respectable doctor working in a medical practice."

"He is a struggling locum, sir, with gambling debts."

"I will vouch for the fact he has nothing to do with it," I insisted. "Why would he come back here if he did?"

"I swear to you," said Baynes, who was pale and shaking, "I had nothing to do with this."

The Inspector ignored him and addressed me. "He came back here because there was more to do. And he may have enlisted you in his scheme. This was concealed hurriedly enough and it so happens we made another find only a short time ago. I can assure you we would have come to you, Mr. Baynes, if you had not come to us. Will you follow me?" He pushed past us out of the room.

At the front of the house was a large and not particularly well-kept garden with a lawn and poorly stocked borders. Inspector Warner escorted us to the bottom of it and on the way he questioned me, dwelling with discomforting eagerness on the fact that I had virtually no patients. Policemen were digging under an ash tree by the wall at the end of the grounds. The work had evidently been going on for a while but it was not visible from the house. Something was covered by a sheet and I recall a thrush sang inappropriately from the tree above our heads. Warner nodded and the sheet was removed.

I had not remotely anticipated what was underneath. The corpse's lower body was partially covered in wet earth but no earth obscured what was left of its head, which was little more than a pulpy mass of blood and tissue. His skull was completely caved in. But I easily recognised that expensive velvet suit and the rings on the hand. It was Garcia.

THE DESPERATE DOCTOR

And so it was that I became acquainted with the dreary interior of a south-coast police station.

In my memory, now, the Garcia affair demands attention partly for its oddity, partly for my direct involvement and also, like the business with the watch, for the insight it showed into the "method." If I had been less engaged, perhaps I would have been able to see that the matter's curious features masked an essential simplicity. But there was one aspect of it which did make a lasting and profound impression: namely the degrading interrogation that came now. The police questioned Baynes and me entirely separately that day. I was in a small room with a desk and chairs, and very little else other than my two interrogators.

These men took gross pleasure in exposing an entirely imaginary corruption. Once they had discovered my practice was near the docks, they assumed at once I was using it for immoral purposes and their tone alternated between an icy contempt, which was bad enough, and a leering innuendo, which was worse. One of them asked repeatedly how many women I employed and whether I ever caught disease from "eating my own apples." Another, who was younger with bright-red cheeks, disparaged my family history (though he knew nothing of it and just as well) and asked if I helped my female "patients" with a powder when they were "inconvenienced." Perhaps their approach was better than the blatant hypocrisy I had witnessed in Edinburgh. But even so, they awoke memories I would rather forget.

There was, however, one curiosity that emerged from the interview. A letter had been found on the dead man from Baynes, accepting his invitation to dinner. This was bad for Baynes, but it was not all. In the corpse's pocket there was a white sheet of foolscap, blank on one side but with a series of numbers on the other. The policeman passed it across to me with a sour look for it was obvious they could not make head or tail of it. I reproduce it here exactly as it was, for I still possess it.

Garcia's document

5 9 13 17 8 16 12 8 7 5 2 11 11 3 7 13 20 5 14 8 10 3 6 6 5 14 21 4 2 7 11
12 12 13 20 8 10 2 14 11 7 5 20 8 15 11 12 5 16 15 7 13 17 13 19 2 7 11
12 8 8 15 5 22 5 10 13 11 5 2 14 2 19 13 6 6 10 2 14 10 8 7 14 8 15 13
14 15 18 13 7 11 5 10 3 6 13 7 6 1 11 2 13 15 20 13 14 10 8 17 1 10 6 13
5 17 11 2 12 13 20 8 10 7 8 13 11 8 15 13 14 8 14 11 5 7 8 6 1 14 8 4 19
2 7 17 2 19 15 7 13 17 13 4 12 5 10 12 4 5 6 6 5 14 19 2 6 19 8 7 8 13 6
18 8 2 18 8 13 14 15 7 8 13 6 16 5 11 3 13 11 5 2 14 16 11 12 8 11 12 5
14 20 16 12 2 3 6 15 12 13 20 8 13 6 5 19 8 2 19 5 11 16 2 4 14 9 3 16 11
13 16 12 8 10 7 8 13 11 5 2 14 15 2 8 16 5 14 17 1 5 14 16 18 5 7 13 11 5
2 14 4 12 5 10 12 5 16 17 13 7 1 4 2 6 6 16 11 2 14 8 10 7 13 19 2 11 16
8 2 5 10 8 18 11 5 2 14 13 6 17 13 14 3 16 10 7 5 18 11 2 19 1 8 1 8 19 7
13 14 23 8 14 16 11 8 5 14 2 7 11 12 8 17 2 15 8 7 14 18 7 2 17 8 11 12 8
3 16 5 13 17 11 12 8 7 8 22 2 7 8 3 16 5 14 20 11 12 8 22 2 2 2 23 13 16 13

23 8 1 11 2 11 12 5 16 10 5 18 12 8 7 11 12 2 3 20 12 5 16 3 16 18 8 10

11 14 2 21 2 15 1 13 14 15 10 8 7 11 13 5 14 6 1 14 2 11 15 2 1 6 8 4 5 6

6 21 8 10 6 8 19 8 7 8 14 2 3 21 12 11 2 15 5 16 8 14 11 13 14 21 6 8 5

11 5 19 11 12 8 1 13 7 8 11 12 8 14 2 19 10 2 3 7 16 8 5 11 13 23 8 11 12

8 10 7 8 15 5 11 5 22 14 2 11 5 19 8 13 7 11 12 8 18 6 13 1 8 7 16 4 5 5

6 6 12 13 19 8 11 2 8 14 15 3 7 8 11 12 8 17 3 11 13 11 5 15 17 3 11 13

14 15 5 16 5 4 5 6 3 16 8 11 12 5 16 10 5 18 12 8 7 11 2 10 2 17 17 3

14 5 10 13 11 8 4 5 11 12 11 12 2 16 8 18 6 13 1 8 7 16 6 5 23 8 21 13 7

10 5 13 4 12 2 5 12 13 19 8 12 5 7 8 15 21 3 11 11 12 8 1 4 5 6 6 23 14 2

4 14 2 11 12 5 14 21 2 19 5 11 16 6 13 7 21 8 7 18 3 7 18 2 10 8 2 7 5 14

15 8 8 15 2 22 11 12 5 16 14 2 11 8 11 12 8 10 2 3 18 13 11 11 12 8 10 8

14 11 7 8 2 22 5 11 5 16 2 22 10 2 3 7 16 8 13 10 2 7 18 16 8 5 12 13 20

8 22 2 3 20 12 11 24 3 5 11 8 6 8 21 13 6 6 1 22 7 2 17 5 11 16 7 5 21 12

11 19 3 6 5 14 12 8 7 5 11 2 7 17 7 16 13 14 1 13 10 13 7 6 5 14 2

6 8 11 11 12 8 18 6 13 1 10 2 17 17 8 17 10 8

I stared at these numbers in amazement. "But it is certainly a cipher or code. Surely this must prove Garcia or his murderer was involved in some subterfuge."

"It is just as likely," said one of them, "that you or your friend placed it there as a distraction. We can make nothing of it." And he returned to his questions.

After several hours, it was dark outside and Inspector Warner entered to tell me Baynes was close to confessing and had been formally arrested and charged. They had little doubt that I was implicated too, but since there was less direct evidence in my case they would allow me to go home, before they resumed their questioning in the morning. I was not surprised when, at first, Warner utterly refused to let me talk to Baynes. But I pressed my case hard. As a doctor, I told him, I wished to observe Baynes's condition. I had heard cases of men being beaten until they confessed. And, given the kind of interview I had just endured, I would not be put off.

He looked at me closely. "Perhaps you merely want to ensure he sticks to your story. I assure you, sir, I do not beat the truth out of my prisoners. But you can have five minutes with him if you wish."

They escorted me down stone stairs to Baynes in his cell. Of course, my main purpose was to speak to him and I felt rather pleased my strategy had worked. I should have realised then that it had proved suspiciously easy.

Baynes was still distraught as we whispered together through the bars. "I warn you," he told me, "heaven knows who is behind this. But I have felt someone watching me for days and you saw what they did to Garcia."

I promised him I would take every precaution and do everything in my power to help him, but one thing had to be settled. I looked round to make sure the jailer could not hear. "Baynes," I whispered, "I know it is hard for you but I must ask. Will you swear on everything you hold sacred that you had no part in this?"

"I swear it."

I replied that I believed him and it was true.

But then he looked at me with a terrible expression of anguish. "Doyle, I am so sorry to have brought this on you. You see . . . I have not told everything. Garcia and I did play a hand. He was a very poor player, among the worst I ever saw. But I won some money, quite a bit."

Of course, I was shocked by this and all my doubts flooded back. "What? But you must declare it."

"I cannot," he whispered. "They would believe the worst. You see, Doyle, he gave me a purse of money and today I thought I was being followed. And I hid it . . ."

"But where is it?" I knew the answer even as I asked.

"In your house."

• • •

At least the street outside my property was dark and quiet as I turned into it. The only thought in my head now was to obtain this purse and either destroy it or give it to the police. If they discovered it on my premises it would be too late.

My so-called practice did not seem particularly welcoming as I entered. There was a howling draft from somewhere, presumably the window which Baynes had used to climb in, but I cared little about that. I lit a candle and went at once to the spot he had mentioned, which was on the first landing. There I bent down and groped under the stair carpet, conscious of how guilty I must look. My hand connected with something and I pulled it out.

The purse was exactly as Baynes had described and I noticed with some horror that Garcia's initials were on it. The sum inside was not inconsiderable. Enough for me to clear my debts, I reflected miserably. And that thought was followed by another, which came so frighteningly quickly I was ashamed and excited. What was to stop me from flight? There was enough here to pay off any debts and I could be sure Baynes would not tell them of it. Without further evidence, would Warner bother to follow me to Edinburgh when they already had the main suspect? I think and hope I would have cast such temptations aside but I will never be quite sure for they were interrupted by a noise from above me.

It was not loud, a soft footstep. But someone was up there. I was sure it could not be the police. They would have made themselves known when I entered. Again it came, a gentle scraping noise.

A few moments later I was advancing up the stairs with my candle in one hand and a sharp knife in the other.

There was nobody on the landing, but the sound had come from a large back bedroom that led off it. For some reason I found myself thinking of that crouched figure I had seen on the bicycle. I had no logical explanation for any of this but supposing it had killed Garcia? It would mean Miss Grace was in terrible danger. And was it now in there, waiting in the dark?

Putting down the candle, I walked forward and flung open the door. It was pitch-black inside; there was no sign of anyone or anything that I could see. Holding the knife steady, I took a pace. Almost at once I felt clawlike hands around my neck. I lashed out, but the knife swished through empty air. The hands tightened brutally. I struggled desperately and they only locked harder. My senses were starting to swim but I was sure these were the hands that had killed Garcia.

With a last effort I managed to use my weight to force my opponent back towards the landing and the dim flame of the candlelight. I could see a little more now, though my vision was clouded. There was the outline of a fierce, hawklike face, gleaming eyes, a fixed jaw. To my amazement I was staring at the countenance of Dr. Bell.

He relaxed his grip, smiling. "Not the most auspicious way to welcome a guest to your home, Doyle." I was still panting for breath. "My apologies for depriving you of oxygen, but that looks like a Sheffield '81 knife. And your consulting room is not too well equipped for surgery."

"I am glad to see you," I said with feeling. Indeed, I felt a huge surge of warmth and relief at the sight of him, especially now when he was so badly needed. "But what in the name of all that is wonderful brings you here?"

"Well, another matter brought me south but I had reason to call and I have observed enough of today's business to see you have need of me. I was reflecting on it while I unpacked some things. Your table is not well stocked, I know, so I purchased a hamper, which I have been opening. Come. You look in need of sustenance. I would say you have lost nine and a half pounds since I last saw you."

In a few moments my consulting room had been converted into a dining room and we were enjoying a feast. The Doctor was as good as his word and rapidly unpacked veal and ham pie, bread, sausage, cheese and butter, not to mention some condiments and a quart of beer. I needed no encouragement and fell to with a vengeance as we sat across the consulting-room table. It seemed like weeks since I had eaten and my spirits soared.

"Yes," the Doctor was saying, "I apologise for not replying sooner. Both your letters were forwarded to me in London where I was doing some examination duty. I decided there was every reason to pay you a call and arrived early today, but there was no sign of you. So I visited your former practice where my other old pupil was full of the Garcia business. Soon I had occasion to speak to Inspector Warner about it and I regret to observe several mistakes have been made." He swallowed a mouthful of pie.

"I entirely agree," I said. "The police . . ."

". . . are extremely astute," he interrupted. "Warner may well be the most capable officer I have ever encountered."

This hardly impressed me. "But they make no headway and suspect Baynes and I were involved!" I protested.

"As well they might," he said, dabbing a morsel of pie

in some mustard. "Has it not occurred to you, Doyle, that if you were dealing with Beecher back in Edinburgh, you would have been deprived of your liberty at once, while Baynes would be on his way to the gallows? No, the Inspector is a shrewd man who, I suspect from what I have seen, plays his hand well. And if I am not very much mistaken, he is outside now. I assumed he would waste no time coming for what he seeks . . ." He spoke nonchalantly enough as he pushed his plate to one side.

I was horrified for, in my pleasure at seeing the Doctor and my delight at his provisions, I had forgotten all about the purse of money, which was still in my pocket.

But the Doctor was not mistaken, for a police cab was visible in the street, and soon there were footsteps in my passage and Warner entered, another policeman behind him.

"We wish to make a complete search, Doyle, for I know you have Garcia's money. I am not so much of a fool as to allow you to confer with a charged criminal out of hearing. The prisoner in the next cell to Baynes was instructed to eavesdrop and I am delayed only because he saw the value of what he heard and tried to bargain with us."

"Do not worry, Warner," said Bell. "Doyle will hand over the money you seek." And to my horror he put his hand out for the purse. I had no choice. I could hardly lie, for the thing bulged out of my pocket.

With some reluctance I got it out and handed it over, hoping the Doctor might save the situation for me. But he merely passed it on to Inspector Warner, who examined it with great satisfaction. "Yes, Garcia's initials are here. Excellent, Dr. Bell. This is conclusive, I think. The prisoner in the next cell did not hear as much of the conversation as I would have liked but at least he heard where the money was. I very much fear your young colleague here has played a major part."

"Undoubtedly he has," said Bell as both policemen stared at the money. And to my intense irritation he left it at that and cut himself some more pie.

THE QUESTION OF GARCIA

I suppose I should have been grateful they did not cart me off to the cells there and then. The Doctor had indicated he would guarantee my attendance when required and was on hand to see I did not abscond. This was not strictly true for he had already established himself comfortably at a local inn and left me shortly afterwards, but he knew quite well I would be there in the morning.

Subsequently I spent a wretched night, fully aware Warner believed he had an unshakeable case against me. Of course, I had been pleased to see the Doctor again but he had treated the whole matter so casually I began to wonder if he was not punishing me for my long silence.

In the morning we had arranged to meet at Cullingworth's surgery, which was as usual seething with patients, but his assistant Hettie went to find her employer, as the Doctor ran an eye over me. "You did not sleep well, I perceive." I was still irritated with the way he had behaved the previous night and the humiliation of handing over the money, and he saw as much. "I can assure you, Doyle, that concealing evidence is never a profitable pursuit. The police are not so foolish as you believe. I want to discover what we can about Garcia here and then we will go to see them."

At this moment Cullingworth appeared from the throng, smiling broadly to usher us inside. "Why, Bell, how good to see you again so soon. I am glad you are helping with this terrible Garcia business. You can certainly count on my expertise. Once, I recall, you told me I'd come on further than anyone in your class."

The Doctor smiled. "In one respect, certainly, your development was remarkable."

"Diagnosis, of course. And so I have more patients than I know what to do with as Doyle here knows! Why, man, you would not give me a few hours of your time and we will whip through my backlist together? I could offer you fifty silver for a couple of days at most." And with supreme vulgarity, as he spoke he took a fistful of silver from the little cache on his desk and ran it through his fingers.

"Oh," Bell said, "I suspect my style might not suit you."

"You are modest, but I know you are almost as quick as ever," said Cullingworth.

I could see the Doctor was controlling himself. "Yes, I find it is useful when encountering the vain and the foolish. Now I would like to see Garcia's notes."

If Cullingworth knew he was being insulted, he showed absolutely no sign of it. He went over to the cupboard, where he kept his medical notes, and produced a folder. "Normally these would be confidential," he said, "but in view of the circumstances I can make an exception. However, I would warn you there is very little to be gleaned here. I have not seen Garcia since Baynes dined with him. He had an appointment with me earlier this week and never appeared. As I think you know, I was concerned and mentioned it to Baynes."

"How did he react?"

"He seemed very worried. But I am sure my locum is innocent."

The Doctor had taken the file and was studying it. "Tell me, Dr. Cullingworth, how long had you known Señor Garcia?"

"A few months. He came to me for a skin complaint. It is all in the notes. I understand he has business interests in Argentina and was certainly of good family. But he had not been in the country for long. Did you visit his house?"

Bell did not look up from scrutinising the pages of Garcia's medical file. "Yes, I was allowed to pay a short visit this morning early. I must say I found it most informative. And I notice this man's appointments with you were always late in the day. Never before two in the afternoon."

"Why not!" answered Cullingworth with interest. "I expect he was a late riser. And there was no family here, the man was a bachelor. I have no idea if he even had any friends. So there is little help to be had from other people as you see."

"Why on earth should I need help from other people?" said Bell, closing the file impatiently, "when I intend to make his acquaintance?"

Garcia's corpse lay awkwardly on the mortuary slab, the head discreetly covered as Bell and I stared down at it. Warner was beside us, keen to make use of the doctor's medical expertise but, I knew, equally keen to continue questioning me.

An attempt had been made to clean the body below us, but there were still ugly patches of earth and exposed flesh, and I found myself recalling Mary Godwin's description of her creature and its skin that "scarcely covered the work of muscles and arteries beneath." There was, I saw, in addition a deep laceration near the subclavian artery.

Carefully, with that air of intense concentration I knew so well, Bell studied it and then slowly drew back the sheet from the head. In the cold lamplight from above, I now saw again the full horror of what had been done here. It was battered so badly that the skull itself was crushed, removing most of the face and leaving just a mess of hair and tissue.

Bell stared in wonder. "Whoever did this used great force. I have rarely seen anything so brutal."

"Then you understand why I am so anxious to get to the bottom of it," said Warner grimly. "It is certainly the most savage beating I ever saw."

Bell bent close to get a better look. "And the weapon?"

"I fear we have yet to find one, though we are still searching," Warner replied and I noted a new respect in his voice. It turned out he had made some discreet and unofficial enquiries into Dr. Bell's previous work in Edinburgh and was impressed. "I ought to say, Dr. Bell, we will be grateful for any further light you can shed on the matter."

"Thank you," the Doctor murmured without looking up. "In the strictest confidence of course."

At last Bell finished his study of the head and replaced the cloth. Then he returned to his examination of the arms. After a time he took a wet linen cloth and carefully wiped away some of the earth that still covered patches of the skin. He was rewarded for this care, leaning forward intensely to examine a mark which had appeared.

"See, Doyle," he said with excitement. "Crown of thorns."

I stared too. "A tattoo?"

"Quite a common one in Spain and South America,

but hardly among the aristocracy." Now he lifted the corpse's hands. "And these are the hands of a labourer. It seems our Garcia has concealed something of his true past. Tell me, Inspector Warner, you are sure you found no passport or papers?"

"No, sir," Warner confirmed. "The money and papers had all gone. We believe they were 'in the box that was ransacked."

"And his landlord?"

"The owner of that house never set eyes on him. The whole arrangement was done by letter. But the purse surely tells us Dr. Doyle and Baynes were involved, does it not?"

The Doctor had finished his examination and straightened up. "Yes, it does," he said. "The matter is becoming clearer."

I was angry enough to try to interrupt but he continued quite unruffled, "I would ask you to wait a day, Inspector. I believe I can be of serious help to you but I wish to go into Southampton and visit the newspaper office there. In the meantime the only condition I would ask is that you leave Dr. Doyle for the moment. I can vouch he will not abscond and he has a patient to see."

This last remark astonished me. Bell had evidently been reading my nearly blank appointments book but I was grateful for I had feared I would have to cancel Miss Grace's consultation. Inspector Warner looked a little doubtful but he was sufficiently in awe of Bell to let him have his wish. I shook the Doctor's hand more warmly before we went our separate ways.

Miss Grace appeared to have absolutely no knowledge of my predicament as she sat in my consulting room, her face dappled with sweet colour by the fading light outside as she looked at me intently. There was in truth little medical business to do until the retinoscope arrived and perhaps she saw I was a little dispirited, for she asked me if there was anything wrong.

"No," I answered. "But a friend of mine is in trouble of a kind. Though I hope it will turn out for the best."

She seemed to understand I could not say more and we left the subject. I was heartened to learn she had not seen our cyclist again, but it also transpired she was too fearful to look back so perhaps this proved nothing. And I reflected how yet again my own problems were impeding me just when I might have been of use to her. It seemed, too, that the nightmares she suffered were worse. As the interview was drawing to a close, she asked if on the next visit she might tell me about them.

I was flattered but I had no wish to be considered a charlatan, so I took some trouble to explain to her that, though it would do no harm for me to hear them, a sleeping potion might be more effective.

She shook her head. "I would like to tell you," she said. And there was something about the way she said it.

After the interview I came back from showing her out to find that the Doctor had returned from his trip to Southampton while I was seeing her and was now leafing through my *Frankenstein or the Modern Prometheus*.

"An interesting book," he said. "Though not one that reflects particularly well on our profession."

"Possibly that is why Cullingworth calls it his bible."

Bell smiled. "There is quite a sadness at the end, though," he said. "When the creature says goodbye and is borne away by the waves into the darkness and distance you feel for him. But enough of that." He put the book to one side. "Have you views on the case?"

"My views?" I replied bitterly. "My views are that the police, as always, have merely picked on the nearest candidates, myself and poor Baynes. Why do they not look into the man's past, into his habits? What was he doing on the day he died? Who were his associates? The thing is a travesty!"

"In some ways," said Bell, getting up cheerfully. "And I will tell you another, which is that for a felon you keep the most abominable kitchen in the world and I was so busy in Southampton I entirely forgot to eat lunch. If you would only produce more of your ill-gotten gains, we might yet dine better."

I was exasperated by his good humour. "You may call me lacking in spirit, Doctor, but an innocent man rots in prison."

"Yet is he entirely innocent? I am not even sure you are. I will debate with you no further, however, and am even prepared to buy you dinner if you promise not to mention the case until we conclude it tomorrow."

I was greatly cheered by this. "Conclude it?" I said. "I will be in your debt if you do."

"Are you sure?" he asked as we left the house. "I doubt you will feel any gratitude if your next meal is at Her Majesty's pleasure. But now let us talk of other things, including the young lady you saw this evening. I look forward with some anticipation to hearing her account of the nightmares."

I stopped dead, more than a little irritated not just by Bell's eavesdropping but also by his typical assumption that anything I did, no matter how private, was accessible to him. "I know you favour unorthodox methods, Doctor, but that surely does not include breaking the Hippocratic oath. You cannot spy on a confidential interview. It is not only unethical, it is treating me like a child."

"Doyle," he said pacifically, "doctors often exchange case notes. What is the difference? But if that topic is barred, so be it. We will discuss *Frankenstein* or Culling-worth, or any other subject you please. I am not surprised your nerves are on edge. But I am quite sure some of the excellent local oysters will mellow them."

"THE WORKSHOP OF FILTHY CREATION"

I am slightly ashamed to say he was right. I felt in a better frame of mind as we returned to the house and, before he retired to his inn, I almost managed to forget my predicament as we pored over the strange message that had been found in Garcia's pocket.

"It is certainly a cipher," said the Doctor, "and a fixed one too. I imagine each number donates the same letter but it is more difficult than it looks. I would wager that '8' is the critical letter within it; follow that letter through, Doyle, and see what you think." He was bending forward, scrutinising the paper with enormous interest. "Yes, I might even go further and hazard that '8' stands for . . ." He frowned. "But the eleventh line is very odd indeed . . . very odd and unlike anything else."

His hand had come to rest on the numbers "1 8 1 8." "You see," said Bell, "from the frequency I would suggest the number '1' denotes a relatively uncommon letter, it occurs only five times in the whole document, '8' in contrast, is about the commonest here, it is on every single full line suggesting to me it must be 'E.' But what possible combination of letters could cause 'E' to be repeated like that with what is certainly a consonant before it?"

"It could be 'M' and 'E' as part of different words. 'Same men,' for example," I suggested.

"Yes, very good," said the Doctor and I could sense the old excitement in him. "Except note that it is bracketed on both sides by '19.' The full section is '19 1 8 1 8 19.' Now '19' is a relatively uncommon number too, a consonant certainly, and the fact it recurs here must rule out your suggestion. Let us suppose '19' is 'F,' which is the fourteenth commonest letter in the language and '1' is 'G,' which is the fifteenth commonest. In both cases these are reasonable hypotheses for their frequency in the text, but by no means certain, and I cite them merely to show you the difficulty. You have 'FGEGEF' or swopping them round 'GFEFEG,' both impossible, and at once you see the difficulties with this confounded '19 1 8 1 8 19.' Try other consonants and the same problem recurs. How on earth can an uncommon consonant denoted by '19' follow what must be another consonant and then an 'E' and repeat the same combination backwards? 'LREREL!' 'TVEVET!' 'JREREJ!' No the thing is impossible! There must be something wrong with that line."

He tossed the paper angrily to one side and stared fixedly at the desk in front of him. Suddenly his face lit up. "Good heavens!" he said, "I think you have given it to me, Doyle."

"I? How?"

"By what we talked about. But now I must think further." And he left me.

Next morning Bell had arranged to meet Inspector Warner at the Garcia house. There was a policeman at the door, who nodded to us as Bell led me inside.

Inspector Warner was in the hall and beside him was a haggard, unshaven figure I barely recognised, but

Baynes stepped forward with desperate eagerness to shake hands. He seemed enormously pleased to see me but his expression told me all was not well and I soon heard why.

"There is enough evidence for me to start formal proceedings today, at least as far as Mr. Baynes is concerned," Warner told the Doctor, who to my disgust merely nodded.

We entered the dining room, which was back to normal, the food and plates removed. Bell looked round it with interest. "And I see the room has been returned to a more acceptable state. Good, for I am now proposing to put some order into this maelstrom. Mr. Baynes, would you be so kind as to go to the postbox and bring me all the letters that have been delivered here over the past three days."

Baynes was rather surprised but he went out, escorted by a policeman. After a moment he came back with a telegram. "A cable for you, Dr. Bell. That is all."

"For you, sir?" asked Warner. "That is remarkable!" Outside in the hall the bell rang and the policeman returned alone to answer it.

"On the contrary, Inspector," said Bell. "My cable is the least remarkable thing about it."

"But I do not follow," protested Warner. "There is nothing else."

"Which is exactly what is remarkable!" Bell explained. "A busy and wealthy man of cosmopolitan affairs. He lives here and yet nobody corresponds with him? It is like everything else in this odd business. So let me come right to the point. In a case with such fantastic aspects, often the obvious suspect is the right one. Doyle and Baynes are both certainly at the heart of the matter. Indeed, I would say Doyle motivated it even more than the young locum."

I could hardly believe my ears. "Good, sir, shall I charge them both?" enquired Warner.

"Certainly," Bell agreed.

I had had enough. "Doctor!" I said, moving forward to remonstrate with him.

Bell raised a hand. "But first, Inspector," he suggested, "I would just ask you to observe one small formality and meet with me a waiter from Southampton."

"I do not follow, sir."

"Bear with me, then," said Bell. "And afterwards you may proceed as you wish." Outside there were voices and steps were coming towards the room. "Ah, may I present . . ." Bell continued as the door opened, "Señor Garcia."

Garcia entered the room. We all stared at him. It was indubitable. Rankly impossible, no doubt, but absolutely certain. The man I had met at the surgery and the man we had seen bludgeoned to death in the grave outside stood there in front of us in his expensive suit and smiled, showing his teeth and pulling his ear lobe nervously with one hand just as I remembered him.

"Quite fit, is he not?" Bell remarked. "For a man who has been dead a week."

Baynes could not restrain himself now. He rushed forward towards the man in an ecstacy of relief. "Thank heaven, oh, thank heaven. You are a wonder, Dr. Bell. Señor, you tell these men, I won the money at cards, did I not? I came here to dine with you."

Garcia smiled and nodded, then gave a deep bow. "Señor," he said in an accent so heavy it was hard to make out the words. "Señor. I understand our small matter is at an end."

"You are quite right," said Bell who was clearly enjoying himself. "Your name?"

"Hernando Gomez."

"And you are . . . ?" Bell asked.

"I am a waiter, sir, at the Majestic Café in Southampton."

"Admirable." Bell was smiling, but everyone else was still at sea.

"So this is not Garcia?" demanded Warner.

"Oh," Bell replied. "It is the man who took that role. There is no Garcia."

"But the body . . . ?" said Warner.

"A Latino seaman who suffered a gruesome accident in Southampton docks some days ago. In truth, he was not so very like our friend here, but it hardly mattered. The container that fell on his head made facial recognition out of the question and, once he was buried in the garden wearing Garcia's clothes, nobody knew him well enough to observe the bodily distinction between the two men."

"But the servants?"

"Merely hired for the evening."

"So it was a fraud," said Warner. "But you said Doyle was responsible."

"No," Bell contradicted. "I said he motivated it. And so he did, though quite inadvertently."

A voice outside in the hall shouted "Hello." It was a voice I recognised and, now that I was beginning to see the truth, I was hardly surprised to hear it.

"And if I am not very much mistaken," said Bell, "here is our perpetrator and the mysterious man who rented this house. I invited him to come."

The door opened and Cullingworth stood there. He took in Garcia and everyone else with a little surprise. But the effect on him was typically outrageous. He merely smiled as if he had been very lavishly complimented and gave a little bow. "Ah, well, so be it. You are on to me, I see."

Warner stepped forward. The policeman was desperate

for someone to hold to account and Cullingworth seemed
the best candidate so he addressed him. "Sir." He gestured
to the waiter who was still grinning fatuously. "Was this
man here your patient?"

"Not really, sir." Cullingworth looked back at Warner
without a flicker of anxiety. "He was a dupe patient. Do
you know the term?"

I did, though I had never heard of such a thing in
England. And now at last the whole matter was becoming
obvious to me and I cursed myself for not seeing through
it.

"The 'dupe patient,' " Dr. Bell was saying, "is a notorious practice originating in America where doctors,
wishing to impress the locals, will sometimes arrange fake
visits from supposedly rich and impressive patients. They
see it, however misguidedly, as an investment in their own
status."

So this was all Garcia had been! Little wonder his English was so bad. He was there merely to impress us and
the idea did not surprise me, given what I knew about
Cullingworth. Here was just another of his mad attempts
to advance himself alongside his bullet-proof armour and
his metal ship protector.

"And after Cullingworth quarrelled with Doyle here,"
said Bell, "he saw a further way of using this so called
patient for an elaborate revenge."

We were in a rough circle now, all of us staring at
Cullingworth, who seemed to take these remarks as flattery. But Warner had heard quite enough and broke out
of it striding forward to Cullingworth. "So you admit responsibility for this, sir?" he charged.

"Yes, I am honoured to accept the credit," Cullingworth conceded with a broad smile.

Warner was almost struck dumb by his insolence.
"You may also accept a sentence," he said, his lips hardly

moving, indeed everything about him was dangerously still. I thought he was about to take Cullingworth by the throat.

"I rather doubt that." Cullingworth was still entirely nonchalant. "It is true Dr. Doyle and I fell out. He questioned my honour and always made inflated claims about his skills. I said I would involve him in my new drama and prove he was hopeless as a detective. It was a kind of . . . wager . . ."

I could hardly believe my ears. "That is a complete lie," I cried. "There was no wager. He was angry with me partly because I questioned the ethics of his practice."

"Oh, yes," said Cullingworth coolly. "He failed as my assistant as well."

But Inspector Warner had begun to regain some composure. "I think you are a little optimistic, Dr. Cullingworth, in assuming you have committed no crime. I cannot arrest you for arranging a hoax, but there is a small matter of the body. I assume you have stolen it from a Southampton mortuary. That is a very serious offence."

"Indeed it is, sir," replied Cullingworth, "but not one I have committed." And he took some papers from his pocket. "The seaman's sister was quite happy to hand the body over to my custody in the interests of a dramatic scientific experiment. She was paid well. And I think we can all agree it was dramatic. Why, you see what I have done? I have brought the dead to life. It is an experiment worthy of Frankenstein himself. I could put this on the stage tomorrow and be turning people away by the thousand!"

Inspector Warner was studying the custody papers in irritation and amazement. "So there is nothing here at all, then? The blood, the strongbox?"

"They were mere props," said Bell. "Like the body itself, buried so obviously. What first alerted me was the fact that hardly anyone seemed to know Garcia. My examination of the house alone suggested the man was a cipher. And it was also curious that he never appeared at Cullingworth's before two, suggesting he was in fact coming from further away. As I suspected, the body did not entirely square with what little we did know of the man. We seemed to face an illusion and the agony column of the Southampton press proved to be the means of recruitment. It also had details of the dockside accident. I had almost all, then, and Doyle here gave me the key to the cipher, which explained the rest."

I told him I could not see how, but Inspector Warner interrupted: "So was a crime committed here or not?" he demanded of Bell.

"As things stand, it is doubtful," acknowledged the Doctor, who seemed now to be wearying of the whole affair. "That is why I was tempted to allow you to commence formal proceedings. At just that point, Cullingworth here would surely face legal action."

"No, no, gentlemen," protested Cullingworth, still every inch the smiling impresario. "This was merely a drama inspired by Mary Godwin's extraordinary novel *Frankenstein*. As in that wonderful tale, I created something with a life of its own. But I had plans to come forward today to prevent any injustice."

"I do not believe that for a moment," I said, still infuriated by the sheer trivia and time-wasting cruelty of what had turned out to be Cullingworth's so-called "drama." "And there is an injured party. Baynes has spent time in prison."

"I will gladly compensate him and I am sure he does not want to pursue the matter."

Baynes agreed, as Cullingworth knew he would. He was still euphoric about his freedom and was in any case hardly likely to challenge his employer.

"But it is perfectly clear what you intended," I pointed out, marvelling at Cullingworth's idiotic vanity, "for you said you wished the thing to take on a life of its own. So you were quite happy to see us both rot."

There was just a flicker of reaction, which made me sure I was right. But the old arrogance returned quickly enough. "I fear, laddie," he said, "your sense of humour is almost as lacking as your powers of observation. For heaven's sake, man, see the fun of the thing. It is a mere fiction played out in the arena of real life, Doyle! Enjoy it."

And he turned to leave.

THE REANIMATOR'S CODE

At least Cullingworth was required, along with the rest of us, to make a long statement to the police. I am sure Warner hoped he would find some charge to bring. But there was nothing. Cullingworth had taken care to have no dealings with the police directly so he had never lied to them. His hire of the body was a cruel liberty, but he had paid the seaman's bereaved sister over the odds through a lawyer. At every turn his money helped him to escape punishment and to my great disgust at the end of the day he walked out of that police station with a reprimand, which I am sure the man took to be a compliment.

Later Bell and I walked on the front to clear our heads. "It is just the nerve of the man," I said. "To think I once liked and trusted him. Is it true you said he was remarkable?"

"I referred only to the development of his egotism. If his medical skills had kept pace, he could have been a legend."

I stopped. We had come to a low flight of steps that gave on to the beach.

The Doctor knew quite well that, after what happened

in Edinburgh, I had always hated beaches. He turned away tactfully and we started to walk back to my house in silence. "Remember," he said very quietly after a moment. "There has been some progress, especially with regard to Chicago, though we still have a long way to go."

"I hardly call it progress," I said. But neither of us continued the discussion. Indeed, it is almost all we said of it during his stay.

There is an awful inevitability in the way one memory triggers another. As we walked back through the streets to my practice, I was powerless to stop them flooding back. Once again I saw in my mind the image of that small upstairs room. In itself that room might once have been ordinary enough but for me it has long seemed one of the most horrible in the world, my own gateway to hell. As I raced up the stairs and into it on that awful night in Edinburgh the first thing I saw was that a fire of newspapers was burning on the hearth in front of the grate. The flames sent flickering shadows dancing around the walls and added to the hellish effect of the place. The flames also picked out a glass jam jar, which lay beside the bed and contained something crimson.

A woman I had seen once before lay on the bed, which was sticky and wet with a clear yet viscous liquid that later I realised was chloroform. Her nightdress had been jaggedy slashed as if by a knife but, not seeing the smaller cuts, she appeared untouched. She was certainly breathing. It took a little while before I saw the second slash in her nightdress below her waist and the redness under it. Yet this was merely another deceit. The redness was natural, obscene only in its flagrant display of her most personal features. It had been cut here for just this display and there was more. For mad ink writing was on the skin beside her exposed thigh and what was above.

One word was "come" and I think the other "in." A twisted scrawled arrow of ink pointed beside it.

And I saw him, as I saw the writing . . .

The Doctor's voice cut into that dreadful memory and wrenched me back to the street and the shops, and a crowd of men laughing by one of the front's public houses. He had obviously seen where my mind was straying and wanted to bring me back. "You perhaps feel I could have taken you into my confidence."

I stared at him blankly. Then I realised he was talking about Cullingworth. Only a few hours ago I had feared for my liberty, now it seemed trifling beside that memory. But I was glad enough of the interruption. "Could you not?" I asked "It would have been pleasanter to know you believed in me."

The Doctor smiled. "But if I had, Doyle, your anger with Cullingworth might have threatened a safe conclusion."

I was about to reply but we had turned into my street and, to my astonishment, outside my house was a carriage and a woman seemed to be approaching the door.

"Ah, see!" said the Doctor. "A patient by the look of it. Your luck may be changing, Doyle."

I was struck dumb. And I could not have asked for a better cure for my own bitter memories than what followed that day. Three patients came to my door and I relished the chance to work. Indeed, I must have given them value for their money, for I remember taking great trouble with each one including a painstaking analysis of a gentleman's digestive complaint, which concluded with the discovery that his cook had misunderstood her instructions and was serving his beefsteak almost raw. It was all a blessed relief.

After I had shown the last one out, I did not wish a

moment of inactivity and walked at once to the grocer to make my own purchases. I chose a fresh loaf, a roast guinea fowl, some butter and milk, and a small cheese and bacon, and even a modest flagon of cider, which the grocer enthused about. I had returned with my spoils and was laying them out in the consulting room when the Doctor entered.

"Three patients, Doctor. My luck has changed and it has enabled me to buy you dinner at last." But then I stopped for his face told me the truth. "No, it is not luck, is it?"

He looked at me very directly. "Well, I have an old colleague who retired here. I asked him to put word around. I am delighted to say news came while you were out that one of your new patients has already given a glowing report."

Perhaps I was a little disappointed that I owed the little start of my new practice not to my own efforts, but to my old mentor again. Yet I put such foolish pride aside. I knew I should be grateful and in my heart I was, and so I thanked him for his help and poured him a glass of the local cider. Dr. Bell's religion was strict, his father had been a member of the Scottish dissenting free church, but he was not a complete teetotaller. And we sat down companionably together.

"There is," he said, as he buttered his bread and cut a thin slice of cheese, "still a last puzzle to examine before we conclude this business." From his pocket he took the cipher we had been scrutinising so intently the evening before and handed it to me.

I stared at the thing up to the line which had baffled the Doctor:

5 9 13 17 8 16 12 8 7 5 2 11 11 3 7 13 20 5 14 8 10 3 6 6 5 14 21 4 2 7 11
12 12 13 20 8 10 2 14 11 7 5 20 8 15 11 12 5 16 15 7 13 17 13 19 2 7 11

12 8 8 15 5 22 5 10 13 11 5 2 14 2 19 13 6 6 10 2 14 10 8 7 14 8 15 13
14 15 18 13 7 11 5 10 3 6 13 7 6 1 11 2 13 15 20 13 14 10 8 17 1 10 6 13
5 17 11 2 12 13 20 8 10 7 8 13 11 8 15 13 14 8 14 11 5 7 8 6 1 14 8 4 19
2 7 17 2 19 15 7 13 17 13 4 12 5 10 12 4 5 6 6 5 14 19 2 6 19 8 7 8 13 6
18 8 2 18 8 13 14 15 7 8 13 6 16 5 11 3 13 11 5 2 14 16 11 12 8 11 12 5
14 20 16 12 2 3 6 15 12 13 20 8 13 6 5 19 8 2 19 5 11 16 2 4 14 9 3 16 11
13 16 12 8 10 7 8 13 11 5 2 14 15 2 8 16 5 14 17 1 5 14 16 18 5 7 13 11 5
2 14 4 12 5 10 12 5 16 17 13 7 1 4 2 6 6 16 11 2 14 8 10 7 13 19 2 11 16
8 2 5 10 8 18 11 5 2 14 13 6 17 13 14 3 16 10 7 5 18 11 2 19 1 8 1 8 19 7

"You had a problem with this eleventh line and its '19 1
8 1 8 19' I recall."

"I did," said the Doctor taking a drink of the cider,
which I was delighted to find was as sharp and fruity as
the grocer promised. "You see, Doyle, in many ways this
is a child's cipher. A serious expert would probably resolve it very quickly indeed, far quicker than I. It is true
that the part which puzzled me would puzzle them, but I
feel sure they would break the cipher quickly even so."

"But how?" I asked.

"Merely," he said putting down his glass, "as I started
to show you last night, by analysing the frequency and
pattern of the numbers which we take to represent letters.
With the exception of that oddity in the eleventh line, the
code appears to be fixed, but it is not sequential. By which
I mean that while '8' is indeed as I guessed an 'E,' it does
not follow that 'F' is '9' or even '7.' It seemed to me at
once from studying the thing that the sequence of numbers
for letters here has been determined not by the order of
the alphabet (which is the most childish of all methods)
but by some other text, presumably a page of prose. So
the nineteenth new letter which appears on that page, or
possibly the first letter of the nineteenth word on it, would
tell us what '19' stands for here."

"Then the thing is impossible, for we have no way of knowing what the page is."

"No, it is not, for even if we cannot discover the key," said the Doctor, "we can, as I say, revert to analysing the pattern and frequency of the numbers. The cipher is open to this method of decryption because the person who created it has constructed it in a somewhat childish way as a fixed cipher. If he had not, I can assure you the numbers would run far higher than twenty-three and many different numbers would refer to the same letter. I have seen treasure-hunting codes with variable keys based around the words of long manuscripts, which run as high as 2000 and higher. These are desperately hard, as so many modern treasure seekers have found."

I laughed. "Doctor, you are not going to tell me you have examined a cipher of buried treasure lately?"

"Certainly I have," said Bell. "A gentleman from Virginia who knew of my interest in such things sent it to me and I believe it to be perfectly genuine too, but I was doubtful I could ever solve it for precisely this reason. It utilises a shifting cipher and its key is a very long piece of text. In that kind of key cipher, unlike the present one, what the creator does is to utilise an entire manuscript and number each word. Then a message is encrypted by taking the first letter of each numbered word as your changing alphabet. The number 500, for example, will refer to the 500th word in that text and if that word is 'yellow' then the 500 will stand for 'Y,' but then if the 300th word is 'year' then the number 300 can also be utilised as 'Y' and undoubtedly many other words can as well. Without the key on that kind of cipher, what hope is there? But this is entirely different."

"I would very much like to see your treasure code," I said. "But on this one you say with each letter fixed, you look for patterns?"

"Precisely." The Doctor seized the piece of paper. "I felt at once there was a strong probability that '8' equals 'E,' for as I said, '8' is the most frequent number here and 'E' is the most frequently used letter in English. Now, once I have made an assessment of what stands for the letter 'E,' the word I look for at once in a cipher such as this is 'the.' And if the encrypter has been fool enough to number his letters using as a key the order in which they appeared in a page of English prose rather than taking the first letters of words, then the chances are he too will have come across a 'the' early and if so, we will get two consecutive numbers repeating themselves before the letter 'E.' Can you see such a thing here by any chance?"

I stared at the page with interest. I was determined to do better than I had over Garcia. "Yes," I said. " '11 12 8' is there early on. And it reappears at least nine times. Here on the seventh, twelfth, and fourteenth line, twice on the eighteenth and another four times after."

"Admirable," said Bell. "This was exactly the point I had reached when my eye fell on that damnable eleventh line. I had decided '11' was 'T,' '12' was 'H' and, as we have seen, '8' was 'E.' I foresaw some detailed work and a long night ahead but I was sure I was on my way. Then, you recall, my eye fell on that line and I faltered. '19 1 8 1 8 19' threw out all my plans. If '8' was 'E,' then unless I was going mad, '1' and '19' from their distribution through the document must surely be consonants. We can state quite categorically the order of commonness of English letters. It is 'e a o i d h n r s t u y c f g l m w b k p q z.' Bearing this in mind, in a document so long '1' and '19' had to be consonants or 'U,' which I had discarded. If, however, you try every consonant in the combination '19 1 8 1 8 19' you will get gibberish. Indeed, I began to wonder if the thing was Latin. I was on the point of giving up in disgust as you recall. And then I looked down at your table here and I had the answer in a trice."

"But how?" I asked, intrigued.

"I will show you," he said. "I have told you it is childish." And he held up the book *Frankenstein* and its frontispiece. At first I could not see what in the world he meant.

FRANKENSTEIN;
OR,
THE MODERN PROMETHEUS.

IN THREE VOLUMES

DID I REQUEST THEE, MAKER, FROM MY CLAY
TO MOULD ME MAN? DID I SOLICIT THEE
FROM DARKNESS TO PROMOTE ME?——
PARADISE LOST.

VOL. I.

LONDON
PRINTED FOR
LACKINGTON, HUGHES, HARDING, MAVOR, & JONES,
FINSBURY SQUARE.

1818.

And then I saw the date at the bottom, and I stared at it and then back at the cipher. And back at the date. And I laughed out loud. "So . . ." I said, " '1818' is not a code at all. It is a date! Left in there to add confusion."

"Yes," said Bell. "But also as a thumping clue. I told you the person who encrypted this was childish. You had been provided with the cipher's key! You already had it here, Doyle, as I saw at once when I made the connection.

I went straight to the first page of the novel, the first sentence, in fact:

You will rejoice to hear no disaster has accompanied the commencement of an enterprise which you have regarded with such evil forebodings.

"As you see, the last word on the first line is 'the.' I was quite sure now I had the key to the cipher. And I studied that page carefully. The sentence gave me most of the cipher key. He had numbered his keys in the order the letters appear in it.

"Y = 1
O = 2
U = 3
W = 4
I = 5
L = 6
R = 7
E = 8
J = 9
C = 10
T = 11
H = 12
A = 13
N = 14
D = 15
S = 16
M = 17
P = 18
F = 19
V = 20
G = 21
B = 22

"I could have proceeded at once," continued Bell, "but, in fact, later in the page I easily picked out his 'K' as '23' here in this sentence down the page:

> *I am already far north of London and as I walk in the streets of Petersburgh, I feel a cold northern breeze play upon my cheeks which braces my nerves and fills me with delight.*

"He did not need a 'Q' or an 'X' or a 'Z.' After that, of course, it was merely a matter of going and writing the thing out and adding some punctuation. He had used the cipher to communicate with 'Garcia' in the personal column so I could now translate the messages myself and the man's address, and summon him to the house. I have the complete translation of the message that was found in 'Garcia's' pocket here if you have to see it, but I warn you it will not please you."

I took it from him eagerly and this is what I read.

> *I, James Heriot Turnavine Cullingworth, have contrived this drama for the edification of all concerned and particularly to advance my claim to have created an entirely new form of drama which will involve real people and real situations. The thing should have a life of its own just as the creation does in my inspiration which is Mary Wollstonecraft's exceptional manuscript of 1818,* Frankenstein or the Modern Prometheus. *I am therefore using the book as a key to this cipher though I suspect nobody and certainly not Doyle will be clever enough to disentangle it. If they are, then of course I take the credit, if not I fear the players will have to endure the game* mutatis mutandis.

> *I will use this cipher to communicate with those players like Garcia whom I have hired but they will know nothing of its larger purpose or indeed of this note.*
>
> *The coup at the centre of it is of course a body I have bought quite legally from its rightful inheritor Mrs. Anya Tabares.*
>
> *Let the play commence.*

As so often, Cullingworth's arrogance took my breath away. Here was still further proof the man would have left me to rot. I was expected to "endure the game *mutatis mutandis*." After I read it, I was so incensed I almost made up my mind to take the thing round to Inspector Warner immediately, but a moment's cooler reflection told me why the Doctor had withheld it. There was nothing here we did not know, it would only mean more questions and more statements, and Cullingworth would no doubt take it all as further tribute to his genius. We were both wearied of the whole affair.

Once we had finished our early dinner I was rather surprised when the Doctor asked if he might do some work upstairs undisturbed in the spare bedroom where I had first encountered him. I did not see him for the rest of the evening, but I heard him moving about and now I recalled hearing some banging and thumping on the stairs earlier in the day while I was absorbed in interviewing my patients. Thinking about it, I decided he probably had some academic materials that needed to be packed for the return trip to Edinburgh and that the inn had not proved a suitable facility for the purpose. If so, I was delighted to be of service.

By eleven o'clock I supposed he must have finished and I went up to see. I had spent some of the evening reflecting on the events of the past few days, and recalling how foolishly I had doubted both his willingness and his ability to help me. Not only had he seen off Cullingworth, but he had helped to establish the beginnings of a practice for me as well. I did not want him to leave thinking I was ungrateful.

I entered the room, which had contained only one mattress and a chair when I saw it last, and stopped in amazement. At one end there was equipment for chemical analysis, including a bunsen burner. There were a desk, some books and other signs of activity, and in the corner a basic but comfortable bed.

"I thought you would not mind if I improvised a place up here," the Doctor said, looking up from where he was writing something. "My old colleague had some things he could spare so I had them sent over today. I think they may prove useful to you."

I was overwhelmed. "He is doubly kind," I said. "I am glad of any furnishings." Now I stared in further wonder at the pile of papers before him. "You are making notes of the Cullingworth business before you go back?" I asked in some bewilderment.

"My dear Doyle, I would hardly bother to write notes of Cullingworth's feeble little joke, I told you when I arrived there was a matter that gave me reason to come here; it was in your letters."

"What matter?"

"The matter of Miss Heather Grace and the solitary cyclist."

I was aghast.

"I am grateful for your intervention, Doctor," I said, trying to make light of it. "And even more grateful for my patients. I scarcely want to see you disappointed. But the cyclist has not yet committed any crime and may just be some timid suitor. I made my own investigation."

"Yes," Bell said, getting up and putting on his coat, "and everything you did was useless while every conclusion you drew was wrong. Come now, the case is as strange and disturbing as the Cullingworth matter was trivial. Baynes has said he will assist us and we should find a cab. Enough time has been wasted. It is high time to see the ground."

THE HORROR OF ABBEY MILL

So once again, this time with Baynes and the Doctor, I found myself at the same strange spot on that wooded road, still puzzled by the Doctor's fascination with what I could have sworn he would normally regard as a minor matter. It was not as if he had set eyes on the cyclist and I had scarcely mentioned his more sinister qualities.

Our cab waited out of sight round the corner and the wood seemed less inviting than ever in the darkness. Baynes was using a lantern to search the trees for clues, close to where I had last seen the cyclist. Meanwhile the Doctor, well buttoned up against the cold, studied the terrain. At last he stood in the exact spot where I had crouched on three occasions. "So," he asked, "was this where you saw the figure?"

"I raced after him to the bend in the road and he was gone. But I had a good sighting and followed your precepts to the letter. Investigation, Observation, Deduction, Conclusion. What could possibly be wrong with that?"

"Almost everything," he said dispassionately, staring at the ground. "First, your hiding place was useless. Had you been behind the hedge, you could have had a proper view of the cyclist. As it is, you can tell even less than your witness."

"But I saw him."

"You saw a vague outline," said the Doctor. "Indeed, the sum total of knowledge you gained from your expedition was the fact that her story was true. What of that? I never doubted it for a moment."

We were interrupted by a shout from Baynes at the turning. When we reached him he was crouched low and pointing at the ground. It was wet but there were distinct marks of a bicycle tyre.

"Well done, Baynes," said the Doctor. "We will make a detective of you yet."

The locum was obviously delighted. "Well, I need something to do before I return to Barts, sir. And I do not much wish to stay on with Cullingworth. His pay is as low as his morals."

"Did he not compensate you as he promised?" I asked.

Baynes shrugged. "Oh, once the police lost interest he merely paid what he owed. He is not to be trusted for a moment. Maybe it is him in the cloak. He was always interested in Miss Grace. I have seen him spying on her."

I was intrigued by this. "And he was certainly enraged when he learned of my investigation. In fact, it was the cause of our quarrel."

Bell had been following the tracks minutely along the ground and now they came to an end. "They seem to lead nowhere," he said with disappointment. For a long time he trudged round and round the point at which they stopped, badly frustrated. "I think," he added at last, "he must have carried it. But where the devil would he carry it to?"

He strode back to the road, looking a picture of disappointment. "I agree with what you wrote in your letter, Doyle. There is a grim feeling about this place. Is it because highwaymen were hanged at that gibbet back there? Or something else?"

He turned. The wind was picking up now, blowing the Doctor's coat around him. "At least I can tell you one thing and that is who your patient feared was following her. His name is Ian Coatley."

I had no idea where he got this but I knew the Doctor well enough not to bother challenging it. "Is he dead?" I asked with an uneasy feeling.

"Oh, yes, he was hanged," said Bell. "The murder of Miss Grace's family at Abbey Mill, which is a few miles away through the wood, was one of the very ugliest crimes of the 1870s."

"My God," I said. "Of course, she told me her parents were dead."

The Doctor had reached the road and turned to walk back to the corner. "Your patient was lucky to escape with her life. The man had killed at least four times."

So now I knew the truth. Little wonder the Doctor had been alerted by the name of Heather Grace. With his wide knowledge of crime, he would have been far ahead of me as soon as he had my letters. Here was why he took the affair so seriously. But now too I saw the full horror of the thing for my patient. Was it any surprise that, faced with this odd persecutor on a bicycle, Miss Grace feared her mind had given way? All the visions of past horrors must have seemed to be flooding back. As I thought about it, I felt an inner fury that anybody could be playing these strange tricks on her. In the circumstances it seemed uniquely cruel.

From that night the Doctor stayed in my house. But his habits, when preoccupied with a case, were still as I remembered. After he had told me of the history, he made it clear he wished to say no more and later he retired to his newly acquired study with the door firmly closed.

• • •

A few days later Miss Grace was sitting in my consulting room, describing the recurring nightmare she had mentioned previously. I would, I hope, in any event have been a sympathetic listener, but knowing the truth about her history made it a very memorable occasion. Afterwards I made detailed notes which are before me now.

> *I am in a corridor in my old home.* [I recall that she spoke quietly, looking down at her hands which were folded in front of her.] *A long dark corridor. At the end of it lies safety, a bright, welcoming room. But I know, always I know with a sickening certainty that I will not be able to reach it. At first I try to ignore this, to hope. I move forward, the light is a little nearer. But soon something is behind me. A figure. I run on desperately but he is closer, and I am barefoot and there is glass on the floor and my feet are bleeding so I cannot move. And the figure is larger and nearer now, and I try to run, but the figure clutches me tightly. He holds me. And I hear him telling me I will never escape, he will always come for me. And then I awake.*

I did not speak for a little while after she had finished. It was indeed truly fearful to think how deeply this dream was rooted in past events. But at last I told her I understood what a torment such a nightmare must be.

"You are the first I ever told," she said.

I wanted so much to offer some reassurance. After we had talked a little more about the dream, I told her my old teacher, Dr. Bell, was going to investigate her cyclist. "I am quite certain he will discover who it is."

She seemed encouraged. "And," I went on, "he said to tell you your cyclist is flesh and blood. He is not Ian Coatley."

There was silence and I wondered if I had made a terrible error. She looked at me, but when she spoke her voice was calm. "It is so strange to hear someone say his name. Of course, nobody does now."

"I can understand that," I said. "But he is dead."

"Yes," she said. "If you knew how many times I have said that to myself. He is dead. They saw him hang."

"I swear to you, then," I said, "it is not him. He is in his grave."

"Please God, he is at peace there."

On a bright yet cold afternoon, some days after this interview, Dr. Bell and I stood on a hillside overlooking Abbey Mill, where Miss Grace had lived when the tragedy occurred. We had arrived by cab and clambered along a path so we were looking down on the place.

I did not care for what I saw at all. I have always hated the notion of living without a view, hemmed in by trees, and below me was a stark, yet grand enough building with woods on one side and rushing water from the old mill on the other. Its windows were mostly shuttered, adding to the general effect of gloom.

The Doctor, however, looked far from gloomy. "Ever since I first read accounts of the crime," he said with animation as we stood there staring at it, "I have always been interested to see this place. It is a school now, shut up for the holidays."

A gust of wind whipped up the grass on either side of our path. "Not one I would choose to attend," I commented.

"Ah"—he was smiling—"but did not Stonyhurst have a similar bleakness?"

"At least we did not fear for our lives," I told him, but I knew we were only putting off the moment. "What exactly happened here?"

"Oh, it followed the pattern of Ian Coatley's other murders to the letter," said the Doctor as we began to meander down the hill towards the place. "His style was unique. He had killed a mother and daughter in cold blood in Middlesex and taken their money. He was renting a room near here and evidently he heard gossip about the wealthy Grace family. They were perfect prey: they had money, they were isolated and they too had an attractive daughter."

"My God," I said, for it was truly horrible to think of a man like that descending like a wolf on the peaceful place below us.

"Yes," Bell continued. "He was a handsome devil and not without charm. He always insinuated himself into the lives of the family and became a friend of the victims. Here, see for yourself. I dug this out of the records." He produced a small photograph from his pocketbook and it gave me quite a shock. The man was good-looking certainly, with long locks of hair, but more than that he looked sweet and even gentle.

We had made a rapid descent and were now close to the building itself. It was not quite as dark and imposing as I had thought from above. An elegant elm tree grew up beside the large window and directly in front was a big door leading, from what I could see through the window, to an ornate hall. There was still something about the place I did not like. Coloured by the knowledge of what had happened, it seemed to lack a vital spark of life and warmth. I looked again at the photo of the man who had made it so. A wolf in sheep's clothing was the phrase that came to me. Just as I was thinking this there came from above us, like some uncanny orchestration, the sound of sweet choral singing.

Over yonder's a park that is newly begun
And all the bells in paradise I hear them a-ring
Which is silver on the outside and gold within
And I love sweet Jesus above all thing

I knew the carol a little, though it is not one of the best-known. The singing was angelic. I looked at Bell and we made our way in that direction.

"Well," he said, "it seems I was wrong about the holidays."

"God forbid," I said for the singing had made me suddenly cheerful as we opened the door and walked inside.

We found ourselves in a large hall, where there were some coloured hangings, beautifully illuminated by the light of the two-storey window. The singing was coming from above us and we went to the stairs. Certainly the effect was merrier than I had expected. But the picture of Coatley was still in my hand and as I looked down at it I could not suppress a shiver to think of what had been done in this place. "So," I said, taking a last look at the photo and handing it back as we walked up the large oak staircase. "This man became a friend. And then?"

"He was increasingly frustrated in his plans. He wished to know where her father kept his money. In fact, although the family was wealthy, there was little of immediate value here. But when Coatley turned, his temper was foul. One night a labourer outside here heard the screams. He had killed the mother on these stairs. Miss Grace was stabbed but managed to get away into the trees. She was in a terrible state, quite distraught."

And in the park there stands a hall
And all the bells in paradise I hear them a-ring
Which is covered all over with purple and pall
And I love sweet Jesus above all thing

We had now reached the first landing and the singing was louder, the purity of those young choir voices making a strange contrast with Bell's words.

And in that hall there stands a bed
Which is hung all around with silk curtains so red
And in that bed there lies a knight,
Whose wounds they do bleed by day and by night

We could see that the singing came from a brightly lit room at the end of a corridor to our left. The Doctor continued his account as we walked towards it.

"They arrested Coatley at an inn some miles away. He had some of Mr. Grace's clothes and he confessed soon enough. What was worse, he even wrote gloating letters from his condemned cell, glad for what he did."

"And the father?"

"If I remember the details correctly, he was found here. In this corridor. He had been stamped to death, there were heel marks all over his skull."

I had no time to contemplate this horror for we had arrived at the room where the choir was singing. It was a very elegant room with two large windows and beautifully cushioned window seats. The choir comprised about eight boys, aged between eleven and twelve, who stared at us as we entered, for their song had just ended. In front of them was a man somewhere in his thirties with a pleasant boyish appearance. He turned and smiled at us without the slightest surprise. It was almost as if we were expected.

"We did not mean to interrupt," said Dr. Bell. "I understood the school was on holiday."

"Oh, it is," said the man, smiling. "These boys have the furthest to go. They set off at dawn tomorrow. You will find the whole place deserted then." He turned to me. "And it is a beautiful place, is it not, Dr. Doyle?"

I reacted with amazement.

"Oh, yes." He addressed me, smiling again, and I found I was beginning to wonder if he did not smile a little too much. "I know who you are. The truth is I have stood outside your house, debating whether to come and see you. I am Guy Greenwell. I hope very soon to be Miss Grace's fiancé. I expect you have heard of me."

We shook hands and I introduced him to Dr. Bell. Disregarding the boys, Mr. Greenwell instantly proposed he should show us round the house and proceeded to walk us through some of the main rooms, though I must confess I could take little interest in the history of the place or its decorations when I thought of what had happened here. Bell, however, seemed most intrigued by everything he saw, asking questions like some moonstruck student of architectural history and drinking in all the sights and sounds of the place. I wondered what Greenwell would say if he knew the real reason for this interest.

As we reached the gardens Greenwell, who had become quite animated, started talking of the song we had heard. "She taught me the song," he said. "Evidently her family sang it." Then again he turned to me, most deferentially. "I know Dr. Doyle must find it strange that I am attached to a place where such awful events happened. But I can assure you, Dr. Doyle, it is a wonderful setting and has, when you come to know it, a serenity that is uniquely its own." We had arrived at a rather pretty little summer house and he opened its door and took us in. "And here is the perfect hideaway."

Copies of *The Times* were strewn around and he told us he was an avid follower of rugby football. He was cutting the scores out each day and mounting them into a book. "Perhaps I will combine them into an almanac one day. Greenwell's, it has a nice ring to it."

I was, I must admit, slightly repelled by his attachment

to the place. "Surely," I said as we looked out from that little house surrounded by Scotch firs, "you would not expect Miss Grace to come back and live here?"

"No," he agreed, "I would never ask that of her. Her family still own the freehold, it is true, but I teach for pleasure and not for a living. I have an estate up the valley here, past the Blythes, called Wade House. You must come and take tea with me there one day."

I noticed Boll's interest at once. "So it is close by her uncle's wood?" he asked quickly.

"Why, yes," said Greenwell. "Miss Grace's uncle and I are very old friends. You will find he has a most wonderful scientific collection. And he is very keen indeed on the match I propose. But even so I have no wish to press Miss Grace too hard for an answer. She suffered terribly in the tragedy here. And not so long ago she was engaged to a military man who left her for another. It was shameful. So I will wait. Otherwise the imminence of her inheritance might seem a motive."

"Is it?" The Doctor could be blunt when he wanted to.

Yet Greenwell took no offence. In fact, somewhat to my surprise he turned, smiling, to me. "I would like very much," he said graciously, "to give Dr. Doyle the answer to that question. Miss Grace's feelings for me have cooled a little since she met you, sir. You would, of course, expect me to dislike you for that. But you would be wrong. I judge her taste to be extraordinary. Therefore I think well of you. And that is what I intended to say had I come to see you. I feel strongly that any woman must be allowed to make up her own mind. Naturally I have every hope she will arrive at a decision in my favour very soon, but it is up to her. I hope that answers the question."

"Admirably." The Doctor seemed somewhat amused by this reply. For myself, I found it impossible to take these words seriously. Certainly Mr. Greenwell's tone sounded genuine but there was, for me, something too smug and self-satisfied about the speaker's mode of expression to be wholly persuasive. I noticed, too, that he ignored the Doctor's reply, making it perfectly clear he was waiting for mine.

"The sentiments are certainly handsome." I struggled to find the words. "But from bitter experience I know quite well how a man can say one thing and do another."

For a moment he looked almost wounded and then again came that smile. It was not a superior smile, rather it was sweet and affecting, so I must admit to bias when I say that I had begun to detest it. "Then I can only ask you to judge me by experience," he said. "I am delighted you are helping to ensure Miss Grace's safety. I have heard these stories that she is being followed. Awful in view of what happened. Almost like . . . some visitation if you believe in such things." As he said this, his eyes seemed to darken and I sensed another aspect to him. Was it fear or something else? "As I say, my property borders on that part of the wood but I have seen nothing."

"And you have no idea," asked Dr. Bell, "who might be interested in her movements?"

"No," he answered. "But I cannot bear to think of her being hurt."

"Good," I said, "for we are determined to ensure no harm comes to her." With that we bade goodbye to him and walked off to where our cab was waiting as arranged.

On the journey back, I could see Bell was turning over what he had heard in his mind but and I was determined to voice my doubts about the man. "I do not trust him."

Bell looked up from his ruminations. A little smile played on his lips. "I wonder if you are not a little biased, but I agree he seems somewhat concerned by our activities. So let us expedite them. Tomorrow, you should return to your observation post on the road, this time, I trust, with better results."

That night, knowing my curiosity about the case, Bell asked if I would like to see some of the documents he had on the Abbey Mill murder. I agreed at once and found that much of it covered the ground he had described. But there was, I will admit, one other item that took me unawares, although the description of Miss Grace's condition when they found her, barefoot and bleeding, was very affecting. It was a copy of a letter that had been seized in Coatley's condemned cell. I still recall the slanted handwriting, the large, childish letters, but most of all how could I ever forget the words, repetitious, almost infantile?

> *I am glad of what happened. I rejoice in what I did to you all. It is a wonderful act and what pleasure it gives me. I go to my death singing, triumphant.*

How desperately I found myself hoping Miss Grace had not known of this. The gloating exultation of the thing recalled memories of my own I had no wish to relive. Of course, it was only a copy, but before I went to bed I took the file containing it and put it back where Bell could find it in the morning. I would cheerfully have slept in a morgue or a cemetery rather than lay my head down anywhere near that note.

THE BLACK HOUSE IN THE WOOD

Next day we had planned that the Doctor should interview Miss Grace at my house and see if he could discover anything of interest, while I took the opportunity to watch her progress on the road as she cycled along it towards the town. Miss Grace's appointment with the Doctor was for two and I set out shortly after twelve. The morning had been sunny but by noon it was overcast and the clouds were gathering ominously as I rode a bicycle procured by Baynes along that grey and unpleasant stretch of road leading to the wood.

I was still stung by the Doctor's scathing comments about my mistakes before and felt utterly determined that this time I would do better. So I laid my plans carefully. First I surveyed the ground, concentrating most of my attention on a lonely strip of hawthorn hedge. I wanted to establish exactly how much of the road was visible from it and soon I settled on a spot behind it that was far closer to the thoroughfare than my previous vantage point. The place was fully protected from view but I could still reach the road itself in moments, for I had already decided that if I encountered the figure again, I would try to get in front of it. Perhaps I might not succeed in forcing it to swerve or stop, but at the very least I would get a close view.

I had more than an hour to wait, so I took up my position and soon found myself lost in my own reflections. I thought of how much I had disliked Guy Greenwell and this in turn compelled me to confront a truth I had been carefully avoiding, namely that my concern for Miss Grace's well-being was no longer strictly medical. She was the first woman I had allowed myself to think of in this way since that time in Edinburgh.

Of course, I was aware such feelings were utterly improper between doctor and patient. But as I lay there and the clouds gathered overhead, I recalled with a smile some remarks made by one of our more perspicacious teachers in Edinburgh, an expert in pathology called Andrew Maclagan. Once, with a twinkle in his eye, he had informed a group of medical students that we could confidently expect all kinds of thoughts and fancies to pop into our heads during our treatment of patients. "You may feel," he announced, "an overpowering desire to box a patient's ears, fall into their arms or kick them down the stairs. In themselves, none of these fancies matters a jot. The mind is a capricious thing and we cannot always hope to control it. Your only task, gentlemen, is to make absolutely and utterly sure that never under any circumstances do such thoughts become deeds."

I knew quite well, as Maclagan had taught, that no doctor can police his own heart. But I was also determined at all costs to observe his practical advice. At that time in my own life, I honestly did not think I could go on living if any feelings of mine should in some unforeseen way hurt or endanger another young woman.

I was so rapt in these reflections that I was almost startled when I saw her cycling into view and realised how much time had passed. I felt foolish for being caught unprepared but I kept low and she passed me, looking intent, her eyes straight ahead. At once I turned my attention to the road behind her. My heart jumped. For the figure was there, just as I had seen it before, travelling at speed about thirty yards away along the road, looking odd and ungainly. The hood and cloak were black while the head made a bobbing motion as it moved.

I ducked down again for if it saw me now it could easily turn round and I would lose my chance. Miss Grace was already at the corner. With my heart beating I waited a few seconds. Then I reared up out of my hiding place and sprang out into its path, desperately hoping I looked braver than I felt.

I was prepared for anything including being run over or attacked, but not for what I saw. The road was entirely empty. There was nobody and nothing there. The clouds had got up a wind and it blew through the grass, and the rooks called out from high in the wood, but again it was as if the figure had never been here at all. In vain I turned in every direction, hunting for some sign of what I had seen. It was useless. There was not the slightest trace of the cyclist.

My first emotion had been fear. Now, as I stood staring around in that road, a sense of terrible failure eclipsed it. Ever since the Doctor denounced my first attempts to observe the cyclist I had been determined to redeem my reputation. Here had been my opportunity and what had happened? At the critical moment, while I should have been preparing for action, I had indulged in a complacent daydream on a subject many would regard as morally reprehensible. As a direct consequence I had been taken by surprise and effectively achieved nothing at all.

Desperate to act, I made for the wood adjoining the road. Some sanity was now returning and I knew that here lay the only possible solution. The highway was clear, the moor empty and there had only been a few seconds in which to disappear. Somehow, as before, the figure had cycled straight into the wood. Yet there was absolutely no sign of any path through the undergrowth and I had heard no noise at all. Bell had spoken of the figure carrying the bicycle, but even so, surely there would be evidence of a trail?

I walked up and down that small stretch of road endless times, forcing myself to observe every detail. This told me nothing very much. But finally I thought it possible that I did detect a soft impression in the moss that might have been made by tyres. As before, these marks led absolutely nowhere but in my humiliation I was prepared to clutch at any straws so I set off boldly into the trees.

I walked for about an hour without covering much ground. I would have given up if I had not been feeling so frantic, for it was hard going. But I knew just a single clue—a match, a footprint, a piece of paper—could make my return easier to bear. The wood was becoming a mass of nettles and brambles. In places the latter were up to ten feet high and twisted together in a way that made it almost impossible to force a way through. Somewhere, of course, I knew there would be an easier path but for some reason I was utterly determined to maintain a line with the tracks I had seen by the road.

Looking back now, there was no conceivable logic to this approach for, even if the cyclist had made those tracks in the moss, why should he proceed in a straight line? But I was in no mood for logic, for I was driven by my own sense of failure. I was, in truth, a slave to that pitiful superstition that *any* heroic struggle, in this case against briars and brambles, must in the end yield its reward. More shamefully, a part of me probably hoped that the sight of my torn clothes and scratched arms would mitigate the Doctor's criticism. If so, I was deluding myself for he would have seen through it at once.

But even the most misguided effort can sometimes be rewarded and on this occasion mine was, though hardly in the way I expected. I had come to yet another obstacle in the form of a holly tree when I heard a noise. It sounded like a bird fluttering in the distance. By itself this was not remarkable as the wood was full of crows, but the noise was too soft and too regular to be a bird. And it seemed to be coming from a short way ahead. I pushed between the holly and a clump of nettles, and straightened up. There was a giant shadow ahead of me. It took only a little time to realise it was being cast by some kind of building.

The light was fading so I moved quickly on, hoping I might have time to explore the place before darkness fell. Soon I emerged from the trees, though the briars were still thick, and could make out the structure quite clearly. It stopped me in my tracks.

The worst operation I ever attended took place in a grim, white-tiled basement theatre in Edinburgh's old infirmary building. The surgeon was a man called Ian Taller, who was often far too leisurely for my liking and on this occasion he was searching without success for a tumour or an abscess in the patient's abdomen. With this in view he had slit open the man's stomach and was burrowing around with his hands, even though it was clear to all of us that the patient was far too ill to sustain the shock of it. The poor man lay on that table gasping for breath and, though he was more or less unconscious, I still recall feeling a terrible sense of his indignity as he lay there dying with his organs horribly exposed to the staring students. Sure enough, he was dead within a few minutes, Taller sewed him up perfunctorily and he was wheeled away.

It may seem an odd story to tell in trying to describe an abandoned cottage, but the structure in front of me had the same air of dereliction, decay and death as that man lying exposed on the table. Some old houses are picturesque ruins; others are piles of bricks. This was neither. The building was still standing and it had two storeys. But although once it might have been a rose-arboured paradise, now you could not for a moment imagine anyone sane wanting to go within a mile of the place.

Even apart from the brickwork, a horribly mottled tapestry of crumbling stone with sightless gaps for windows, everything in front of me was dark and decayed and dismembered. It was enough to make you wonder how any structure on earth could ever have grace if it could be broken and degraded in this way. But at least the noise that had brought me here was louder and I could see its source. Someone had tied a strip of material to the upstairs window and it was fluttering and flapping in the wind.

I was glad there was still some daylight as I entered the cavity which had once been a door. But inside the place it was dark enough. There was no floor to speak of, but broken masonry and glass crunched under my feet as I tried to grope my way towards the staircase. The dereliction around me was bad, but the pathetic touches of humanity that remained seemed even worse. I brushed past some hanging patterned wallpaper that was wet and faded but still clung to the black wall.

The stairs seemed to be solid and I could still hear that flapping noise above me. I shouted a hello, more to keep up my own spirits than in the expectation of any reply. My voice echoed a little but it met with utter silence. I climbed the creaking stairs slowly and they held my weight, though the banister was broken and offered no support.

At last I reached the top. Ahead was a dark landing

with three rooms leading off it. From what I could make out, the cloth I had seen was hanging from the room at the end of the landing. Slowly I walked towards it, turning to look in the other rooms as I passed. The first was empty except for the dirt and debris that lay everywhere in that foul place. The second had the ancient shell of a bed and mattress, though nobody now could possibly have lain on it.

Finally I reached the door of the last room and stood there staring in. It was just as dark and intimidating as all the others but tied to the remains of the window frame was what looked like a strip of jet-black cloth, which swirled and fluttered in the wind. I moved forward at once to get a better view of the thing.

The noise erupted from behind me just as I reached it, a horrible gutteral scream. I whirled round but already the thing was on me. I saw just a glimpse of cloak and hood but little of a face; indeed, I had the uncanny impression that the eyes were socketless folds of skin.

Then I lost my balance and was reeling back against the glassless window. My hands clawed for support but there was none and I fell headlong. Next there was searing pain in my legs and arms, and the air was knocked out of me. A sharp dagger stabbed at my cheek, narrowly missing my eye.

Even as I struggled to get up, I thanked God, for I had landed in more of the briars I had been cursing earlier. They slashed my face and legs, but my thick coat protected me from the worst of them and they saved my life, for they broke my fall from that window.

Once I had staggered to my feet and established no bones were broken I am afraid all thought of further self-justifying bravery went clear out of my head. There was, as I had suspected, an easier path back, with brambles that reached only to my knees rather than over my face. I had never dreamed I would be so glad to see that road.

An hour or so later I was standing outside that hellish house again in the darkness and rain, taking great gulps of brandy from a flask offered me by Baynes, as police carrying lanterns weaved around us.

"I still say," said Baynes, "you could have seen Cullingworth. He is perfectly capable of donning a hood and he was out all day."

"If only," I said, feeling better for the brandy, "I had seen more of him." I was actually thinking that, had I not been pushed, I might well have dived out of the window on purpose rather than face the figure in that room at close quarters, but given the circumstances I did not think in my heart that made me a coward.

Not far away from us, dressed warmly against the night, the Doctor was studying the ground by the door with the benefit of a lantern. He kept shaking his head and eventually he came over.

"The ground is devilishly hard to read here because of the rain, Doyle. But you may consider yourself fully redeemed as an investigator and I think we can now agree the case is serious."

"Yet I still failed to see him," I had not forgotten my sense of humiliation earlier in the day.

"Hardly your fault. It certainly seems to me he will not let anyone close. And we can only thank providence for these bushes or he would surely have broken your neck."

We were interrupted by Inspector Warner, who announced there was nothing at all to be found in the house. "I am sorry for what happened to you, sir," he said. "But whoever was there has gone."

The Doctor was not surprised and turned back to me.

"Before we go, Doyle, I wonder if I could ask you to face this house once more with a couple of stout policemen and a lamp? I want to be precisely sure of what you saw."

So it was that I found myself again in that upstairs room, standing opposite Bell by its glassless window. It was, so far as I could tell, exactly as it had been before.

"Our friend was obviously behind the door," said Bell. "But what took you to the window?"

It was only now that I realised I had forgotten about the fluttering cloth. "There was a black piece of cloth, a scarf possibly. It fluttered here, making a noise in the wind."

"We found no black cloth," said Warner.

But Bell was already making a minute examination of the window and its frame. "Yes," he confirmed. "There are some tiny strips of material here." He gathered them up with considerable care and evident satisfaction.

Later, back on the road as we prepared to leave the place, Bell had a final talk with Baynes and myself. Knowing the signs of old, I could see he was extremely excited by the day's developments. "It is," he said, "as suggestive a case as I have ever seen. Tomorrow, Doyle, we must of course call on the young lady's guardians."

Baynes was evidently itching to be given something to do. "Should I not keep watch on the road, sir. I would love to have a chance to prove my theory."

"Very well," Bell agreed. "I would be very grateful if you did, Baynes. But be careful. You know what happened to Doyle here. On no account whatever—and I mean that—on no account go into the wood."

THE COLLECTION OF MR. CHARLES BLYTHE

The Doctor was anxious to set out on our visit early next morning and with some regret I had to explain to him over breakfast that, unless he went alone, this was quite impossible. My list was growing, I had a number of postponed patients and I could not possibly be ready before lunch. He was not pleased, but he had to make the best of it and retreated to his room with some words about keeping my appointments as short as possible.

The phrase seemed to work as an evil charm for I have rarely known such long and arduous consultations. A local publican with a stomach complaint insisted on taking me through two week's worth of meals in order to prove he was allergic to eggs. A mother, who quite erroneously feared pleurisy, wished me to make a study of her family tree. And finally, with only one patient left, a neighbour rushed in begging for help with her infant son who had a coughing fit. None of these cases was remotely serious, but all needed attention. I was glad when finally I shook hands with my last patient, a querulous builder's wife called Mrs. Caine, who wished to use the cloakroom and insisted I need not trouble myself as her maid was waiting and would see her out.

I had returned to my consulting room to put my notes in order when I was interrupted by a piercing scream and it was only then I remembered that Bell was liable to use the downstairs cloakroom for his own purposes. Sure enough, a few minutes later I was apologising to a shaken Mrs. Caine who had evidently peered behind a bath screen, only to see the Doctor, standing in the bath under a maze of test tubes wishing her "Good Morning."

I shut the front door with relief and after a moment Bell appeared, grinning. "A trying patient, Doyle. And she constantly quarrels with her husband, who is a wealthy builder."

"Do you know the Caines?" I asked in surprise.

"Of course not, but her wedding ring shows a married woman of means and the specks of fresh cement and carpented wood on her insole told me she has recently visited a building site, while the name Caine is on various sites in the town. She also stamped her foot twice in a rage in my presence. No surprise that the toe of her right shoe was worn."

I was amused, of course it was all true. "I hope you will not scare away all my patients, Doctor."

"In her case you might thank me, but I fear she is the kind who always comes back," he said. "Now, a cab is waiting for us outside and at last we can make our visit."

And so, once again, we drove up that long and desolate road on to the hills, where a fierce wind was blowing the trees about. Bell leant back in the cab, his eyes half closed in that odd way he had when he gave me his view of a case, prompted on this occasion by the previous day's interview with Heather Grace.

"All my instincts warn me," he began, "that your patient is at serious risk and this risk is in some way connected to the imminence of her inheritance on her twenty-fifth birthday. Her uncle is very keen on the match to Greenwell, the teacher we met, partly because it seems she had been engaged before to a naval captain called Horler who jilted her and went abroad. But I know you will be interested to hear I have made my own enquiries about Mr. Greenwell. It seems he is not such a wealthy man; indeed, there was some land speculation in which he lost money. It could therefore be said he has a motive for frightening Miss Grace into marriage."

This interested me considerably but there was more. For Bell had pressed Miss Grace on the matter of the cyclist and learned something new and somewhat disturbing.

Once, at night, on that road she was returning from an errand to the farm when she became sure she heard the cyclist very close behind her, closer, that is, than ever before. Then, as so often, this reminded her of her dream and the memory made things far worse, for in the nightmare she frequently stumbled and fell. In her terror she had swerved and lost her balance, and tumbled from the bicycle. She was not hurt but she lay there in desperate fear, her eyes tightly closed, not daring to open them. In that awful moment she was sure the figure was on her, and she could feel his hand touching her and even whispering. She did not dare open her eyes for fear but at last, when all was quiet, she made herself look and there was no sign of him. Finally she had decided his closeness must have been imaginary. It was all in her mind, which was why she had not told me before.

It so happened that as the Doctor was recalling this, we were passing that stretch of road and as I stared out at those dank trees I hardly wished to contemplate the terror she must have felt. But my companion was far more worried by the implication. "I am not at all sure," he said, frowning, "it *was* in her mind. That is what concerns me."

At last we reached the ivy-clad rectory. It was, as I

have said, a pleasant enough building, comparatively shel-
tered from the elements by its position and surrounded by
a well-kept garden and parkland.

Bell had sent word through Miss Grace that we were
coming and we were admitted by a maid as a small elderly
woman appeared, with neat grey hair and a somewhat
worried expression, and we made our introductions.

"I am Heather's Aunt Agnes, gentlemen. Her poor late
mother's sister," Mrs. Blythe said as she led us deeper
into the house, which was far more spacious than I had
realised from its exterior, with large, well-furnished
rooms. "It is my hope our niece marries Guy Greenwell
as soon as possible and all this stupidity will end."

"Stupidity?" asked Dr. Bell.

Mrs. Blythe stopped to reply and I noticed she had a
nervous habit of wringing her hands. "Why, the poor girl
has such fancies! My husband has little patience with
them. She was engaged before, you know. To Captain
Horler, who treated her shamefully."

We continued down a short corridor to a green baize
door, which she opened somewhat timidly, I thought. "If
you will wait in here, my husband will be with you
shortly."

At first I found it difficult to take in very much, as the
door shut behind us, for the room was not very well lit.
Then I began to realise we were standing in the middle
of some kind of collection. All around us were large glass
tanks, reaching well above our heads. The one closest to
me was full of fish, but it was untypical for soon I came
to beetles and then snakes, and at last I was staring at a
nest of what looked like scorpions.

"Interesting companions," commented Dr. Bell.

"For some," I said, because "interesting" was not the
adjective that came most readily to my lips.

The Doctor had, however, moved on to a display case

full of spiders and was studying it avidly. "*Latrodectus hesperus*... A long time since I have seen you, my friend."

Quite suddenly a figure appeared behind the case, standing bolt upright. I still have no idea, as I think back to that room, whether he had been in there the whole time or had entered while we were staring at the cases. My suspicion, partly arising from later events, is he would lurk in the shadows of the place, musing over its contents.

Blythe was a big, bull-necked man, bursting with energy. "Which one of you," he asked with evident hostility, "is Doyle?"

"I am," I answered with more casualness than I felt.

He turned to me. "My niece, Heather, is not here. But I am glad you have called as she said because I wanted to talk to you. I believe, sir, you have designs upon her. You must stop all dealings with her at once."

"I am sure she can make up her own mind. And you seem unaware that I am her doctor."

He glared at me. "Which makes the impropriety all the grosser."

Dr. Bell had been watching alertly and stepped forward now to intercede. "I can vouch for my young colleague here, Mr. Blythe. We are visiting you on a matter I believe to be of importance. It seems to me your niece is in danger."

Blythe stared rudely at Bell. "There at least we can agree. Who are you, sir?"

"I am Dr. Joseph Bell of Edinburgh University."

"The Dr. Bell, head of operative surgery, who wrote the monograph on the adaptation of the eye to distance?" His tone was excited.

"The same," said the Doctor.

"Why did you not say so, Dr. Bell?" Blythe smiled warmly. "I studied botany and zoology in London until I withdrew to supervise my own collection here, which I may say I have plans to expand. Have you noted it?"

I was amazed. He wished to expand what was already so large, but it gave me a good idea of the man's ambition. "Indeed," the Doctor was saying, "I admired it. Though I was surprised by the *Latrodectus*."

"Ah, yes," said Blythe, with what seemed almost like paternal affection. "A deadly little man." He moved over, put his hand in and the spider crawled on to it.

The Doctor looked alarmed but Blythe merely smiled. "Venomless," he explained. "I extract the venom. It is one of my hobbies. Oh, I am a dabbler, a mere picker up of shells on the shores of the ocean of science. You, of all people, would understand. Indeed, your orbital development is so pronounced that a cast of your skull would be an ornament to any museum such as this."

"Thank you," said the Doctor. "I am not yet ready to donate it." He paused. "We are here because I fear your niece is at risk. There is a figure that follows her . . ."

Blythe, who was putting the spider back now, looked a good deal less interested and interrupted the Doctor rather rudely: "My niece has two great defects, Dr. Bell. She is grossly over-imaginative and may soon be very rich. The latter causes men to follow her and to fight over her, while the former conjures up even greater threats. You should think twice about any account she gives." Blythe had moved over to his desk and now indicated a pile of legal correspondence. "I am attempting, for her own sake, to retain supervision of her inheritance and advancing my legal claim to do so. She has a nervous affliction which makes her ill-suited for the money."

I sensed the magnitude of the Doctor's interest though he barely moved a muscle. "And I imagine," he said mildly, "the interest on it is of considerable help in servicing your collection?"

The inference of the Doctor's remark was so unmistakable I almost expected Blythe to move across the room and attack him. But, strangely, this fierce man became suddenly passive and very still. In fact, his voice dropped. "I shall not take that as an insult. My wife has means of her own. In any case as soon as my niece marries Mr. Greenwell I will settle them both with the money for she would be out of harm's way and in proper hands. So I fear your errand here is pointless." He moved forward to usher us out, indicating that the interview was at an end. I am sure he would have been happy to talk science with Bell all day but these other topics were not to his taste.

As we reached the door, Bell stopped. "Mr. Blythe," he said. "I see you have an elegant line in outdoor dress. The hood must be useful." Hanging on a peg were two black coats with hoods. I stared too, for they looked familiar.

Blythe stopped and ran his fingers along one of the cloaks. "Oh, I collect specimens at all times and in all weathers, Dr. Bell. You will excuse me now if I return to my studies but there is a fine nest of *vipera berus* in the wood below my house. I like to take the adders' skins while they are alive and also sometimes I milk their venom. Perhaps one day you would care to join me?"

We said our goodbyes and the door of that room shut behind us. "What a man!" I exclaimed to the Doctor as we came out of the corridor and made our way back to the entrance hall. "You saw that cloak . . ."

"Certainly," said Bell, "he has a motive for undermining his niece if he wants to keep his hands on her money. But in itself I fear the cloaks prove nothing. They are common enough garments." At the time, as we moved out of that house and back into the wind, I wondered if Bell was not being overcautious.

On the road we stopped the cab to talk to Baynes, who

was crouched behind the hedge and had as yet seen nothing on his watch. The Doctor urged him to give it up and Baynes agreed to take advantage of the lift into town. "But I will try again one last time in the morning, Dr. Bell," he said with a grin as he settled in the cab. "Sometimes it takes a while to draw an ace but one comes in the end."

That night, perhaps prompted by my own fears, it was my turn to have bad dreams. I saw Heather Grace moving through a house infested with spiders and snakes and cruelty, and I tried desperately to take her from it. It is a dream that has often returned over the years.

THE DARK WINDOW

The following day I had an appointment with Miss Grace, in view of her uncle's rude words to me, I wondered if she would be allowed to attend. I waited in my consultation room, making some adjustments to the apparatus for the study of her eye condition when, to my pleasure, I heard voices outside and Bell showed her in.

He left us and I got to my feet and shook her hand, telling her the machine was ready. I had already decided to say nothing of our interview with her uncle but she looked a little distracted and her shoes were muddy. She told me she had been walking and thinking. Then she sat down in the chair I had placed in front of the light. The retinoscope is essentially a machine for reflecting a beam of light from a mirror into the eye in such a way that enables the physician to study areas of shadow as the mirror is rotated. Now I set about positioning the light so it would illuminate her eyes and soon I was looking deeply into them.

I have written that I found it hard not to be distracted by my patient's eyes when I first met her. Now that I was staring into them at such length this was doubly difficult. As I looked at those beautiful eyes and made my notes, I found myself thinking about my dream the previous night and also about her strange uncle and the figure who pursued her. She looked so vulnerable, but thank heaven I sensed a strength in her too.

I told her I intended to make such examinations regularly and compare the results. "There are areas of shadow, which strike me as unusual," I said as I stared, "and pools of darker colour. But I believe they are slightly smaller than when I last observed them with the naked eye."

"And yours," she said with a smile—for, as I stared into hers, she was inevitably looking into mine—"I seem to see conscience and faith in them."

"Sometimes I feel little enough of either," I told her, taking my eyes away with difficulty and altering the angle of the mirror. "I was brought up a Catholic and I believe in something, but I cannot always find clarity in it."

"Yes, I want so much to be clear in myself too." The medical consultation was coming to an end, but if she wanted to talk then I saw no reason to stop her. "You see, when my parents died I was young and I often wondered if I would ever move beyond what happened. Find love. Then there was the one man I loved."

"Captain Horler?"

She nodded. "And I must admit when it ended and he left me I thought nothing would ever make me whole. Never, ever. That I would not find someone again."

I told her that I knew this feeling, but wounds could heal.

"I wish so much . . ." She stopped. "But will you not tell me more of what happened to you?"

It was not a subject I much wished to dwell on. "It was a long time ago," I said.

"That makes no difference, as you said yourself."

I thought of the events of that awful year in Edinburgh,

the year marked by my unopened box. I would not have been prepared to answer anyone else's questions on the subject but I answered hers.

"There is little to say." I spoke quietly. "She died. Dr. Bell failed. It was a vicious crime. Even now we hope one day we will see justice."

"I understand. And you keep thinking over and over, is there something I should have done? Was I a coward?"

"Yes," I agreed. "I know it."

"I was sure we shared it." The light from the retinoscope was still casting odd shadows as she spoke and our faces were very close.

"I feel," she said, "I have always felt—and you must forgive me this—as if I could read your thoughts."

I do not know how long we looked at each other. It is indeed as strange for me to look back on that moment now as it was to live it then. She was, as I have said, the first person I had ever talked to about what happened to Elsbeth and I felt such a sense of release to know someone else could understand my feelings. I still feel the intensity of my exhilaration to this day.

In any case we were interrupted by the ringing of my doorbell. It was the next patient. But that was my last appointment and Miss Grace readily agreed to wait so I could see her safely home.

She had not come by bicycle, so a little later we were climbing out of a cab at the rectory gates and she was insisting I should come in and take tea. We had been talking merrily enough about our early lives and I confessed to her I had not wanted to be a doctor. Weaned on tales of a great-uncle who led the Scottish brigade at Waterloo, I would probably have become a soldier, but my mother overruled me.

"I think your mother was right to guide you then," she said. "But it is not always so. Sometimes it can be stifling if decisions are made for you. I will be honest, Dr. Doyle, there are times when the marriage my people propose feels to me like a prison."

"Then why proceed?"

We had stopped quite close to the house when our conversation suddenly became more serious again, her hand playing with the collar of her coat as she stared up at me. "Because," she said, "at other times I think it may be right. You know what fears I have."

"I have counselled you against them."

"And I am glad we have met. There is so much I want to tell you. I feel safe when we are talking." She paused, her eyes turning to the house. "But if . . ."

"But . . ." I spoke almost simultaneously.

We both stopped, knowing exactly where we were leading, and it seemed my place to say it. "I was merely going to say that if we became close friends then it would be best for me to stop as your doctor."

"Yes, I was the same," she said and her face fairly shone to know we were one of mind. "Sometimes I walk out on afternoons like this, if one day . . ."

But I was never destined to hear her proposal. For quite suddenly and literally in the fading sun a shadow was cast over us. A figure had stepped out from the side of the house.

We turned to face Greenwell. He stood there, neither scowling nor even, for once, smiling. When he spoke, it was in a more abrupt tone than I had ever heard from him on our first meeting. "Miss Grace, I was waiting here for you. We must have a word as I am sure you will understand."

Her change of expression was terrible to behold. "Mr. Greenwell."

He turned to me. "Dr. Doyle, take my carriage if you wish. It is round the other side."

"I do not want it," I said firmly. "I was invited to take tea with Miss Grace and I think when we last met you said you wished her to make up her own mind."

His manner softened a little. "But of course she must decide," he said. And he turned back to her with the same smile I remembered so well. "Miss Grace? Your uncle is aware I am here."

Her eyes filled with tears and she turned to me, evidently powerless to do anything. "I am sorry, Dr. Doyle," she said. And nobody who cared about her would have wanted to press her further in such circumstances.

I bade my farewells and they went inside. I certainly had no intention of taking Greenwell's carriage, nor could I bring myself to leave immediately. So I wandered into the trees on the edge of the lawn to calm my own furious passions. I stood there a few minutes, reflecting on what had happened. At least, I told myself, while Heather Grace might be bullied in the matter of afternoon tea she had as good as told me she would not be bullied into a more permanent state of misery. Therefore I determined I must keep my dignity and take the now familiar and arduous walk back into the town.

I emerged from the trees and was just turning back towards the drive in the gathering darkness when my attention was caught by a window at the side of the house. It was not brightly illuminated; indeed, the room was partly in darkness, but I could see two figures in the flicker of candlelight. Drawing closer, I made out Miss Grace and Greenwell. It was impossible to hear what was being said but she stood there with a terrible stillness as he remonstrated with her. He looked angry but then, and somehow this was even worse to behold, the whole tone of the encounter seemed to change, and his manner became softer and he smiled that awful smile. His anger appeared to vanish and I wish I could say Miss Grace's mood changed too, but it did not. Some of her tears left her, but she seemed paler and more unhappy than ever as he continued to speak. Just then a servant entered and the exchange came to an end as the blinds were drawn.

The memory of that change, especially, haunted me as I walked along the dark road. I wished then that I had not seen the second part of the encounter. It disturbed me even more than the first. I was feeling very weary when I came back to the house that night, but I will acknowledge too that my conscience was starting to prick me. I tried not to think about what the Doctor was likely to say if he knew that I had been close to some kind of passionate declaration to a woman who was not merely at the centre of his current case but who was also my own patient.

As I climbed the stairs I could see through the half-open door that a candle burned in the upstairs room Dr. Bell had taken over as his study and he was working at his desk. He knew I had elected to escort Miss Grace home and I was reluctant to face any questions. So I went quietly past his door to my bedroom. Knowing the sensitivity of his hearing, I am sure he heard me. But he did not call out.

And so, for the first time in these temporary quarters, we went to our rest without exchanging a word. Judging from past events, I should have known this would prove an ill omen.

THE STAND-UP GRAVE

I woke early, knowing I would sleep no further, and got up even though it was hardly light. Looking out of the window, I saw it was one of those days where day struggles to come at all and, moreover, there was a whipping wind, gusting the rain against the glass. I walked down the stairs, intending to write up some notes, for I was sure the best way forward on such a day as this lay in work. But I jumped, for there was a figure in my consulting room, staring out of the window. It was Bell. "Why, Doctor," I said in a friendly tone, for I felt guilty about avoiding him the night before, "it is still early."

He turned and his face was ghastly, his voice quiet. "No, it is not early, it is not early at all. It is late. I was about to knock on your door. Are you ready?"

"Ready?" I asked and now I saw the message in his hand.

"We must go at once. As soon as I heard, I sent word to Warner. Baynes did not return to his lodgings last night."

Within an hour Bell and I were at the same spot on that dreary road, well ahead of anyone else. We knew the place Baynes favoured for his lookout—it was not far from where I had waited twice myself—but there was no sign of him at all.

We at once began to explore the wood itself. It was a miserable day, but at least there was enough of a dawn for us to make out the ground as we tramped among the trees. I could see absolutely no signs of any trail in the vegetation and, though the Doctor stopped a few times to examine the ground, I was sure he too found nothing.

After much fruitless walking around in circles, I began to hope for a better outcome. Perhaps Baynes had merely abandoned his post and gone into Southampton for a game of cards. Possibly he was even now back at his lodgings or would appear on the road.

But as I looked back through the trees, I saw Bell had slowed his pace and was staring over to his left. There was something on the ground in that direction I could not make out. I watched Bell walking smartly towards it. Then his pace slowed and he stopped dead. "*Doyle*!" I doubt I will ever forget the way he shouted my name.

Something soft and pale was sticking out of the foliage. I raced back through the trees towards him as he bent down and started to pull at the earth around it. I got there, panting for breath, and began to help him. The thing was soft and fleshy under the mud, though at first we could see no more of it than that. Then, as we scrabbled to get more earth away, I found my hand touching something protruding from the muddy mass and recoiled with an exclamation. For now I saw what this was and the Doctor's grim face told me he already knew. I had touched a human ear. What we were excavating was Baynes's head.

We clawed our way on to try to discover more and slowly the features became visible, limp and lifeless, the eyes staring. At any moment I dreaded to find it had been severed. But in fact what we uncovered was far worse. For soon, below, his shoulders too were visible.

I could see how upset the Doctor was. "I should have given him more warning," he said.

"But what has been done to him?"

The Doctor was running his hands over what we had so far disinterred. "He has been dead for hours. His hands must have been tied."

"But he is standing."

"Only because the earth supports him, his feet will be restrained. The police should be by the road now. Will you go and get them?"

It took two and a half hours to drag poor Baynes's body out of the terrible narrow grave in which he stood. I will never forget the sight as they lifted him. Two men had to clamber down into the hole, others pulling from the top and gripping him under his arms, as they hoisted him out. By then he was almost rigid but I still recall (and wish I did not) the head lolling back as he was raised up.

They laid him face upwards under the trees. Of course, there was mud on the corpse, but not enough to obscure the full horror of the sight, especially the fact that, because it was filled with earth, the mouth was gaping wide open. Just as Bell had predicted, the feet were weighted down with stones and the hands bound tightly with knotted twine.

As soon as it was excavated the Doctor, who had been waiting and watching with ill-concealed impatience, bent down to examine every detail of the corpse. He paid particular attention to the knots, studying them with great concentration for what seemed like hours. Finally I saw him take one and preserve it carefully. In the pockets he found only the gaming dice Baynes always carried. There were no marks on the body, other than where it was bound, so it was soon clear enough that the cause of death was what we dreaded: Baynes had died of suffocation.

The Doctor and I stood watching as the police raised up the corpse on a stretcher to carry it away through these trees. Because of the undergrowth they were forced to hoist it very high and the last thing I saw of Baynes was one of those dexterous hands hanging limply down. A policeman reached up to move it out of view before he was borne solemnly away.

Throughout the rest of that long, grey morning the Doctor studied the ground quietly and methodically within a broad radius of the grave. He said almost nothing but I saw on this occasion little of the excitement that usually surrounded him at a murder scene. It was obvious to me that he was furiously angry with himself for allowing Baynes to take such a risk.

At last he was done and Warner was waiting for us at the road.

"So his feet were weighed, his hands tied," he said as he led us to a police cab. "What sort of killer is it who buries his victim alive and standing, Dr. Bell?"

The Doctor stared at him almost as if he did not hear. "One who at least is not afraid to leave flamboyant traces," he replied bleakly.

"And we already know, Mr. Baynes here was a gambler who regularly lost money at cards in Southampton," said the Inspector. "Perhaps the solution lies there."

"Perhaps," agreed the Doctor. "But what strikes me most about the crime is its drama. And the man Baynes himself suspected has a great weakness for such things."

It was agreed that Warner would investigate Baynes's gaming associates while we made enquiries nearer at hand. After we had left him, Bell sat in grim silence as the cab took us to Cullingworth's practice. Although Inspector Warner was anxious that news of the murder should not yet spread too far, Cullingworth had been informed, for technically he was still the man's employer. Like Bell, I was very curious to see how he had received the news.

There were no patients at the practice when we reached it and his maid informed us he was in his study, working on his magnetic ship protector, and could not be disturbed. Bell simply ignored her and moved forward down the passage to Cullingworth's study. He reached the door and opened it.

The room was in semi-darkness and there, across at the far wall, Cullingworth stood bolt upright, pointing his pistol right at Bell's heart. He was smiling.

"I am at your heart, Dr. Bell."

"So I see."

"But have no fear. For my magnet by the door will draw the bullet well off to the left."

I was just behind and to one side of Bell. "If it does not," replied the Doctor, "you will be arrested for my murder. And possibly Baynes's as well."

"Yes, I had word of the tragedy. Well, the man had gambling debts as you know. He was not careful of the company he kept at the card table. No doubt you will find his murderer in the slews of Southampton."

"It was you," said the Doctor, "who tried to cheat him out of his money. He also caught you spying on Miss Grace. Have you been following her?"

As he spoke, Bell was quietly moving to one side, closer and closer to the magnet.

I could see Cullingworth's frustration at this but there was little he could do. "That is no good," he exclaimed, "you are almost on the magnet. The bullet will hit you."

"Exactly," said Bell heartily, "and then you will be killing me for no purpose." He was at the magnet itself now and Cullingworth threw the gun to one side and sprawled on the sofa in disgust.

"Let it wait then, Doctor." He waved a hand to indicate we should join him.

Neither the Doctor nor myself was in any mood to do so. We remained standing. "You take a great interest in Miss Grace, do you not?" asked Bell.

"Perhaps I do," Cullingworth agreed carelessly. "The truth is I never knew a woman could be quite so . . . forward. Of course, I am aware they find me attractive."

I was annoyed enough already, and now he had the gall to turn and address his remarks to me with a superior smile. "It has been a curse, laddie. Though at times a pleasant enough one." And he gave a little snigger that made me want to punch him in the face.

Bell probably sensed my anger for he went on quickly, "Did you make advances to her?"

"Is that what she says?" he asked in a coarse and jeering tone, which reminded me of the policemen who had interrogated me.

"Well, like any woman, she wanted my attention and I had to resist her charms. Besides, she was engaged to a fellow who went off to Natal. It was really rather shocking of her to flaunt herself at me."

I had had more than I could bear. "You have not the slightest notion of decency," I shouted. "And now you blame her to cover your own lechery! You know quite well how angry you were when she asked to be my patient."

Cullingworth got up carelessly, as if to end our visit. "Oh, well, you are welcome to her, laddie. We know what she is. Though it is Greenwell who has set his heart on her money and will surely get it. But perhaps I should think of arranging another of my little dramas around Miss Grace. The last was a small enough affair, I grant you, but it was still a minor triumph, did you not think,

Bell? Only be warned, this time I might not make it so easy for you."

Cullingworth was so puffed up by his own boasting that he had not observed the Doctor, cane in hand, edging closer to him as he was talking. And quite suddenly, at this last remark, Bell flung himself right at him.

The attack came so fast and Cullingworth was so ill prepared that he could do nothing but step back and the Doctor seized the advantage at once, using his cane horizontally and viciously to trap Cullingworth's neck against the wall.

"Now you listen to me, *laddie*," said the Doctor with such fierceness and intensity that I felt the hairs on the back of my neck standing. "These are serious matters and they involve people, not toys. Your stupid Garcia game may well have been a deliberate attempt to scare Doyle off Miss Grace. Perhaps it was you who murdered Baynes and seek to cover your guilt. But even if it was not, I tell you now that any further 'dramas' and I will personally see you are disbarred from practising medicine anywhere in these islands. Given that I know of your medical ethics, I am sure that could be swiftly achieved."

The Doctor's eyes were flashing with a rage I had rarely, if ever, seen before. All the feeling that had been building up since he saw Baynes was pouring out of him and he was quivering with so much energy that I was half frightened his cane would break Cullingworth's neck.

The man was gasping for breath. "I cannot breathe, sir."

"Do we have an understanding . . . laddie?" shouted Bell, increasing his pressure.

I could see Cullingworth was now truly frightened. "Very well." He managed to get the words out at last. Bell moved back and Cullingworth panted for breath, rubbing his bruised neck.

"I think you had better go," he said at last, evidently trying to recover some shred of dignity. We made our way to the door. Cullingworth had regained a little colour and some of the old guile was back in his eyes as he rubbed his neck. "But," he whispered, still short of breath, "you are in deep waters, gentlemen. I wonder if you have grasped how deep."

We had already decided our next call would be on Miss Grace at the rectory and, as if to mock us, the weather, for so long inclement, was becoming clearer. Bell was silent and pensive as the cab took the road out of town again. I do not think either of us was quite sure what to make of our encounter with Cullingworth. His last remark had hinted at something beyond our investigation that I did not entirely understand.

We reached the rectory and were greeted warmly enough by Miss Grace and her aunt, who had not been out and appeared to know nothing at all of what had happened. Evidently Miss Grace had woken up fairly early the previous night with a bad dream and spent most of it in her aunt's spare bed.

The Doctor made no mention at all of the events in the wood; indeed, he took some trouble to be as normal as possible, but he did indicate matters were a little more urgent and the police were taking the affair of the figure seriously.

"Mrs. Blythe," he said courteously, "as you know I have been a little concerned by the fact that someone appears to be following your niece. I am quite confident we can resolve the business but even so I think it is prudent to take every precaution. In such circumstances I have certain foolish rituals and regarding them I would ask for your patience and indulgence. One would be to see Miss

Grace's bedroom, just to satisfy myself it is secure."

They both looked a little surprised, but the Doctor was calm and reassuring. "Of course," said Mrs. Blythe, "I am hopeful you will not find anything amiss. If you will follow me?"

We climbed the stairs, passed through a carpeted passage and then Miss Grace and her aunt led us to a large, light and airy room with two big windows and a wonderful view of the surrounding countryside.

"This is my room, Dr. Bell," said Miss Grace cheerfully as we entered and looked around. "I feel foolish enough. I had been better but last night again the same nightmare. He pursues me. A cloaked, sightless thing. I called out and fortunately my aunt was here so quickly that I got over it."

The Doctor went first to the windows. He seemed pleased and I knew why. We were three storeys up overlooking woods and fields and there was no way on earth anyone could have climbed up here along a sheer wall. Even if they did, the windows were shut fast. He pretended his pleasure derived from the view and then went to the fireplace, but that too seemed to offer little prospect for intrusion.

Mrs. Blythe's face showed no expression as she watched, for I think she had been deceived by the Doctor's manner into assuming, as he intended, that he was merely a little fussy and eccentric. Miss Grace, however, knew better. "Nothing has happened, has it?" she asked.

I felt at once that we could not maintain this charade and it would be better to tell them. The Doctor and I often disagreed about such things, for it was second nature to him to say as little as possible until all the facts were assembled. I was about to find the words but the Doctor read my thoughts and got in ahead of me: "We are following various avenues and there are always odd connections. I hope to have a solution for you in due course."

Again Mrs. Blythe seemed to accept this but Miss Grace had noticed his glance at me and it clearly concerned her, for in that moment of anxiety her hand went, as ever, to her locket and found only thin air. She was not wearing it.

The Doctor observed this at once. "You have no locket, I see." he said.

Her aunt stepped forward, clasping her hands. "Oh, yes, it is very peculiar. She woke up today and it was gone. It was her parents' locket."

"And it was removed from here?" asked Bell, coming over to them. His tone was deliberately flat but I could see well enough how concerned he was.

"I cannot think what happened to it," said Miss Grace, turning to her dressing table with agitation. "Last night I put it in my jewellery case here and this morning it had gone. Of course, I thought I might have been distracted and it was on the dressing table or even the floor, but it seems to have vanished."

At once Bell moved to examine the small but pretty engraved case, which sat on the dressing table. He opened it and a familiar tune played, "Over Yonder's a Park," known also as "All the Bells in Paradise," the same haunting carol we had heard at Abbey Mill. "This is very fine," said Bell. "Now you are quite sure it was here?"

"I am certain," she frowned as she tried to remember. "But I was very tired and I suppose it is possible I took it off elsewhere and merely thought I had put it away."

"That is surely the explanation," Bell stated firmly and she looked much happier. "I am certain it will turn up. This is a very lovely air, is it not?" And he turned to the box, as if listening to the carol. I was, however, beside him and could see quite well that he was actually studying that whole section of the bedroom with urgent attention:

the table, the wall, even the ceiling. I thought of Blythe and his strange menagerie of snakes, scorpions and God knows what else, and could well understand what came next.

"It is a delightful tune," said the Doctor with a twinkle as he closed the lid. "Tell me, Mrs. Blythe, would you have any objection to moving a servant in here to keep Miss Grace company? It seems a shame to leave her even for a moment if she is having nightmares."

"Why"—Mrs. Blythe went over to her niece— "I will sleep in here myself and lock the doors and windows. We will be snug."

She was not the most effusive of women, but I did see a tenderness in her eyes and Miss Grace's expression was happy too. "I am foolish but I think I would feel much better," she said. "Thank you."

Here at least, it seemed, was some genuine affection. And I was relieved for if Mr. Blythe did have some awful design on his niece and her fortune, surely he would think twice before exposing his wife to any danger?

As if echoing my thought, Bell was now asking Mrs. Blythe with great courtesy whether it might be possible to have a few words with her husband.

"I have no objection," said Mrs. Blythe, turning back from her niece. "But he has been on one of his long speci-men hunts. In fact, I have not seen him since last night."

Bell and I exchanged a discreet glance. "Well," said the Doctor, "with your permission we would be glad to see him if he is available."

Mrs. Blythe and Bell began to make their way to the door, but Miss Grace lagged behind and looked at me imploringly.

I turned to Mrs. Blythe. "With your permission, ma'am, I wish to talk with Miss Grace about her symp-toms. I will be along presently." The Doctor looked impassive. Mrs. Blythe merely nodded and exited with him.

And so I found myself alone with my patient. At first, of course, I thought it prudent to make some pretence of medical discussion. For a few minutes we talked about her symptoms and the results of my tests. I asked if she had been drinking more water, for I had suggested this as a common panacea for eye trouble.

She showed me a carafe by her bed and picked up the glass, smiling. And in this way we got around to more personal matters. "Dr. Bell seems so concerned," she said with an apprehensive smile. "I hope after our last conversation you might be able to take me into your confidence if something has happened."

"Yes." It was not, after all, such a difficult decision. I had wanted to tell her though I had no intention of going into details. "A man, whom I do not think you know, has been murdered in the wood."

Because I had wished to inform her in the first place I was much too abrupt. She turned and stared at me as if not understanding and then I saw her sway. The glass dropped from her hand, shattering into pieces on the floor.

I moved quickly to comfort her and she fell into my arms, her whole body trembling as we clung to each other. I felt the softness of her skin below me, her hands clasping me so tightly. Perhaps it was a gross abuse of my position, but I did not care about that any more than I would care about getting my clothes wet when a person was drowning in front of me.

She was sobbing now, her face pressed against my shoulder. "He died and it should have been me."

"No," I answered vehemently. "We will discover why."

"But do you not see?" she went on wildly, still holding me as if I would vanish in her grip. "I cannot bear it all coming back. It is my dream coming true."

"No, I swear it is not." I held her more tightly, as if I could force the fear away.

"I was foolish to think I could ever leave it behind. If I marry Mr. Greenwell, this nightmare will stop. The dead will be dead. I will be free. He has told me so."

"That is not a reason," I said, shocked. "It is more like a threat."

There were steps outside the open doorway. We moved apart and the Doctor stood there. Of course, he knew at once he had hardly interrupted a normal interview between doctor and patient, but he said nothing except that Blythe appeared to be out and we must be on our way.

As we walked back through that rambling house to the stairs, he still said nothing and I had no wish to start a conversation for I knew quite well where it would lead. So we descended the long staircase in silence and I believe I saw the figure at the bottom just before he did. We stopped, expecting to see an angry Blythe.

But it was his wife who stepped out of the shadows and, much to our surprise, her whole demeanour was quite altered. In the bedroom she had been placid. Now her expression was anguished and she was ringing her hands.

"Gentlemen," she whispered, "I am glad I have caught you for I have just had something of a shock. Will you come with me?"

She showed us into a small yet comfortable parlour by the stairs, which she evidently used for household matters. There were a desk, a small sofa with some cushions and embroidery, and a table covered by a red cloth. Letters were scattered on the table and she led us to them. "My husband often takes the mail to his study when he comes in," she explained. "He is not the tidiest of men and occasionally letters for myself or my niece only reappear a few days later. I have rebuked him for it in the past."

Bell looked interested, but I could hardly see the rele-

vance of this until she picked up a letter that had been
hidden under another. "These are already a few days late,"
she went on, speaking very quickly in her agitation, "and
after leaving you I came down here to go through them.
Oh, it is lucky for me I did for there was one . . . Well,
you will see for yourself. I will say nothing of it to my
niece for it would only terrify her. It must surely be some
joke, a silly trick. If you would take it?"

The Doctor accepted the letter eagerly. It was an en-
velope on which someone had cut out type from a newspaper. On the front in disparate letters, it read:

miss grace

the rectory

Bell studied it. The postmark was local. Then he lifted
the already opened flap and took out a plain piece of paper
with a message gummed to it. This consisted entirely of
words also evidently cut out of a newspaper. They read:

your grave

waits In the wood

THE MAD NOTE

That night I felt doubly grateful to Mrs. Blythe, not merely for keeping watch over her niece, but also for ensuring this mad note had never reached her, for I dreaded to think what effect it might have had.

The Doctor was galvanised by the new evidence and, before beginning a full-scale chemical analysis, ordered me to try to collect every national daily newspaper for the past fortnight. It was by no means a simple task but I was fortunate. A co-operative newsagent on the front had a large collection of back copies and was able to meet almost all my needs. I took these to Bell and then completed the collection with a trip to the station and a hotel.

When I returned to his converted bedroom on the second floor with my last armful, he had already separated most of what I had brought before and was directing his attention solely to *The Times*, which was my final burden.

"Well done, Doyle," he said, taking them from me, evidently cheerful to have concrete evidence at last. For the moment, at least, this latest development had entirely distracted him from questions about my involvement with Miss Grace, but I knew they would come soon enough. "That is them all," he was saying as he sorted through them furiously. "And here is where my hopes lie. In *The Times* leader."

He tore one paper open, then another, then another, all at the leader page. "No," he said. "No." Then his eye settled on one like a hawk. "Yes, Doyle!" he said. "Read this paragraph here. It concerns free trade."

I started to read:

> "In *the last analysis, a protective tariff is the* grave *of free enterprise for my protection soon becomes* your *dense* wood *of obstruction. Yet it is* missi*ng* the *point to see free trade as some state of* grace. *It a*waits *only . . ."*

I broke off in amazement for I could see the paragraph contained all the words of the note even down to Miss Grace. Only the address of the rectory had defeated its sender, who had resorted to single letters.

"Yes, all the words but how in heaven did you go straight to this one?"

"Oh, because type is an important part of criminal work and there is as much difference between the leaded bourgeois type of a *Times* leader and the thin face of the *Herald*'s fount as between oil and water. But there is more. This was cut with nail scissors, for the cutter had to take two snips over 'in the.' Moreover, it was done in great haste—see, the words are not gummed in an accurate line. Perhaps he feared interruption."

Both our thoughts lay now with Guy Greenwell for we remembered the summer house filled with copies of *The Times*, and his daybook of cuttings. But in the event he proved a difficult man to find. Knowing the school was closed, we made a fruitless journey in the dark to his property, Wade House, which was shuttered and empty. On the way back an ageing ground keeper came out of a cottage on the drive to ask our business and from him we learned Wade House was being sold urgently because of the same debts Bell had already uncovered. Its owner was staying with friends in the town, but only the absent housekeeper could provide details and we would have to call back for these in the morning.

The Doctor was thoughtful as we made our return journey. "Well, it would seem," he mused, "that Mr. Greenwell has been guilty of one small deception at least. Of course, it may purely be pride on his part but the wealthy estate owner teaching only for pleasure rapidly gives way to a debtor who must procure money wherever he can."

We had done all we could for the day but I was not to escape Bell's strictures so easily. After we had made a late and hasty meal in my consulting room, he broached the subject I had been hoping to avoid. "Tell me," he said as he leant back, putting his fingertips together and half closing his eyes, "have you considered the dangers both to yourself and your profession of becoming too close to Miss Grace?"

I suppose I should have confided in him properly and told him all that had occurred between us, but it was the kind of subject I avoided with the Doctor. So I said little.

Now his hawklike eyes were full on me. "Do you not understand?" he pressed. "It is not merely a question of some romantic attachment. She is part of a case."

"If she is at risk," I answered carefully, "it would hardly be honourable to withdraw on those grounds. Do you not see that she is terrified of Greenwell and what he will do? Even to us he talked of some visitation of the dead. And from what she said to me today it seems clear he is trying to convince her that Coatley, the man who murdered her parents, has come back from the grave. I think we should seriously consider whether we can leave her in that place." The Doctor did not seem inclined to argue the point further but he made it clear he was far from happy.

He was still silent the next day as we returned to the rectory to interview Charles Blythe. I hoped to see Miss Grace, but the servants informed us she was visiting the town with her aunt. They did not know whether Charles Blythe was available or even if he had returned so, with our cab waiting, we were again led into that grim, darkened display room while they attempted to discover.

The door closed behind us and the place seemed to be empty. Once again I peered into those glass cases, filled with every kind of poisonous insect and reptile. Bell directed my attention to a *Hadrurus Arizonensis*, which sounded innocent enough until I saw it was an orange scorpion about five inches in length with a vicious sting in its tail which it pointed towards me as if it would dearly love to get at me through the glass.

I was staring at the thing, when suddenly there was movement behind it and a huge caped shape rose up in front of me. Charles Blythe had been lying on a low sofa that bordered part of his collection and he stared at me angrily.

But then he saw Bell and, as on our first visit, his respect for the scientist seemed to overcome his dislike of me, though he was still fairly abrupt in his tone. "Dr. Bell," he asked, "what are you doing?"

Bell was for the time being as charming as could be. "We must apologise for the intrusion," he said, coming over to face Blythe. As he did so, I could not help comparing the two men. Bell was tall but Blythe was almost a foot taller. Bell was lithe and wiry, while Blythe had weight and stamina. I would not have much cared to predict the winner in a wrestling ring.

"Of course," the Doctor was continuing smoothly, "I am always glad of the opportunity to revisit your collection, but there have been certain events close to here and we are helping the police with their enquiries. So you have been in the wood I see?"

"Yes," Blythe replied. "I have been on a marathon hunt, returning late last night. I did not wish to disturb the house so I slept in here."

Blythe would have moved away but the Doctor kept his gaze fixed on him. "Did you see anyone?"

"Oh, yes," answered Blythe. And he took a small box out of his pocket and opened it lovingly. Inside were an assortment of beetles and a lizard. "I saw these pretty friends. Nobody else, though."

Now, for the first time, I could sense the Doctor's impatience and irritation. "Nobody? A man has been murdered in the wood."

To our mutual astonishment, Blythe did not even look up from his "friends" at this news. "Is that so?" he remarked gently. "We live in a barbaric age, do we not?" With that he went over to one of his glass cabinets and opened the door.

"Indeed we do." Bell's anger was restrained but I knew he was thinking of Baynes's body lying in that blasphemy of a grave. Even if Blythe was not responsible, his indifference to human suffering was still monstrous. "Tell me, Mr. Blythe,"—the Doctor had moved closer to him and his glass cabinet—"do you recall the night of the Abbey Mill murders?"

This had some effect, for Blythe paused a moment, before continuing with his preparation of a display case for his new finds. "It is not something one forgets," he said.

"That old case has always interested me," Bell told him. "There were many inconsistencies. But what I had never realised before making a full study of the trial transcripts was that on that terrible night you were here with

Guy Greenwell. So both of you had alibis."

"We hardly needed one." Blythe had taken a small metal spadelike implement about a foot long and was using it to transfer some earth and grass into the case before he added his insects and closed the door.

Bell's tone softened, which usually meant he was going for the jugular. "I am not so sure," he mused. "For of course it turns out you both benefited handsomely. You have had eight years of interest and now, with your encouragement, Greenwell stands to gain the principal."

If, as I suspect, Bell was intending to provoke Blythe and force him to engage with us, he had at last hit his mark. For the man now turned like an angry bull. His muscles were tense and his reddening colour was a wonder to behold.

"That is quite outrageous, sir! You imply a false alibi. And you must know Coatley confessed."

"I know it well," said Bell with infuriating mildness, evidently pleased by the reaction. "But I am equally aware that someone or something threatens your niece now."

Blythe moved over until he was within inches of the Doctor. He still held the metal spade in his hand and I thought for a moment he would launch a physical attack. I feared it too, for though I have said the two men were evenly matched, Blythe's brawny arms were of the kind that could certainly snap a limb before they were restrained. And now, as if to prove this, he took the spade in both hands and bent it into a curve. "I would ask you to cease meddling in my affairs," he said and, though his tone was not loud, there was a harshness in it that could have shattered glass. "I can assure you my niece is not of sound mind. She was confined once before for her own good and we may do it again."

But the Doctor stood his ground, not moving a muscle through all this as he looked up at him. "Yes, rather than see her money disappear I am sure you would. But we intend to protect her and discover who is doing this."

It was Blythe who finally turned away, tossing the spade to one side and moving back to his work. "I have made myself clear I fancy," he said. "Now I have matters to settle. Indeed, Bell, you should leave your wild notions and help me here. You waste a good scientific brain."

"I imagine that is my privilege," replied Bell. "Though some might go so far as to say people are worth almost as much attention as insects." But Blythe did not even look round as we took our leave.

I had been horrified by Blythe's blatant threats against his niece and, once we had ascertained Greenwell's whereabouts from his housekeeper and were travelling back into the town to find him, I poured out my feelings. It seemed to me there was clear evidence of a conspiracy between Miss Grace's uncle and her suitor. If Miss Grace succumbed to the pressure and married her uncle's close friend and ally, Guy Greenwell, the estate would effectively be his to reward her uncle as he wished. If she refused to marry him, even under the terrible pressure, then they could send her back to the asylum where she had evidently been confined for a short period after the terrible events at Abbey Mill and enjoy her estate between them. Both men had every motive for scaring the wits out of her. Indeed, perhaps our cyclist was not one man but two, for they could take turns as the cloaked figure.

The Doctor was most interested by my logic, but occasionally he frowned and tapped the fingers of one hand against the other, adding there were other separate questions that puzzled him. By now we had reached the windswept esplanade where, the housekeeper had informed us, Greenwell was taking a small sketching class. We alighted and walked a little way until we reached the pier where we caught sight of a group of boys, about the age of twelve, who were sketching while their master pointed out aspects of the landscape. He turned with some surprise as we approached and came over to us.

Bell was on to him at once. "Mr. Greenwell, we wish to talk to you urgently. It is serious."

He looked most uneasy. "What is it?"

"We know you take *The Times*, do you not?" the Doctor asked. "Did you see the leader on free trade last Monday?"

There was no smiling now. He looked upset. It seemed to mean something to him. "Why, yes. But what do you say?"

"That," said Bell, "you are guilty of intimidating Miss Grace."

One of the boys looked over at us and Greenwell insisted we move away further. "I utterly deny that. I am in love with her," he protested.

"It is a very strange kind of love that causes such fear," I said.

"I do not like your tone, Dr. Doyle," he came back harshly. "It is you who have caused so much misery in her. Raising hopes that cannot possibly be fulfilled. Do you not understand her birthday is soon now and her uncle will challenge the settlement unless she accepts me? She may even be sent back to an asylum. You should not have interfered. Even if she cares for you it is only a passing infatuation as before. There is no question she will marry me in the end."

His words caused a confusion of emotions in me. He almost seemed to accept that she did care for me and yet he was also trying to threaten. But I had no time to reply for a boy had come over to show Greenwell his drawing.

"A moment, Anderson," he said and the boy returned to the group. Greenwell regained his composure. "We cannot have this out here. Perhaps you disbelieve in the supernatural, gentlemen? Well, then, come to the Mill this evening. I will show you how much evil has returned. Then you will see why she needs my protection."

He moved smartly back to his pupils and, with some reluctance after such an extraordinary interview, we turned away. "My God, Bell!" I said. "Did you see the guilt when you mentioned the article? He must have sent it. I never believed all that painful honesty for a moment and now we see the truth."

The Doctor, too, was greatly energised by what we had heard and I could see his mind turning it over and over as we walked rapidly along the front. "I will need some time alone to think, Doyle. There is much I have to consider, not least the nature of Mr. Greenwell's involvement, for clearly he has an involvement. I will see you tonight for our expedition to the mill."

"But surely now we cannot leave her where she is?" I persisted. "I have to go to her."

He turned to me severely. "If you bring her to town, you may only put her in greater danger. I have begged you not to become involved." His sudden anger was no surprise. Like me, he was thinking back to past events in Edinburgh.

"You must understand that is my affair," I said, moving away to find a cab.

I reached one within a few minutes, for there was a rank close by the pier, and looked back as I entered. Despite the weather the front had a good share of horse-drawn traffic and there were even a few brave boats in the bay beyond. But one figure was utterly unmoving. Bell still stood beside the railing, staring down at the sea. He was utterly still, more like a portrait of a figure than a man. For the moment, at least, I could see he had forgotten our quarrel and was immersed once more in his beloved data.

THE DEATH IN THE CORRIDOR

I was lucky when I reached the rectory in the late afternoon, for there was no sign of Charles Blythe and a servant showed me into the sitting room. Heather Grace was standing on the other side of the room, half turned away. A fire burned fiercely in the grate, sending flickering shadows to the wall behind her. She looked pale and tense, her eyes were a little red and she did not smile to see me.

"I am glad you are here," I said. "Is your uncle . . . ?"

"No." Her voice was strange. "He is not here. He is out." At this I moved towards her, but she backed away. "Please." She turned her head away, the shadows from the fire dancing behind her. "I do not want to be near you."

I stopped abruptly. Her tone was so different. Now I remembered that this was the room where I had spied her with Greenwell. It was not a cheerful memory.

"I am sorry," she went on. "I have had time to reflect."

"I understand. But you must know I come only to help you." I spoke as gently as I would to a child.

Still she would not look at me. "Then please," she said, "get away from here now. I am a coward. You have probably heard I entered an asylum for a short time. It is obviously where I should be."

It was horrifying to hear this from her. I could see they had succeeded in sapping her will and everything in me rebelled against it. "No!" I spoke with some feeling. "There is no surprise or shame in it after what happened to you. Do not let anyone say you are mad. You are not."

My words did seem to have some effect. "No?" she questioned. "I want to believe it so much but . . ." I could see her struggling.

Then a woman's voice called, "Heather?" and her aunt entered the room, carrying some embroidery. She looked relieved to see her niece. "Ah, here you are. I was worried." She saw me and stopped in surprise. "Doctor!"

"He is leaving," said Miss Grace, giving me no choice. But as she moved past me she whispered, "For both our sakes, do not try to help me."

On my return, Bell was locked away in his room and there was no further communication between us until we set out for Abbey Mill after nightfall. In the cab, the Doctor must have sensed I was in no mood to talk, for he carefully avoided asking about my visit to Miss Grace and instead outlined his plans for the night. Naturally Greenwell had instructed us to meet him in the main house where we first encountered him and his choir, but Bell had decided we should first investigate the summer house.

After the cab had let us off, we walked across the lawn to the little building. It was one of those uncannily still evenings you sometimes get in early winter, lacking even the sound of pigeons or crows from the nearby wood, so we refrained from talking until we reached the summer house and found its door ajar. Entering, the Doctor struck a match to light its candle and we fell to examining the copies of *The Times* that were strewn around.

The paper, which had been the source of that evil letter,

was nearly two weeks old. There were three weeks' worth of papers on the desk but it was not among them and I suppose we both now assumed that it had been destroyed. But I went to a shelf at the back where there were some other much older copies of local papers. And my heart leapt when I saw an isolated copy of *The Times* had been hurriedly thrust under them. It was the edition we sought, though I could hardly believe it had been hidden so casually. I brought it to the table, and the Doctor turned to the leader and gave a cry of excitement. For the column had been mutilated with nail scissors and many words removed.

"Let us see what Mr. Greenwell has to say about this," I said in triumph. "What a conceit the man has that he leaves it here."

But the Doctor had turned over to the rugby football scores. And now he frowned. They were unread, untouched even. "But he said he cut the scores out daily."

"Then he lied," I said. "He seems to be fond of the practice. I know his arrogance is breathtaking but this is enough. We must get to him."

There was still little sound as we walked back across the lawn towards the lighted windows of the Mill, but I heard an owl hooting somewhere behind us. A moon had appeared and the pale light made the building in front of us even more grey and mysterious. I can still recall the elation I was feeling that all my doubts about Greenwell appeared to be vindicated. I had never liked the man and was now quite happy to believe the worst of him, even down to the stupid arrogance of leaving that newspaper for us to find. In any case, I reflected, since he did not know the letter had arrived, what reason did he have to conceal it? Once again Mrs. Blythe's discretion appeared to have worked in our favour. Surely now we could prove he had committed a criminal offence?

The big door leading to that ornate hall was open and Greenwell had left candles burning to guide our way. Climbing the stairs of the main house, Bell told me he had asked Inspector Warner to join us here.

"You think we can arrest him?" I asked with hope. But the Doctor frowned and raised his hand for urgent silence.

At once I knew why, for I could hear voices from above. One was Greenwell's and he sounded agitated, even terrified. "No!" he was shouting now. "I do not wish to give it to you . . . I had thought you . . ."

Now came choking and then a horrible rasping sound like someone slashing cloth.

Bell and I began to run. Reaching the landing, I was first along the corridor, which led to the music room and there, ahead of me on the wooden floor, a crimson puddle was spreading. Above it a dark shape slumped against a wall, clutching what looked like some sort of notebook. It was Greenwell. The broad gash in his throat was pumping blood and certainly mortal. Bell ran to try to staunch it but I could see there was no hope. Quickly I moved into the room ahead. It was largely in shadow and at first I could make out nobody. But then I saw it.

The figure from the road was standing on the edge of the window seat. There was blood all over its cloak and it threw back that horrible bobbing head, as if it were laughing, but no sound came. Then it stepped out of the open window.

I ran toward to the sill, and saw it had clambered down the ivy to the ground and, without pausing, I followed at once, clutching wildly at branches which burned my hands as I scrambled down them.

Once on the ground, I could see the figure was ahead of me and already two-thirds of the way to the trees which bordered the Mill. It moved with a horrible bobbing motion, and at times weaved an erratic course as if it were sightless. Even so, it covered the ground rapidly.

I raced after it, and my days on the rugby field served some purpose for I was moving faster than it and gaining ground, yet still I was not close as it entered the trees.

When I reached the wood, I did not stop but plunged in. This was foolish, for in these thick trees it was pitch-black and I could see very little. I blundered on for a few moments until I stumbled on a stone and was forced to stop and listen.

It was eerily quiet in the darkness, especially on so still a night. From far behind me back at the Mill there were distant shouts and the faint flicker of torches. Warner and his men had evidently arrived and were coming after me, but all my senses were taken up by what lay ahead. I strained to listen. There was a slight sound, perhaps a twig breaking, or a branch in wind, for I thought I felt a waft of breeze. I could just make out a large tree I took to be an oak. Was there a shape beside it or had the figure moved on and away? If it were truly sightless, that would perhaps be an advantage in this blackness. Already I was having to use my hands to feel my way.

As lightly as I could I moved forward to that tree and the shape beside it, ready to do battle if necessary. I managed to get quite close, making as little sound as possible, half crouched in case the figure fell on me. Soon I was near enough to make the shape out. But it was only another of those infernal bramble bushes. I relaxed, disappointed.

In that moment I heard a sound, turned and saw the figure a few inches from me, something raised in its hand.

And then everything was truly dark.

THE BEDFORD COUNTY CIPHER

The next thing I knew I was in a darkened room, staring at the arm of a chair. Panic gripped me. I shouted out.

The door opened and a shadowy shape stood in the doorway carrying something. For an awful moment I thought of the figure in the wood and shrank away in terror. But it moved forward and I saw it was the Doctor, who smiled reassuringly. He was carrying water. "I only went to get some more liquid. You are concussed."

I looked around now and slowly realised I was in my own barely furnished bedroom at the practice.

"What has happened?" I asked, trying to sit up. The room became a blur again and I sank back, dizzy with the effort.

The Doctor came over and looked down on me, obviously assessing my state. "Greenwell did not recover," he said grimly. "You were luckier. Your attacker could not linger for we were getting close. They would have you in hospital, but I thought I had better take charge of your case. Meanwhile, of course, they are stampeding over the scene of the crime like elephants."

I smiled, knowing how much it must have cost him to leave the place and return here with me. But then a thought darkened my mind. "Heather?"

"Have no fear," he said. "I had word a short time ago. She and her aunt are perfectly well. Indeed, Warner had a man with her and the aunt all evening. He is staying there till daylight just to be sure. But again, Doyle, note the uncle was out."

"Thank you." I was immensely relieved. "Tomorrow . . . ?"

He knew what I was going to say. "Yes, I agree. We will make new arrangements for her. But what did Greenwell have to show us, Doyle? If we only knew that. His notebook is most uninformative, nearly empty apart from a number, a word and a sign that means absolutely nothing." He showed me an almost blank page in a small, tattered pocketbook, which I recognised as the one Greenwell had been clutching when he died. As he said, there was a number "1," a word and a strange letter.

I stared desperately at this but could make nothing of it, though the word looked like "love."

"He was evidently rushed when he wrote it," said the Doctor. "See the writing and he broke off more than once."

The Doctor took it back up and stared at it himself for a moment, before returning with it to his seat by the window.

I lay there, looking at him, reflecting that the room was indeed one of the emptiest in the house. My mattress lay on bare boards and, apart from the plain but comfortable chair that the Doctor had placed by the window, there was nothing else other than the clothes that hung from a length of string I had nailed in a corner, and a small jug and basin. I noticed that a mass of papers lay by the Doctor's chair and assumed these were his notes on the case. But as he lifted them I could see that they were ciphers, not unlike the one Cullingworth had concocted. For a wild moment I thought perhaps he had found them at Abbey Mill, but the Doctor laughed at this suggestion.

"No," he replied. "I have told you how little there was to find. But I have spent two hours looking at Greenwell's notebook without the slightest enlightenment as to what it means or could mean. Yet I am sure it has a meaning. And sometimes, in such circumstances, I find it helps to reinvigorate the mind by turning back to old successes of a similar nature. Solutions, I have found, can sometimes present themselves while you are not struggling." So saying, he put the papers down and came over to insist I drank some water before I went back to sleep.

I slept for two more hours, and when I awoke I was alert and quite unable to lie quietly any longer. I felt less weak but my mind was overactive, and I found myself turning over and over the mystery which faced us and asking Bell endless questions. Who could possibly have hit me? Was it Blythe? Or Cullingworth? Or another, though I dreaded to think who that might be for I had heard enough of Miss Grace's dreams. Did the fragments in Greenwell's notebook contain some pointer we had missed? A letter, a word, a code, a strange hieroglyphic? If so, Bell's expertise in ciphers would surely lead him to an understanding of it sooner rather than later.

I worried over Greenwell's notebook for some minutes and got nowhere at all before my mind went back to Miss Grace. From his seat by the window Bell, who was still recharging his mental batteries by examining earlier ciphers, could see well enough that I was becoming agitated but also that I was unable to sleep. A more orthodox physician would have insisted I stay quiet. But after a time he clearly made up his mind that would not work.

"Doyle," he said reasonably, "We know she is safe tonight. It is even possible this notebook is irrelevant. In any event we are not going to solve it by beating our brains in so laborious a way. If you wish to know more about such things then I will show you. It will be a distraction and I think you will find it diverting. Either that or I insist you take a sleeping draft."

I refused the latter option, but I accepted his point. I was willing to be taught.

He pulled his chair over to the bed and thrust a paper at me. "In any case, when we discussed the Culligworth cipher you said you would like to see this. So here it is."

"What is it?" I asked.

"A genuine treasure map."

He lit another candle and I turned the paper over at once, glad of anything that would get my mind away from our predicament for I could see I was doing myself no good. This is what I read.

THE TREASURE (Joseph Bell's 1881 copy*)

115 73 24 807 37 52 49 17 31 62 647 22 7 15
140 47 29 107 79 84 56 239 10 26 811 5 196
308 85 52 160 136 59 211 36 9 46 316 554 122
106 95 53 58 2 42 7 35 122 53 31 82 77 250
196 56 96 118 71 140 287 28 353 37 1005 65
147 807 24 3 8 12 47 43 59 807 45 316 101 41
78 154 1005 122 138 191 16 77 49 102 57 72

---

*The Beale cipher is widely regarded as genuine and was first discovered around the 1880s.

34 73 85 35 371 59 196 81 92 191 106 273 60
394 620 270 220 106 388 287 63 3 6 191 122
43 234 400 106 290 314 47 48 81 96 26 115 92
158 191 110 77 85 197 46 10 113 140 353 48
120 106 2 607 61 420 811 29 125 14 20 37 105
28 248 16 159 7 35 19 301 125 110 486 287 98
117 511 62 51 220 37 113 140 807 138 540 8
44 287 388 117 18 79 344 34 20 59 511 548
107 603 220 7 66 154 41 20 50 6 575 122 154
248 110 61 52 33 30 5 38 8 14 84 57 540 217
115 71 29 84 63 43 131 29 138 47 73 239 540
52 53 79 118 51 44 63 196 12 239 112 3 49 79
353 105 56 371 557 211 505 125 360 133 143
101 15 284 540 252 14 205 140 344 26 811 138
115 48 73 34 205 316 607 63 220 7 52 150 44
52 16 40 37 158 807 37 121 12 95 10 15 35 12
131 62 115 102 807 40 53 135 138 30 31 62 67
41 85 63 10 106 807 138 8 113 20 32 33 37 353
287 140 47 85 50 37 49 47 64 6 7 71 33 4 43
47 63 1 27 600 208 230 15 191 246 85 94 511
2 270 20 39 7 33 44 22 40 7 10 3 811 106 44
486 230 353 211 200 31 10 38 140 297 61 603
320 302 666 287 2 44 33 32 511 548 10 6 250
557 246 53 37 52 83 47 320 38 33 807 7 44 30
31 250 10 15 35 106 160 113 31 102 406 230
540 320 29 66 33 101 807 138 301 316 353 320
220 37 52 28 540 320 33 8 48 107 50 811 7 2
113 73 16 125 11 110 67 102 807 33 59 81 158
38 43 581 138 19 85 400 38 43 77 14 27 8 47
138 63 140 44 35 22 177 106 250 314 217 2 10
7 1005 4 20 25 44 48 7 26 46 110 230 807 191
34 112 147 44 110 121 125 96 41 51 50 140 56
47 152 540 63 807 28 42 250 138 582 98 643
32 107 140 112 26 85 138 540 53 20 125 371
38 36 10 52 118 136 102 420 150 112 71 14 20

7 24 18 12 807 37 67 110 62 33 21 95 220 511
102 811 30 83 84 305 620 15 2 10 8 220 106
353 105 106 60 275 72 8 50 205 185 112 125
540 65 106 807 138 96 110 16 73 33 807 150
409 400 50 154 285 96 106 316 270 205 101
811 400 8 44 37 52 40 241 34 205 38 16 46 47
85 24 44 15 64 73 138 807 85 78 110 33 420
505 53 37 38 22 31 10 110 106 101 140 15 38
3 5 44 7 98 287 135 150 96 33 84 125 807 191
96 511 118 40 370 643 466 106 41 107 603 220
275 30 150 105 49 53 287 250 208 134 7 53 12
47 85 63 138 110 21 112 140 485 486 505 14
73 84 575 1005 150 200 16 42 5 4 25 42 8 16
811 125 160 32 205 603 807 81 96 405 41 600
136 14 20 28 26 353 302 246 8 131 160 140 84
440 42 16 811 40 67 101 102 194 138 205 51
63 241 540 122 8 10 63 140 47 48 140 288

"So this is the treasure cipher you mentioned?" I asked.

"Yes," answered Bell. "Faced with the puzzle of the notebook, I thought it might help me to look at my own earlier work in solving such things. This is the first of two ciphers I was sent, one provides a background, the other more details."

"How on earth did you come by it?"

"Oh, I had been in correspondence with a Virginian doctor in Lynchburg, a Dr. Murdoch, about my *Manual of Operations for Surgery*. We discussed various aspects of diagnostics as well as treatment and in the course of our correspondence he told me how a local man called James Ward had famously spent all his time and money in an attempt to solve this cipher. Evidently it was left to him by a man called Thomas J. Beale who claimed to have found a rich vein of gold in the West and had supposedly moved this horde by wagon back to Virginia.

Beale deposited the ciphers in a strongbox with instructions they should be opened after ten years."

I stared at the numbers. "So is this a key cipher based on a text as you mentioned?"

"Certainly," said the Doctor, "but it cannot be analysed in the simple way I analysed Cullingworth's prank, for we have reason to suppose these numbers correspond to the words in a long document. If the tenth word is 'Your' then '10' will be the letter 'Y' but if the hundredth word is 'Yesterday' then '100' will be 'Y' as well. Many of these numbers may well therefore refer to the same letter."

"Maybe it is gibberish?"

"I grant that was always a possibility, but it is not."

"Then you have deciphered it?" It was a relief to be considering an abstract problem that might yet help us find rules we could apply. Even without my throbbing head, it was obvious by now that we would get nowhere in this business through sheer brawn. In so odd and awkward a case, it seemed certain that only mental skill, ruthlessly applied, could possibly help us avenge Baynes for that awful grave on the forest floor and end the horrible climate of fear surrounding Heather Grace. And so I listened eagerly to what the Doctor had to say about solving such things. Indeed, I have rarely been a more willing pupil.

He was smiling modestly, touched by my enthusiasm. "There was word from my correspondent that the key to this one might be a text that would be familiar to every American. It seemed to me at once this must mean a historic text of peculiarly American importance. It was not very hard to arrive at various candidates. This will show you the amount of labour involved." He handed me another sheet.

Now I stared with true amazement at the Doctor's copperplate for I could see at once the detailed work. He had taken a famous historical document and numbered every word of it, and I include the first and most relevant part here.

DECLARATION OF INDEPENDENCE (Joseph Bell's marked copy)

*When(1) in(2) the(3) course(4) of(5) human(6)
events(7) it(8) becomes(9) necessary(10) for(11)
one(12) people(13) to(14) dissolve(15) the(16)
political(17) bands(18) which(19) have(20)
connected(21) them(22) with(23) another(24)
and(25) to(26) assume(27) among(28) the(29)
powers(30) of(31) the(32) earth(33) the(34)
separate(35) and(36) equal(37) station(38) to(39)
which(40) the(41) laws(42) of(43) nature(44)
and(45) of(46) nature's(47) god(48) entitle(49)
them(50) a(51) decent(52) respect(53) to(54)
the(55) opinions(56) of(57) mankind(58)
requires(59) that(60) they(61) should(62)
declare(63) the(64) causes(65) which(66)
impel(67) them(68) to(69) the(70) separation(71)
we(72) hold(73) these(74) truths(75) to(76) be(77)
self(78) evident(79) that(80) all(81) men(82)
are(83) created(84) equal(85) that(86) they(87)
are(88) endowed(89) by(90) their(91) creator(92)
with(93) certain(94) inalienable(95)
rights(96) that(97) among(98) these(99) are(100)
life(101) liberty(102) and(103) the(104)
pursuit(105) of(106) happiness(107) that(108)
to(109) secure(110) these(111) rights(112)
governments(113) are(114) instituted(115)
among(116) men(117) deriving(118) their(119)
just(120) powers(121) from(122) the(123)
consent(124) of(125) the(126) governed(127)*

that(128) whenever(129) any(130) form(131)
of(132) government(133) becomes(134)
destructive(135) of(136) these(137) ends(138)
it(139) is(140) the(141) right(142) of(143)
the(144) people(145) to(146) alter(147) or(148)
to(149) abolish(150) it(151) and(152) to(153)
institute(154) new(155) government(156)
laying(157) its(158) foundation(159) on(160)
such(161) principles(162) and(163)
organizing(164) its(165) powers(166) in(167)
such(168) form(169) as(170) to(171) them(172)
shall(173) seem(174) most(175) likely(176) to(177)
effect(178) their(179) safety(180) and(181)
happiness(182) prudence(183) indeed(184)
will(185) dictate(186) that(187) governments(188)
long(189) established(190) should(191) not(192)
be(193) changed(194) for(195) light(196) and(197)
transient(198) causes(199) and(200)
accordingly(201) all(202) experience(203)
hath(204) shown(205) that(206) mankind(207)
are(208) more(209) disposed(210) to(211)
suffer(212) while(213) evils(214) are(215)
sufferable(216) than(217) to(218) right(219)
themselves(220) by(221) abolishing(222) the(223)
forms(224) to(225) which(226) they(227) are(228)
accustomed(229) but(230) when(231) a(232)
long(233) train(234) of(235) abuses(236) and(237)
usurpations(238) pursuing(239) invariably(240)
the(241) same(242) object(243) evinces(244)
a(245) design(246) to(247) reduce(248) them(249)
under(250) absolute(251) despotism(252) it(253)
is(254) their(255) right(256) it(257) is(258)
their(259) duty(260) to(261) throw(262) off(263)
such(264) government(265) and(266) to(267)
provide(268) new(269) guards(270) for(271)

their(272) future(273) security(274) such(275)
has(276) been(277) the(278) patient(279)
sufferance(280) of(281) these(282) colonies(283)
and(284) such(285) is(286) now(287) the(288)
necessity(289) which(290) constrains(291)
them(292) to(293) . . .

"Yes, it was the work of many nights," said Bell as I stared at his labours. I could sense from his tone the excitement the topic held for him. Though he was fairly modest about it at the time, I know now that his work on the Beale cipher took many years and that he regarded it as one of his most triumphant moments of pure analytical deduction. I think that was why he wanted to present it to me that night when we were at a low ebb.

"Perhaps I could have been better employed, Doyle," he continued, "but once I started with the Declaration of Independence I was sure I was on to something. The devil was in the details for the author must have been using a shortened form of the Declaration. This means there are serious mismatches in the higher—but not thank heaven the lower—numbers. From my researches, I calculate his version of the Declaration was around sixty-eight words shorter than the one we know. This is perfectly possible for the key text may have been in a newspaper and the story is that Beale intended to provide it, but never appeared to do so. I could even see where he had difficulties. In the whole of the Declaration, there were no words beginning with an 'X.' Beale resolved this by using '1073' 'extends.' You will find it as '1005,' it is indeed one of the numbers most altered by the shortened text he used."

"So where is your translation?" I asked eagerly.

"Here is the result of my labour." And he handed me the following with a flourish.

> *I have deposited in the county of Bedford, about four miles from Buford's, in an excavation or vault, six feet below the surface of the ground, the following articles, belonging jointly to the parties whose names are given in number three herewith: The first deposit consisted of one thousand and fourteen pounds of gold, and three thousand eight hundred and twelve pounds of silver; deposited November 1819. The second was made December 1821, and consisted of nineteen hundred and seven pounds of gold, and twelve hundred and eighty-eight pounds of silver; also jewels, obtained in St. Louis in exchange for silver to save transportation, and valued at thirteen thousand dollars. The above is securely packed in iron pots, with iron covers. The vault is roughly lined with stone, and the vessels rest on solid stone, and are covered with others. Paper number one describes the exact locality of the vault so that no difficulty will be had in finding it.*

I have written that I sometimes found it hard to reconcile myself to the Doctor. But in one thing he was completely consistent, and that was his regular ability to amaze me. Here was such a time. I was, after all, lying in an ill-furnished bedroom in a humdrum villa in Southsea. And in order to further what was a desperate investigation he had produced a genuinely deciphered American code of buried treasure! If only we could apply the same technique to Greenwell's notebook, surely we would reach a safe harbour.

"It is extraordinary," I said. "But surely you have deciphered details of an immense fortune? What did your correspondent say? What about the other code?"

"Yes, I admit," he said, smiling, "there was quite a flurry

of letters from Virginia when I sent Dr. Murdoch the decipherment. And yes, there were many questions about the other cipher. But the treasure interests me a great deal less than the puzzle itself, which is a remarkable one."

"You have the other cipher?"

"I do but I fear it presented greater difficulties." And he handed it over.

THE LOCALITY OF THE VAULT*

```
71 194 38 1701 89 76 11 83 1629 48 94 63 132
16 111 95 84 341 975 14 40 64 27 81 139 213
63 90 1120 8 15 3 126 2018 40 74 758 485 604
230 436 664 582 150 251 284 308 231 124 211
486 225 401 370 11 101 305 139 189 17 33 88
208 193 145 1 94 73 416 918 263 28 500 538
356 117 136 219 27 176 130 10 460 25 485 18
436 65 84 200 283 118 320 138 36 416 280 15
71 224 961 44 16 401 39 88 61 304 12 21 24
283 134 92 63 246 486 682 7 219 184 360 780
18 64 463 474 131 160 79 73 440 95 18 64 581
34 69 128 367 460 17 81 12 103 820 62 116 97
103 862 70 60 1317 471 540 208 121 890 346
36 150 59 568 614 13 120 63 219 812 2160 1780
99 35 18 21 136 872 15 28 170 88 4 30 44 112
18 147 436 195 320 37 122 113 6 140 8 120
305 42 58 461 44 106 301 13 408 680 93 86
116 530 82 568 9 102 38 416 89 71 216 728
965 818 2 38 121 195 14 326 148 234 18 55
131 234 361 824 5 81 623 48 961 19 26 33 10
1101 365 92 88 181 275 346 201 206 86 36 219
324 829 840 64 326 19 48 122 85 216 284 919
```

*Never officially solved.

861 326 985 233 64 68 232 431 960 50 29 81
216 321 603 14 612 81 360 36 51 62 194 78 60
200 314 676 112 4 28 18 61 136 247 819 921
1060 464 895 10 6 66 119 38 41 49 602 423
962 302 294 875 78 14 23 111 109 62 31 501
823 216 280 34 24 150 1000 162 286 19 21 17
340 19 242 31 86 234 140 607 115 33 191 67
104 86 52 88 16 80 121 67 95 122 216 548 96
11 201 77 364 218 65 667 890 236 154 211 10
98 34 119 56 216 119 71 218 1164 1496 1817
51 39 210 36 3 19 540 232 22 141 617 84 290
80 46 207 411 150 29 38 46 172 85 194 39 261
543 897 624 18 212 416 127 931 19 4 63 96 12
101 418 16 140 230 460 538 19 27 88 612 1431
907 716 275 74 83 11 426 89 72 84 1300 1706
814 221 132 40 102 34 868 975 1101 84 16 79
23 16 81 122 324 403 912 227 936 447 55 86
34 43 212 107 96 314 264 1065 323 428 601
203 124 95 216 814 2906 654 820 2 301 112
176 213 71 87 96 202 35 10 2 41 17 84 221 736
820 214 11 60 760

"But the numbers are huge!" I said, " '2906.' This surely must have defeated you."

"Yes," admitted the Doctor. "Actually, you have put your finger on one of its most interesting features, Doyle. '2906' is one of only two numbers above two thousand in the entire text. It must be a rare letter indeed if he had to go so far into that key text to find it. The Declaration has no '2906,' so I knew at once it was a longer document than that. I could also on those grounds exclude many other key American political documents like 'The Bill of Rights,' the Gettysburg Address from President Lincoln, even the basic American constitution, all too short. The Bible was another obvious starting point. The first book I

tried was Genesis. It was a natural beginning, but I got
nowhere. I tried other biblical texts. Exodus was no more
successful than Genesis but Kings had its points. The
Book of Samuel had great potential but in the end it was
discarded. Of the Gospels, Luke proved most interesting,
but I could not finally persuade myself there was hope.
Pickwick Papers seemed a likely candidate, given its success around the time the thing was compiled but it was
of no use at all. I believe I still have the first few lines,
based on *Pickwick*, let me see."

He shuffled some papers. "Yes, here. 'TFFO H ACA';
not a promising start. And then I took the bull by the
horns. I do not think I have to tell you, Doyle, of a story
by Edgar Allan Poe called 'The Gold-Bug.' "

"Of course, I know most of Poe!" I cried. "It is about
the finding of Captain Kidd's treasure. But your story of
the Beale ciphers reminded me of his at once. Are they
connected?"

"I believe so," said the Doctor. " 'The Gold-Bug' was
the most popular of Poe's tales and on its original pub-
lication in 1843 this story secured fame for its author that
in later years was second only to 'The Raven.' It also
originated from the same part of America as the Beale
story. It is my honest belief that the whole Beale thing
was inspired by 'The Gold-Bug.' "

"But you say you solved the second cipher?"

"Yes, I have gone some way towards it and I will tell
you how. You were drawn to the same figure, as I was
'2906.' It caught my eye as soon as I examined the cipher.
Surely this must be a rare word or letter, for there is no
other number nearly so high as this anywhere else. My
first task on approaching 'The Gold-Bug' was to try to
find a word around this part in the manuscript that looks
likely. And Poe's texts have bedevilled the thing. Some
miss words, it is not easy to get an agreed version, and

there is also the huge problem of whether to count hyphenated words like the 'gold-bug' itself as one or two. But at approximately the right place in the Poe manuscript for our '2906,' we find two very interesting possibilities: 'excitable' and 'anxiety.' I prefer the former."

"Then you have done it?" I asked.

"I have the start of one. I believe that, unlike the other, the numbers denote a combination of words and letters. The readings are variable on account of the problems I have mentioned, yet the thing translates. I could hardly believe my eyes when I first began work and almost at once I had for '48 94 63' 'City of Carolina.' But although I was making sense I soon saw it lacks the proper flow of the other cipher and is more of a cryptic message. Much of it remains obscure but the full beginning of the cipher seems to be: 'It is a white beach three miles from the City of Carolina.' Then later: 'Make the point three miles from the glass.' "

"But that is exactly what the treasure message is like in the story itself!"

"Precisely," the Doctor agreed. "I suspect that is the point of the thing. The treasure message in 'The Gold-Bug' begins as follows: *'A good glass in the bishop's hostel in the devil's seat forty-one degrees and thirteen minutes— . . . shoot from the left eye . . .'* Now, this seems to be gibberish, yet in the story the hero uses it to deduce how to find Kidd's treasure. Perhaps I am forgoing a great opportunity, but I am driven to the conclusion that, despite the similarity of the message I have decoded, no such option is available here. The code is genuine but I have finally come to the belief, I regret to say, that the Beale cipher, while partly translatable and not without serious interest, is probably a hoax. It may even be a Masonic one for the first cipher text I deciphered has various links to Masonic ritual, with its talk of a stone vault and iron."

Despite the lack of pirate gold, I was persuaded by this solution and thrilled to find a direct connection to a writer who had long been my hero. But above all I was impressed by the Doctor's scrupulous decoding and now we reapplied ourselves to the object of the exercise and stared again at that a page of Greenwell's notebook. "Is it possible," I asked, "that the letters and numbers are not some kind of cipher but rather a cipher key?"

The Doctor sighed. "That has occurred to me. If so, numbers of the code would equal the letters here: '1' would be 'I'; '2' would be 'L'; '3' would be 'O'; '4' would be 'V' and so forth. Not many letters, but then perhaps they are all you need to break the rest, especially if you have 'E' and 'O.' But I fear that in this case our position is hopeless, Doyle. What use is a key without the message itself? Perhaps that is what was taken and without it we had as well throw this away. And yet . . ." He stared back down at the notebook. "It is that one odd symbol where hope lies. If we could read that I am sure all would be clear. Well, I will keep on trying and I hope you have found some instruction."

I yawned and lay back in my bed. "Certainly," I said, "perhaps it will come to me in my sleep."

"I will be quite happy," said the Doctor, picking up all his papers, "merely if you sleep."

I could see his approach had had the desired effect for my mind was less agitated. "As for Beale," I asked, feeling very drowsy now, "will the second cipher, you think, ever be completely decoded?"

"I do not know. It is certainly intriguing," he answered, standing over me with a smile. "In fact, I may come back to it one day. Perhaps if men invent thinking machines, which can tabulate and quickly cross off all permutations, we will get further. But the truth is I have a suspicion we never will and this cipher is on a level of difficulty that will always ultimately defeat us, at least beyond my modest efforts. Now I will put away my games though I am glad they have diverted my patient. It is time for you to sleep more and we have much to do tomorrow."

Certainly, as I recall the memory of that strange night, I note his words have proved true. Despite much ink and erudition, nobody has got further with Beale's ciphers than Joseph Bell.*

---

*Note: This is still true. The Beale cipher has been subjected to endless computer analysis by cryptographers throughout the twentieth century, but the "locality" cipher remains entirely mysterious and, unlike Bell, nobody has achieved any translation at all.

SWALLOWED BY MIST

Next morning, the Doctor would have me rest but I felt far stronger and absolutely insisted I should accompany him back to the rectory, where he intended to persuade Mrs. Blythe that the time had come for some urgent precautions. Whatever the resistance of her husband, Bell planned to make sure that Heather Grace was away from that place.

It was the mistiest day I had yet seen; a white pall hung over the trees and the edge of the road, as our cab turned into the wooded road. "So," the Doctor was saying as we went along, "we have a list of boarding establishments quite near us, which seem to be safe and dull in the extreme if she can stand the tedium."

He suddenly broke off and I could see why. For ahead of us were lights, and I recognised Inspector Warner and other police. Clustered around the side of the road, they made an eerie sight in that ground mist, for their feet were hard to see and it looked almost as if they were floating. Nearer the wood two other policemen stood looking down at the ground.

We climbed out of the cab and I was hardly surprised to see how worried Warner looked, for now he had two unsolved murders on his hands. "Dr. Bell, Dr. Doyle," he greeted us, turning to me with special attention. "I am glad to see you better, sir, it is a terrible business. I am very sorry."

"Yes," said Bell. "We have decided it would be best to bring Miss Grace into town here, where she would be safer. You have found nothing?"

Warner looked concerned. "But I don't understand. I sent a sergeant round to you with the news."

Bell spoke sharply. "We made a call at the telegraph office. I had to send some telegrams, so he would have missed us. What is it?"

But as he spoke, I made it out. One of the policemen on the edge of the wood moved and I saw the handlebars. It was Heather Grace's bicycle.

"She was on her way to see you," said Inspector Warner.

I do not have a very complete memory of the events of that day. My concussion of the previous night, together with the awful news of the disappearance, combined to send me into a fever of activity. I know that while the police themselves searched, the Doctor and I combed through large areas of the wood and that I must have walked almost three miles, trying to find anything around the spot where the bicycle was found. The mist had lifted a little by the time I reached the ugly abandoned cottage in the clearing where I had been pushed out of a window. It was empty and I moved on. But wherever I looked, I found nothing and saw nothing except those accursed brambles and briars. I was sick to death of that wood now and hated the sight of every tree in it.

There was no better news when I went back to the road, so I returned to search further. More hours passed, the light was starting to go and I was ploughing through thicket after thicket until they all looked the same. Bell had been following a nearby path but his fixed frown told me his mind was elsewhere.

Eventually Inspector Warner came to us both. He looked grim and exhausted. "Gentlemen, we have been through the area twice now. You can do no further good by staying here. I will put some men on watch overnight and we will try again at first light. It is all that can be done."

"What of her uncle?" I asked.

"We have questioned him. He seems upset."

"Of course, what do you expect?" I said angrily, thinking of his display of strength in his study the previous day, the awful gleam in his eye and his tactical withdrawal. "He is an actor. Give me time with him alone."

"We cannot do that, sir."

"Well, I am not leaving." I strode back into the wood.

The Doctor did not follow me at once, but stayed talking with Warner. Some time later I was standing, steeped in misery, looking fruitlessly at the ground around a copse of ash trees, when he appeared. We stood there for a moment in silence.

Finally, I broke it: "So, Doctor, have we lost?"

He was quiet for a moment. "I do not know."

"I wanted to bring her back earlier, you recall, if only we had done so . . ." This was unfair of me but I felt such bitterness at the thought of the missed opportunity.

"That too I do not know. If her uncle is responsible, he could probably have abducted her from a boarding house."

"So it is as before. We have failed again, Doctor." The mist wafted at my feet almost like a tangible proof of my despair.

"We have not failed yet." He fixed his eyes on me. "And as you know, we have had our successes."

"But what is the good if we lose when it matters?"

We stood there a moment. The sun was casting its few last rays through the branches of the ash trees in the copse. I know my words were harsh but it is difficult to convey the sheer weight of my anguish. I felt that all the shadows I had been dodging since that awful case in Edinburgh had now returned to haunt me. It was as if I were doomed to see all the things I loved mutilated and destroyed. And was this not some kind of punishment for the hubris Bell and I had shown in thinking we could solve even the worst crimes?

"Perhaps mistakes have been made," conceded the Doctor. "In the most serious cases they often are. It is part of the pattern. But we have not yet finally lost." I was about to scoff, but he went on with more severity, "And currently, Doyle, I am afraid to say you are impeding my progress."

"That is arrogance." I was ready to walk away.

"No, it is fact." He was less angry now, more patient. "Last night there was active work I could have done on the question of Baynes's death, a matter I need to re-search. Have you ever heard of Majuba Hill." He had turned and was looking away into the trees.

"The Boer massacre." It was rare for him to throw out a hint like this in the middle of an enquiry and it says something of my state of mind that I was barely interested.

"Exactly. I have had to content myself with cables in order to stay by you and see you were all right. That is as it should be. But now you are physically whole I cannot possibly waste my time nursemaiding you. Let me get on with the case, which I accept is a very difficult one, and in some ways agonising or else"—and here he turned back to me—"we part for good."

I could see something in his eyes. There was anger, of course, but much more. It was pain. I realised now of course what I should have seen before, if I had not been so caught up in my own feelings. The Doctor was in many ways as emotionally engaged as I was. I felt somewhat chastened. "Very well," I said simply, "if it helps your progress."

"It may. And you should not lose heart. Believe me, in the darkest hour sometimes . . ."

"But that was just how she felt," I interrupted with passion for I wanted the Doctor to understand how she had suffered. "It is what makes it so sad. If only this man Horler had not treated her so badly. He was her one great love. But she had hoped to move on from it."

While I was talking, Bell had fixed his eyes on something in the tree in front of us and now he started and turned to me. "What did you say?" he asked somewhat flatly but quickly.

I was surprised by this odd tone. "That he was her one great love and she hoped to get past it. Why? What is it?"

For the Doctor appeared to have lost interest again and was moving closer to the tree. He was excited. "Yes! Yes, of course. You have heard of lovers carving their initials? A pledge of their love."

I looked and saw he was staring at some ancient letters someone had carved in the tree, dated 1801. They could not possibly have any bearing on our case, for they were almost a hundred years old.

"But these initials are ancient. They can have nothing to do with this case."

"You are quite right," said the Doctor. "In themselves they can have no relevance, but I am still grateful to whoever made them. You see, Doyle, if you follow two chains of thought, you will at last find some point of intersection that should lead you approximately to the truth. And here on this tree is our intersection. I am grateful to you, extremely grateful for bringing me to it." He had taken out

Greenwell's notebook, and was studying the page with the strange symbol on it. "You have helped me understand something," he stated with some satisfaction as we walked back together to the police on the road.

I suppose the Doctor's excitement should have renewed my hopes but it did not. I spent an awful night, thinking of that dank wood and of Heather Grace. When morning finally came, the news was as bleak as ever. The officers, posted by Warner, had seen and heard nothing. A massive search had resumed at dawn with absolutely no result. And now the mist had come down again.

Bell was nowhere in evidence and I heard this news when I reached the road, accompanied by one of Warner's men. He had no inkling that I was close to the missing woman and assumed I had been called merely as a doctor in case they found her. "You will not be needed, Doctor," he told me with an air of confidential importance. "The word is we have no hope of finding her alive. Even if her abductor spared her, last night was bitterly cold."

The mist was so thick now that we could hardly see the trees from the road but I insisted on entering the wood all the same. I stood there alone in the mist and thought of his words, and wondered if she was lying anywhere near me. I did not search very much, if at all. But when I walked back to the road I was cold and numb. And the mist round the trees seemed more than ever like a tide flowing around a dank beach.

THE HUNTER IN THE DARK

Another day passed, during which the Doctor was consumed with his researches, and I barely saw him until he came in hastily with news that Warner had decided to subject Charles Blythe to a further interview.

I was anxious to attend, but to my surprise the Doctor was even more so, weaving through the noon crowds on the pavement with fastidious urgency. Despite our haste, the interrogation had already begun when we reached the police station, a flat grey building so close to the railway station that I had walked past it when I first arrived at the town. Blythe sat opposite Warner and two other policemen, as Bell and I were shown in to sit behind them.

Blythe certainly looked a changed man. All the arrogance and fight seemed to have left him. He was haggard and he trembled slightly. I was glad to observe Warner had changed tactics and was now questioning him very aggressively.

"I keep telling you," Blythe said as they went back over events, apparently for the fourth time. "I have no idea what has happened. As I say, I have abandoned my attempt to block the inheritance."

"Perhaps, sir," suggested Warner, "because you know

her money is already yours. It will be if she is dead."

There was no rage from Blythe at this suggestion, quite the opposite. His hands shook more. "You think I want her dead?" he asked. "First poor Guy and now her. It is awful."

I was trying to decide if any of this was genuine, when the Doctor intervened. "Tell me, Mr. Blythe," he said politely without a hint of the argument they had had in Blythe's study, "does the name Majuba mean anything to you? Do you know someone who suffered there?"

Blythe started. "Why, yes, I do," he answered, evidently surprised. "But it was supposed to be private. He is a poor devil. But he went back overseas."

"No, sir," said Bell quickly, "I believe that poor devil is part of this. And you must tell me how they first met."

"Very well." Blythe seemed unsure of where this was leading. "He was stationed near our house. The Royal Marines. They were engaged in exercises all through the wood."

"Yes?" Bell leant forward with what I could see was enormous interest. "What was his field?"

"He was a munitions officer."

The effect of these words on the Doctor was extraordinary. He was out of his seat in a trice. "My God! Then why the devil are we wasting time? We may already be too late. Come, Warner, at once."

Inspector Warner was baffled, "But I do not . . ."

"There is no time for understanding! We must get back to the scene now. And I need the tools of the geologist. An axe and above all an *auger*." The Doctor all but ran out of the room and we scrambled to follow, leaving Charles Blythe, his mouth wide open with astonishment, staring after us.

Warner was still at sea, but his respect for the Doctor outweighed any doubts he may have had. Within an hour

we were back at the wood with a full complement of men.
I had rarely ever seen the Doctor so energised, and he
looked quite a spectacle as he moved into the mist and
the trees, brandishing an axe as if he were about to com-
mit murder himself. He made for the spot where I had
first seen the cyclist, close to where poor Baynes had orig-
inally noticed the tracks and where Miss Grace's bicycle
had been found. Here he stood and surveyed the ground,
though there was little enough to see. Meanwhile the police cabs, carrying spades and other items he had re-
quested, moved along the road to be as close as possible
to him.

Warner went back to them while the Doctor stood, concentrating fiercely on the terrain. For a moment I thought
nothing was going to happen and then quite suddenly he
went into action. He tilted his axe upside down, moved
to where the bicycle had been found and started to walk
from this spot into the wood, banging the axe head hard
against the ground as he went. His eyes were half closed
and he had his head to one side as he listened intently to
each blow.

There was a loud clank from behind us on the road as
the police started to unload spades. He looked up at me
sharply. "Doyle, tell them to keep quiet at all costs. We
may already have lost her."

His tone renewed all my worst fears and I ran back to
the road where Warner was supervising the unloading. He
saw my urgency and silenced his men at once.

Warner and I moved into the trees a little way and
watched the Doctor. He was still banging that axe head
against the ground and listening intently as he weaved a
trail back and forth, which took him slowly into the wood.
The spectacle was an odd one. I could see that Warner
for one could not make head or tail of it. "What is this
now?" he murmured to me. "I have followed him faith-

fully, but I hope he has not taken leave of his senses."

"It will happen to us first," I said ruefully. It was not that I was in any way sure of his success but I knew the Doctor well enough to be certain there was some kind of serious method in these antics. His ruthless logic and speculation had often led to disagreement between us, but once he acted as resolutely as this there was generally good reason for it.

The Doctor was now a little closer for he had weaved back across once more. Suddenly he stopped, turned, then shouted, "Here, Doyle!"

I moved over to him. He had dropped the axe and turned to pick up the auger, a long-handled instrument with a corkscrew at the end, which is used by geologists for taking earth samples. The Doctor bent over, pushing it carefully into a patch of exposed earth where the vegetation was not so thick. Fortunately the frost had gone and the ground was soft. But as I reached him he was not obtaining the results he wanted. "Nothing," he said as I came beside him. "Nothing, but I am certain . . ."

He broke off, for as he was speaking the earth seemed to give way under the auger and it sank some inches into the ground without resistance. The Doctor's face flushed with triumph. "There," he said. "There! I knew it."

He studied the hole he had made. It was clear now that below where we stood was empty space. The Doctor angled the instrument one way, then another so he could find that space's limits. "We just need to find the line of it," he muttered. Then he looked up again at the terrain. "Yes, I am sure! That copse. It will be the entrance." He straightened up and strode towards a clump of bramble bushes and trees. There was, I now saw, a relatively bare area of twigs and earth and dead plants beside one of the bushes. Again he plunged the auger down and this time it hardly moved at all. It seemed to hit something quite solid. "Here!" he said with a great cry of excitement, which brought Warner over at once.

"This is one entrance," said Bell, "but we need tools to get it open. Any handle there is will be on the other side." Warner stamped his boot down where Bell had been working and felt the hard surface at once. "Yes," the Doctor confirmed, "it is wood."

Inspector Warner was amazed. "But how could he get a bicycle down there?"

"He did not need to," said Bell. "It seems there were munitions stores and old tunnels all over here. There will be other entrances and he has probably covered most of them up for good. This one, though, we can prise open."

Now a frantic unloading of further equipment began. The Doctor himself grasped a pickaxe as soon as it was brought to him, I had a sharp spade and, together with others, we began a furious assault on what we soon saw was a wooden trap.

It astonished me how little there was to see at first, but soon the entrance was obvious though, as the Doctor had warned, there was no evident means of opening it. Two of the men had chisels and managed to force them underneath, and eventually with a great splintering of wood the trap was open.

Below us, sure enough, we could now see a tunnel space. It was not very wide—indeed, there could only be room for one man to crawl at a time—but it led away from us into the wood.

"This," said the Doctor, "will take you to him under that abandoned cottage. It will not be pleasant but two men with lamps must follow it. I am sure there will be another way in from there, probably under the stair. Doyle and I must find it."

The tiny tunnel below was hardly an appetising prospect but even so, I would have been glad to get down there at once. The Doctor, however, insisted I would do more good with him.

The two of us made our way back to that wreck of a house in the clearing where the figure had pushed me from the window. All around us the wood was a fever of activity. Men with lanterns ran to the tunnel, for Warner had decided at once to put more than two down it. Now he had a goal, he did not want to risk losing his prey and he was nearly as energised as the Doctor.

Bell and I reached that dark ruin, which was as gloomy and dilapidated as when I had first seen it. Inside it seemed quite as still and deserted as ever. Bell was holding a lamp and took it straight to the moth-eaten panelling under the staircase. Certainly, it seemed solid enough to the eye and there was no obvious sign that we could penetrate it but, holding the lantern high, Bell brought his face within an inch or two of the wood and studied it minutely. At first, quite clearly he could see nothing. He moved back and forth, appraising the entire surface. He ran his hand over it, still without conclusion. Then he stopped and his hand moved back.

"There is paint here and it is not so old. It serves to cover the line. We need a chisel or better, a compass saw."

I had a bag of instruments with me but the best we could find was a chisel and hammer. Bell showed me where to aim my chisel and soon we were exposing the line of some kind of join in the wood. At last I managed to get some purchase and a part of the panelling splintered open, revealing an aperture behind.

"Yes, he has nailed it down from inside," said Bell with excitement. "But we can force it."

I kept working with the chisel; the Doctor took up his axe, using the blade this time to smash through the wood. It was not easy work, for we could see what we were uncovering was a cellar door of thick oak that had been disguised on the outside and nailed fast on the other, but soon more wood was splintering and we had a hole. I had the lantern now and held it up to peer inside. What I saw made my heart leap.

"Bell, there are steps!"

And then it came from somewhere below. A woman's muffled scream.

"My God!" I shouted. "It is her." I seized the axe and gave it all my strength. This time I smashed a hole close to where the lock must once have been and the door was beginning to buckle under the weight of our attack. At last, after more blows, there was room to get through.

We moved on and into that space. I held the lantern high and we began to descend the steps, which were covered with dirt and moss, but still, as we observed, showed signs of recent use. The lamp sent ghastly flickering shadows around us but beneath all was pitch-black.

I called her name but there was no reply. Still we could see nothing at all below.

We rounded a corner and the steps became steeper. "My God," I said, "if we are . . ."

But I broke off, for now at the bottom I saw a lair with makeshift signs of occupation. The beams picked out an old mattress, bits of food and some clothes and blankets, and then a shape on an ancient mattress.

She was there. Her face was deathly pale, her eyes wide and half terrified and pleading, for all she could see was the light. But she was alive and conscious. She muttered a word I could not quite make out and then I think she saw me and I moved towards her.

There was a warning cry from the Doctor: "Careful, Doyle."

In that instant I saw the shape come at me out of the darkness. It was cloaked and carried a long knife like a machete, which it swung at my neck.

I just managed to avoid the knife and, turning, threw my lamp full in its face. It did not hit its mark but connected with its arm and the weapon went flying as my lamp crashed to the ground.

The cloaked figure had sprung back and I ran for the blade as the flame from the lamp found some old straw and clothing, and fire flickered up.

As the figure turned, weaponless, its hood fell back and in the dancing light of the flames we caught our first glimpse of its features. It was an unnerving sight. Only a part of the face was there at all and it was clear now why I thought it had no eyes: one was missing entirely and much of the skin on that side appeared to have gone with it.

But our glimpse was fleeting for the figure turned and ran like a trapped beast towards the far corner of the lair. I could see there were two or three entrances to tunnels and he might well have eluded us for good, but already more lanterns had appeared and his way was blocked. Warner himself had taken the low road and now with two policemen he moved on the figure. They tackled it hard, and held it as more police clambered down the steps behind us.

I had already turned back to the mattress where she was. "You are all right?"

Now I was sure she did recognise me, but I could also see she was fevered. She made an effort to get to her feet and almost did so, despite the cord that tied her.

"Oh, Mr. Doyle I think . . ." she said in a tone that told me she barely knew where she was, and then she fainted dead away.

The Doctor was beside me now. "She has only fainted. We must get her up and out."

Quickly he applied himself to undoing her bonds. "See the knots, Doyle, just as on Baynes! It was what first told

me our man was naval. That and the tarred twine and that
fragment of his Royal Marine scarf. It was only then that
I saw the full significance of Natal. But what bedevilled
me was this. If this man had left her, why would he have
returned? The initials on the tree were what gave me the
answer."

I could follow some of his logic and knew I would
soon be clearer about the man but the last observation
about the initials on the tree baffled me completely. "I
cannot see why," I began. "You have already admitted
those initials were nothing to do with the case." But I had
lost his attention. Bell had spied something on the ground
and gone to pick it up. I did not see what it was but when
he turned back to me, I was shocked to see how worried
he looked. "What is it, Doctor?" I asked. "Is she all
right?"

His features had composed themselves again. "We are
very fortunate," he said. "As far as I can tell she is quite
unharmed."

Now a stretcher was ready for Heather, other police
were lifting her on to it and she was being borne out of
that hellish place. I was still overwhelmed with relief and
turned back to the activity over by the tunnels. The figure
was lying handcuffed, the police torches shining on him.
As I stared down at the wretched creature, who had so
long eluded us, I found myself thinking of how poor Baynes must have felt to see such a man attack and bury him.
I was beginning to recall, too, where I had heard of such
a punishment before.

Meanwhile, Warner had turned to Bell. "Who is he?

"He is Captain Horler," said Bell, "of the heroic British
defence at Majuba Hill in Natal. The Boers took half his
face and most of his mind, it would seem. But his skill
with munitions had not left him and he became fanatically

jealous of his former fiancée whom he had left here. Now we must get him out."

Our party must have made a strange spectacle as we came back through the wood in the gathering shadows. Our rescued heroine was in the lead, borne aloft on a stretcher. Behind came the police party pressed around the odd, shambling figure of Horler, his hood now replaced for he seemed easier with it. Lastly there was myself and the Doctor. But I spared time for one last look back at that hideous old cottage, whose sightless windows even now looked strangely impervious to the rays of the setting sun. How fervently I hoped I would never have reason to visit it again.

When we reached the road, Miss Grace was carried to a vehicle as Captain Horler was safely secured in a Black Maria. Inspector Warner looked on with what was clearly great satisfaction.

"If only I had your brains," he told the Doctor, "I would have made the connection to Natal. The Boer massacres caused enough sensation here; you can see the unhappy results on every street corner. On Majuba Hill were not the poor devils attacked by surprise while they slept?"

"Yes and the burial with weighted feet was meted out to traitors in the same campaign," added Bell. And now I recalled I had once read of such a thing. "But please remember, Inspector," Bell went on as he gave a look of concern at the Black Maria carrying our fugitive away, "this man was severely wounded fighting for his country. He must be treated properly."

"Yes, I will remind my people tonight. My congratulations, Bell."

"Thank you," said the Doctor. "I do not deserve them."

"Well, we should have been on him quicker I suppose, but at least it is wrapped up very nicely. We have the blade. There can be no doubt he killed Baynes and Green-well."

"Oh, none at all," said Bell. "He killed them, and brutally."

Knowing the Doctor as I did, I was quite sure he was irritated that he had allowed the murderer to stay so close to him and not been able to prevent the deaths. As before—in fact, as so often in my cases with Bell—I thought I knew everything.

I did not. Indeed, I knew nothing.

THE DANCE ON WATER

The Doctor and I visited the rectory that night, where the Blythes could hardly have been more welcoming or relieved. It was certainly the most hospitable greeting we had yet received at that place. My advice had been that Miss Grace should be taken to the infirmary for a thorough medical examination but this had revealed nothing at all serious bar a few bruises and general exhaustion. She was sleeping peacefully and would return home in the morning.

"It is quite wonderful," said Mrs. Blythe and her husband seemed genuinely grateful too. It was remarkable to see the change in him, as he smiled at us both—yes, even at me—and offered glasses of his favourite sherry. But then I recalled how volatile the man had shown himself even from our earliest meeting when blatant hostility had suddenly given way to flattery. Later I had watched as he bent that spade in a rage, evidently about to strike out, then suddenly thought better of it when he saw the steadiness of his opponent. Blythe, I decided now, was an eccentric bully with a fierce and erratic temper who had been chastened by this experience. His understanding with Guy Greenwell was probably tacit but I am sure Greenwell offered every hope that, after marrying his niece, he would help Blythe with the expansion of the collection. However, with Greenwell gone such hopes were dashed. And, for the moment at least, I was glad to see that Mrs. Blythe seemed to have regained some power in the marriage. "My husband's hope that Heather should marry Guy led to some actions that were wrong-headed," she said quite openly in front of him, as Blythe merely pursed his lips and recharged our glasses. "Now Guy is gone there can be no point at all in opposing the settlement."

Watching Blythe as he chatted animatedly, I guessed he was one of those men who find supposedly principled reasons to mask their own greed even from themselves, but who quickly change tack when their hypocrisy is effectively challenged. Now his greatest wish was only to talk science with the Doctor and he invited Bell to make a lengthy tour of his collection. Rather to my surprise, the Doctor agreed, for I had absolutely no desire to go with them. Mrs. Blythe had been a far truer ally to her niece than anyone else in the family and I was quite happy to sit hearing her stories of Heather.

But, as he got up to leave the room with the Doctor, Blythe did proffer some interesting information. "Yes," he said. "I was the only one who had seen Captain Horler since the massacre and knew of his condition. Some months ago I received a confidential letter from a London doctor, who informed me Horler was his patient and I visited him there briefly. The man was obviously off his head but I had no idea he had conceived this obsession with Heather. Naturally I never told anyone and I understood he was returning to Natal almost at once. I genuinely thought he had gone back."

"I quite accept that," said Bell cordially as they were leaving the room. "Still, while we are exploring the ocean of science I do have some other matters to discuss with you."

"Of course, you have earned it."

"The first is trivial," Bell began as the two men exited the room. "You take *The Times*, do you not?"

"Yes, what of it?" I heard Blythe reply as their voices drifted away down the corridor.

In the days that followed I did not see very much of the Doctor. I visited Miss Grace twice after she returned home from the infirmary and found her shining with gratitude, but still quite weak. I had already made arrangements to hand over her medical care to another doctor of my selection who seemed eminently honest and very suitable for the task. Since I have already written here of hypocrisies that we hide from ourselves, I might as well admit that he was elderly and married with four children.

On my second visit, I found Miss Grace sitting up in her bed in her old room, smiling happily as I entered. I could never have disguised how pleased I was to see her and we chatted about nothing in particular for a while. Her birthday had been celebrated extremely quietly the previous day and she laughed to tell me how her ancient lawyer had talked to her of "entails" and "deeds" and other things she barely understood. "I like him very much, but he believes in conveying every single clause and comma, and he was so serious, Dr. Doyle. My hand ached from signing all his papers. I think there is every chance I am going to be the silliest and least practical woman of independent means in England."

"That would be quite an ambition," I said. "I would hate to think your new-found status is already leading to pride."

We laughed at this and other trivialities for both of us,

I think, wanted for the moment to avoid being serious, but in the end she had enough of it and looked at me in that way she had. "I miss our talks," she said gently.

I did not reply. For I was glad she said it, but I had resolved to leave any serious discussions until she was up and about.

"And therefore I have something to ask you," she continued. "I know we are being light-hearted and I want that. You and I have known sadder things and it is good to escape them a while. But I have decided that when I am better I will leave here and go to London. Then I would like you to come and visit me and we will see if you still find me as interesting as a person as I was as a patient."

"I think you know," I said slowly, "that I do. For it is why you have a new doctor."

She smiled radiantly at that. How vividly now I see her smile, the way it dimpled her left cheek, the way her eyes closed slightly, the way a lock of hair curled just over her ear. Sometimes at moments like these, when I visited her, sheer joy overwhelmed her, and she would throw her head back and laugh as if she were no more than fifteen years old. I loved her; I might as well acknowledge it, but never more than in those moments.

I do not think either of us felt we needed to say more, and when Agnes Blythe entered she found us chatting merrily again and in my heart I danced with happiness.

I returned home that evening with a spring in my step and walked up the staircase to Bell's makeshift quarters. I was in a merry enough mood, and he had asked me to report on my former patient so I entered his room eagerly to tell him of her recovery.

"Doctor," I said, "it is all good news, she . . ."

But I broke off for I was surprised to see how dark it was. Bell was sitting bolt upright at his makeshift desk. "What are you doing in the dark?" I asked. I went straight to the lamp and turned it up, noticing the mass of papers in front of him.

Now at last he turned from them. "Merely preparing to ask you a favour."

"Of course," I said. "You wish to stay for another month? I will be delighted even if you scare away all my patients."

"No, no," he replied. "I have trespassed on your hospitality long enough. I will be returning to Edinburgh in a few days."

"Then what do you want?"

The Doctor turned and leant back listlessly. I had been a little concerned by his manner but now it looked to me as if this was just the normal apathy that I had seen settle on him more than once after a particularly difficult case.

"Oh, I am sorry, Doyle. It is just that sometimes the aftermath of a case bores me, as you know. Now, how did you find her?"

"Her recovery is as good as I could possibly hope." I continued with a fuller account and he seemed interested and pleased. "But what is the favour?" I asked when I had finished.

"Not a large one. I merely wish to return with you to the scene of Greenwell's death before I go . . ."

"Of course." I was perfectly willing to help him and I knew quite well the Doctor was often fastidious about tidying up small outstanding details. "But surely we know what happened there."

"Oh, yes, I am quite satisfied Horler was responsible. Still, there are a few small points to resolve."

"Very well," I said. "I have no objection at all, though it is not a place I wish to revisit."

I bade him goodnight and turned to leave. As I did so, I noticed what he was studying.

It was the file on Ian Coatley.

THE SKULL BENEATH THE SKIN

I did not much relish my return to Abbey Mill, but it was a small enough price to pay for all the Doctor had done for me. And so it was that late on a dull November afternoon we made our way by cab down the school's elegant but somehow forbidding drive. As we approached it the sun was setting and I decided to be cheerful and put its horrors out of my mind, for Miss Grace was now restored to full health and making active plans for her departure.

I had seen very little of Bell in the days since our conversation in his study. He had taken to leaving the house early and coming back very late. Once I did observe him on his way out carrying a great mass of papers and guessed they were the extensive notes he would be providing to the Crown for Horler's prosecution. Bell always avoided any contact with criminal prosecutors, preparing his evidence in a series of anonymous briefs. This might seem odd, for naturally he hated to see his investigations compromised by sloppy court work, but the practice was second nature to him following the desperate aftermath of the Chantrelle case where he was so badly compromised. Because I knew this, it had come as no surprise to me to see him constantly scurrying around in the aftermath of Horler's arrest with scribbled notes and forensic reports.

But now it seemed he had finally finished his work for he carried nothing more than a notebook as the cab let us off a little way up the drive and we walked down to the Mill in the fading light. Why did we walk? I believe the Doctor said he wanted to enjoy the evening air. But in my mind now that walk seems to last for ever as if it were a walk into another kind of world.

We came to a stop below the window of the room where we had first met Greenwell. And then, to my amazement, the sound of the piano and a voice rang out above us.

> *Over yonder's a park that is newly begun*
> *And all the bells in paradise I hear them a-ring*
> *Which is silver on the outside and gold within*
> *And I love sweet Jesus above all thing*

At first, I did not recognise the singing, but I was still overwhelmed by its beauty and then, of course, I knew.

"Yes, I contacted the owner," Bell told me. "The new owner, that is!"

My heart leapt. "Why did you not say?"

As we walked on, listening to that song, tears came into my eyes and Bell himself was moved. I have never described the Doctor as an unemotional man. He could be logical at times and at others severe, but his feelings ran deep enough: there was a look in his eyes as we listened I had rarely seen before.

Now I know, as I did not then, that the beauty and power of that singing reminded him of his wife Edith and of those awful hours he fought to save her from peritonitis, almost exactly four years before we met. Once, in Edinburgh, during my own sadness, he showed me his diaries of the night he lost his wife. I expected to see a long and painful account of what I knew had been a titanic struggle. But there were only seven words written with a terrifying plainness on a grey white page. *"On 9 November at 8:05 p.m. Edith died."*

> And in that park there stands a hall
> Which is covered all over with purple and pall
> And in that hall there stands a bed
> Which is hung all round with silk curtains so red
> And in that bed there lies a knight,
> Whose wounds they do bleed by day and by
>   night

Little wonder, then, that he was moved by that singing now. We entered the house and stood in the hall as that magical music continued from above.

> At that bedside there lies a stone
> Which our blest Virgin Mary knelt upon

"Now, are you glad you came?" the Doctor asked as we walked upstairs and into the corridor.

"Even so, you should not have asked her. She comes back rarely enough and think of the memories it has."

> At that bed's foot there lies a hound
> Which is licking the blood as it daily runs down
> At that bed's head there grows a thorn
> Which was never so blossomed since Christ was born

Probably it was the corridor itself that made me suddenly feel a flicker of apprehension. The site of my patient's recurring dream, the place where she was always trying to escape was not somewhere I walked easily. But there was something else, too. For lurking in my mind was the glaring and obvious truth: that Bell never arranged anything like this without a very serious reason.

"Bell, you do not think she is still at risk? Is that why you bring her?"

He turned to me and I could see at once that his reply would provide no reassurance. "I cannot be sure," he said.

And in that moment I saw all the foolishness of my false confidence. My mind went racing back to Blythe and Cullingworth, and even Agnes Blythe. Was there collusion after all? I remembered Greenwell's supernatural fears of a visitation. For the first time, I found myself wondering if it was possible that Ian Coatley still lived, that another man had hanged. None of this speculation was at all pleasant and a part of me cursed the Doctor for bringing me to it in this place.

It was dark now and, as we entered, I saw she had lit the candles in that beautiful room with its large windows and window seats. Heather broke off from her playing at once and came to be by our side.

She was flushed and animated, and I wanted for her sake to try to put all my fears aside. I only hoped Bell would have the tact either not to talk of the case at all before she left us or treat it lightly. She shook my hand with a smile of happiness and I noticed with pleasure she had found her locket for it was in its usual place. Then she turned to my companion. "Dr. Bell," she said, "I was glad to come and see you for I have had no occasion to thank you personally for all you did."

"Thank you. I did my best." He went to the window seat. She smiled at me and was about to make some remark. "But a part of me feels I have failed," the Doctor continued.

She turned back to him. "I do not see how you could

have done more. But I suppose the mark of success is someone who accepts his failures."

"Of course. Like your wonderful song," said Bell. "It is very sad. The knight who bleeds. He bleeds for others. I feel that the song means something. Here in this room, even this spot. Did you sing it here?" He laid his hand on the window seat.

She jumped a little. "Yes, of course I associate it with this room."

This was hardly surprising. "Doctor," I protested, "I wanted to help you but why drag Miss Grace back to this house? There is no need and I would like to see her home before we continue . . ."

Miss Grace interrupted. "No," she said bravely. "I am happy to stay. I want to hear whatever the Doctor says. I owe him that."

"Thank you," replied Bell graciously. "I was heartened to see how well you have recovered."

After that we went on to pleasantries. She offered us some refreshments, talked of her music, of the evening air, of anything except what had brought us here.

But Bell came back to it soon enough.

"I must ask you, Miss Grace," he said at last. He had moved away from us and gone to the window. "I have spent some time thinking about Captain Horler and why he came back. You were engaged to him, were you not? And he broke off the engagement?"

"I was a fool." For a moment she turned away, then came over to him from where we had been standing by the piano as I followed.

"Because," said the Doctor, "I saw some letters on a tree. They had nothing to do with the case. But they made me understand an important part of it. Which is this: everything would make far more sense if out of some ancient loyalty you had broken off the engagement with Horler."

She frowned. "What?"

". . . And broken his heart," continued Bell. "Just as the Boers later broke his mind and body. If he had spurned you, why would he be here? It was only when I realised you had spurned him that I knew he could well be our cyclist."

Miss Grace did not seem as offended by this intrusion as I was. "What are you saying?" I could see the effort it was for her to go back to it. "That I could have stopped him pursuing me?"

"No." The Doctor's tone was deadly serious. "At first you were very frightened. You genuinely did not know who the figure was and feared it was only in your mind. But once you realised it was Horler you sensed he could be used."

"How can you mean 'used?' She looked sad and incredulous. "You think that I wanted him to imprison me?"

"Of course not," said the Doctor. "You were held against your will but that was the limit of it. You knew he would not harm you."

She seemed puzzled and anxious. But I could not contain myself. For by now I knew the Doctor's game and I had rarely felt such fierce anger. Here was one of his famous mental contortions. First to have troubled me with fears on her behalf, and now to be torturing both of us with this kind of senseless and twisted logic. I had seen him wrong before and I knew quite well he was wrong now.

"You are mad." I strode towards him. "I truly believe you have taken your method too literally and spun yourself into the stupidest of corners. But I know where you are leading and I want you to give it up. How could she have had anything to do with Baynes's death? Or Greenwell's? For the first she was in bed having a nightmare! During the second she and her aunt were with one of Warner's men!"

He was quiet for a moment. But he was merely measuring his way. "I agree," he said softly. "All of that is true. She was not at the scene of the crimes. But she was still involved."

"No!" I repeated, concentrating on his face by the window, not wanting to look at her for I knew the Doctor's ways but she did not and I could not bear to think of how it would affect her.

"Yes!" he came back quicker, his eyes fixed on me. "Baynes died because he had seen her and Horler together. She regretted that, but still she did nothing because in her heart she knew she had found a way to escape Greenwell who was blackmailing her into marriage. And in the end I very much fear she played on the jealousy of her mad suitor, Captain Horler, as skillfully as she plays that piano!"

I turned now, for I had to. The pain in her face at this was hard to bear. "That is unfair," she protested. "It is cruel."

"She is right." I faced Bell. "And what possible motive could she have? There is none."

"Ah, the motive," said Bell. "Yes, we come to that." He moved towards the door as I followed. "And with some regret I will show you it."

And he flung the door open on that terrible corridor.

I almost expected to see Coatley standing there. Of course, it was empty, but as its wood gleamed in the candlelight it had never before looked so horrible or so menacing. "What happened there in that corridor, that is your motive."

"Bell!" I wanted only to stop him. I heard her steps behind me. She came beside me.

"It was not Coatley," he said to her. "*You* broke your father's skull and stabbed your mother."

Heather Grace recoiled from his words. I was so horrified by them that I almost wished to strike him.

"How can you say that?" There were tears in her eyes.

"He confessed, Bell!" I shouted.

"Yes, but the man knew he would hang anyway," the Doctor replied. "They had him for his earlier murders. He hanged for her."

"This is blind assumption and lies," she said fiercely.

"Very well," said Bell. "Will you do something for me, Miss Grace? Will you open your locket?"

The effect was dramatic. All the colour drained from her face. Her hand went to the locket. "It is personal."

"I know," he agreed. "For I have seen what is in it. It lay beside you in the cellar of that house."

She bowed her head and opened it.

Staring out at us was not, as I had always believed, a picture of her lost parents, but the same handsome boyish features I had seen in the photo Bell showed me at Abbey Mill. It was the face of Ian Coatley. Nor was that all. Scribbled below it was the strange symbol from Greenwell's notebook. A very odd letter that looked like a heraldic H. And two words, which filled me with apprehension, for I had heard them before: "One Love."

I did not look at her face as she closed it and turned away behind me but I felt her eyes on the Doctor, as mine were. "The symbol is a lover's pledge," said Bell, speaking now in the soft tone he reserved for his most intensely worked revelations like my father's watch. "I and H— Ian, Heather—intertwined. One love. Those letters on the tree jogged my mind and at last I saw their significance. He cared for her deeply, as so many others have done. And when I realised that I gradually unearthed all the discrepancies of the trial. Every account mentions her barefoot, bleeding. Again and again, I asked myself, why? And where were her shoes? The grounds were searched for days, no shoes were ever found. They had been buried or destroyed. And Coatley's shoes were free of blood."

As I watched and listened to this, I was very conscious of her behind me for I heard a rustle of her dress but I felt I would be lost if I looked round. "Even his letters from prison did not gloat," the Doctor continued and my mind flashed back to that awful letter: *I am glad of what happened, I rejoice in what I did* . . . "No, they are veiled love letters, though one was mistranscribed. He did not say 'to you all,' it was 'for you.' They refer only to his pride in the sacrifice he was making for her."

"But even if this were true," I said for, though I could not bear to look at her, I would not grant him an inch, "the case is closed, why would it matter now?"

"Because her uncle had his suspicions, as did Greenwell. Neither of them wished to reopen the case and besides, there was no evidence. But the question of her inheritance was quite another matter. Greenwell snatched the locket and wanted us to see it the night he invited us to the Mill. To him it proved she was possessed, and he thought it gave him a hold over her and her money. They had put her in an asylum before and, if she did not marry him, they would have done so again. She had struggled with this, even to the point of sending that anonymous letter to herself and trying to blame it on Greenwell. But the cyclist, when she found out who it was, came as a godsend. He was a way out, a possible path to freedom. As you were, Doyle, as you were."

Now for the first time I saw the full sense of what he was saying and felt a sudden awful pang of doubt at my core. I made myself turn round to Heather Grace.

And all my worst fears were realised. For her eyes

were filled not with outrage, but sadness and anger. "You are too late." She spoke very quietly.

Bell had his eyes fixed on her and now I realised why he had been so affected by her singing. I could see how much this must have cost him. The worst event of his life was the death of his beloved wife. Afterwards, he had worked very hard to moderate his children's suffering. The idea of a child murdering her mother and father—in effect, ending a family—was desperately hard for him and you could see it in the eyes. "I know that," he replied, obviously controlling his anger with difficulty. "No court would follow me. Even Warner would have none of it. Without evidence, I can do nothing to see you receive justice. But I tell you, if you do not plead with the jury for clemency for Horler, then I will risk my own career in an attempt to expose you."

She spoke almost in a whisper. "I have no wish to hurt him. I never did. I was horrified by what he had endured in Africa."

"But . . ." The Doctor waited. I had turned away, listening, but no longer looking at either of them.

"But I realised I had power over him and so when I became desperate perhaps I did provoke his attack on Mr. Greenwell. But I swear I never desired the death of your friend. I could not always control Horler, as you saw when you rescued me. I will be happy to see he has clemency."

"So we are agreed. We need say no more," said the Doctor with a curious flatness which enraged me.

I had had enough. "Say no more!" I turned to her. "But what happened here? What happened in this house? Were they cruel?"

Now she looked directly at me and some of the old emotion was back in her. I could see she was finding it hard to express what she wanted to say to me.

"No," she said at last. "But they . . . that is, there was

little love . . . It was like a prison. But I did love. I did. They would never allow it. Never. I wanted so much to tell you . . . I tried." And she came forward towards me as if I could absolve her.

"Coatley," said Bell.

"Yes," she said. "Coatley. They found us that night. In this room. There." She was looking at the window seat. "It had been the happiest night of my life, I never knew such happiness. Never. What was I to do? What?"

She turned back to me. "It is why the song means so much. It was he who sang it. He was my bleeding knight. And he did bleed. He died for me. And then, when it was over, I made up my mind what I wanted. I had waited for it so long and they were going to stop me. My uncle and Guy. Take my independence, my freedom. All the things you know as a right. Have you any idea what it is like to lose them? Can you not see what it means?"

There was no answer. All my hopes had turned to ashes in my mouth. I had been used, as the Doctor perceived. "And your eyes?" I asked, feeling like the most trusting little fool in the whole of the country.

"It was real, I swear. As were my dreams. My eyes are always the same. Around this time of year, when they died."

THE STRAIGHT LINE AND THE MINOTAUR

Doctor Bell once observed that the final and most danger-ous stage of a Greek labyrinth is a single straight line. It is on that last apparently simple stretch that many thinkers and detectives lose their reason. I had occasion to think of this more than once after that night at Abbey Mill. In ret-rospect, the climax seemed to have an awful inevitability: suddenly we emerged from the maze and on to the straight that ended in that room. And there I found my heart's sick-ness just as once before I had found it on a beach.

Of course, rationally I knew that Heather Grace's crimes, brutal as they were, could hardly be compared with the mad acts in Edinburgh. But there was still a hid-eous irony about this outcome, which twisted the knife in my soul. How slowly and painstakingly I had rebuilt my heart, only to lose it to someone who was herself guilty of murders. Here was my Minotaur, and I never dreamed of how it would look until we arrived at the end and I saw it.

In the days after that awful night at Abbey Mill the Doctor was at his very best. He rarely referred to the matter, but considered only my welfare, even delaying his departure north, though by now he had urgent business in

Edinburgh. For a time he even took over my patients, telling them I was indisposed, and he would have happily performed this task all week but I was determined not to let him. For the work was a useful distraction.

In the evenings, usually on the Doctor's urging, we would engage in games of reasoning and deduction. He would propose a real or imagined puzzle, another cryptogram, some strange feature of a case, or a particularly abstruse clue from his vast store of recollections and then we would use it to test my skill. Sometimes we merely sat at the window and watched passers-by, attempting to deduce their occupation or family life or mental and physical condition. Once or twice, when I was listless, I am convinced he would deliberately put himself in the wrong by planting some ludicrous piece of speculation just to see if I would pick it up.

There was one occasion, for example, when I was particularly low in spirits as we sat at the window, discussing the character and occupation of passers-by. The Doctor insisted that a woman with young children was their mother, supporting his case with a series of extremely abstruse observations about her coat, her hands, her show of affection and a ring on her finger. I was quite certain from the age of the eldest child, the items the woman carried and, indeed, her whole demeanour that she was a governess. The debate flew back and forth with gusto and finally we rushed out and followed them.

Bell pretended to be confounded when five or six streets away the true mother greeted the party at her front door. But I had my doubts and, as time went on, I became increasingly certain that most of these carefully crafted "mistakes" were little more than an attempt to restore my spirits.

After a few days I walked out alone on the beach I had always avoided and made myself think of the woman I had lost in Edinburgh. As I looked at the waves, in my mind's eye I suddenly saw her very clearly. She was dead but there was her face, framed in its halo of hair, her impish smile. And as the surf pounded on the sand in my ears, she seemed to be telling me I should try to see the cosmic absurdity of it: a man sees his first love murdered, then finally, after many years, renews his affections for another woman, only to discover his new love has murdered twice or even (on the worst construction of her role in the death of Greenwell) three times.

I have no idea if it was sane or healthy or proper, but I threw back my head in the wind and rain and laughed with Elsbeth's ghost. Then I laughed and cried a little more, without any disrespect for those who had died, and I felt better for it as I turned to come home.

After another week the Doctor saw he could leave me and a date was arranged for his departure. Meanwhile we learned that Miss Heather Grace would be leaving the town to live in London as she had always intended.

The Doctor had arranged matters so he would depart on Monday's mid-morning train, before connecting to the north and we became aware she would be taking this train too. I suppose, looking back on it, the Doctor had designed this coincidence to allow for unfinished business and test my own nerve. No doubt if I had protested he would have made other arrangements, but he knew quite well I would never give in to such cowardice and our plans remained as they were.

And so, just as the affair of the Miss Heather Grace's eyes had begun on that station platform when James Heriot Turnavine Cullingworth accosted me, months earlier, so it ended there.

We appeared, to find that a crowd of friends and well-wishers had gathered to see Miss Grace leave the town. She was, after all, now not only a rich heiress but also one who had survived two attempts on her life. The matter of Captain Horler had not been given wide publicity and the man himself seemed likely to spend his days in an asylum, but word of it had spread. Through this throng, I glimpsed her in the distance, solemnly kissing her aunt and uncle goodbye. From her appearance and her luggage and servants, it was possible to see how she had been translated by independence into the epitome of a rich and emancipated woman.

The Doctor and I nodded at Inspector Warner, who had already paid his respects. I even passed Cullingworth, who smiled faintly when he saw me but avoided looking in my eye. Not for the first time, I thought of the man's odd warnings about his former patient: did he perhaps after all have some dim perception of the truth?

It was Mrs. Blythe who saw us first and came over to greet us warmly. "Look at the crowds, gentlemen," she said happily. "We are so thankful to you, Dr. Bell. She is greatly loved. Oh, she is leaving a present for Dr. Doyle, something she says she no longer wants."

Miss Grace concluded her instructions for the loading of her luggage and came over. I could see she was much more groomed and still extremely beautiful. Her eye was on me, but first she came to the Doctor. She would have put out her hand but saw from his expression he would not take it, so she merely nodded. "I have made a statement to Inspector Warner," she told him gravely. "I understand from him it seems likely the Captain will be deemed mad and spared the gallows."

"Yes, he told me," said Bell. "I will not thank you but you may conclude our agreement stands." And he moved off, leaving her to me.

She came over to me, now, and stood close by me, her eyes intense. "You remember once I said I saw something in you. It was all true."

There was something very appealing and genuine in her expression but I held her gaze. "It was a lie," I said.

"No, it was not. Most of what I told you was the truth. What I felt for you was true. I knew we shared something. And you ought to realise . . . I was seventeen and what I did, however awful, I did for love . . ."

I could not reply. For all the high hopes I had entertained were gone and here at the end of them was just this single moment. And again I asked myself the same question as I had once before: is it pride that brings me here? Is it the godlike pride that we can solve great mysteries, where others have failed, that brings me to this bitter sense of my own failure and of human frailty?

"Will you say nothing?" her voice interrupted my thoughts.

"Only that I believed in you once."

"Then you must face something," she said. And she leant forward and I could feel her softness and warmth, all the sweetness I had once held, as she kissed me on the cheek and whispered without artifice, "A part of you always will . . . *my own*."

Then she was gone.

Her words had such an effect I do not think I saw her enter the train, but a servant was handing me a parcel.

Blindly I followed where Bell had gone further up the platform. I reached him and we said nothing. I was relieved to see he had secured a compartment far away down the train, where there were few people.

"As to what you are thinking, there must be a way," he said.

"A way?"

"To apply the method as rigorously to human character as to forensic detail. Let me think about it."

"I would be glad if you did."

For some reason his words comforted me. I had indeed

been trying to apply some rudimentary analysis to Miss Grace's extraordinary character. She believed what she said, I was sure of that. But did that make it true? On that afternoon when she was recovering from her ordeal, she had asked me to visit her in London and we had all but declared ourselves. Suppose the Doctor had never made his startling revelation, would we have renewed this happiness? Or would I have endured the slow agony of seeing her slip away in yet another direction? Perhaps it was only a desire for consolation, but I strongly suspected it would have been the latter. And even now, in spite of the fact that she seems never to have properly married, I must try to believe it.

The Doctor was safely in his train now and appraised me humorously, standing at its window. No more words were needed on the subject. The guard raised his flag and a whistle was blowing. "To our next case," he said, as the train began to move . . .

"To my further education," I countered.

He said something but I could not catch it. The train was carrying him away.

I could see him smiling as he leant out of the window. "What?" I shouted.

"And to mine. And to mine," the words floated back.

And he was gone. I stood there on the now empty platform. Then I remembered the parcel.

I sat down and opened it. There, in my hands, was her small musical jewellery case. I lifted the lid and once again I heard that carol.

And in that bed there lies a knight,
Whose wounds they do bleed by day and by night

I have the case beside me now. But I will not open it. I return it to its box and close it.

EPILOGUE

11:05 P.M., 13 OCTOBER 1898

The fire is low now and it is late. Louise has been asking for me and I must go to her.

But I have had another parcel. The maid did not wish to disturb me while I was working and has brought it in only in these past minutes. I stare at it now, as yet I cannot bring myself to open it.

But I know from the string and the address, handwritten this time, that all my fears have foundation. Something has come back. Something which should by all that is sane have ended for ever with a black flag outside Newgate on a drizzling Tuesday in October nearly ten years ago. Good God, even the clothes were bought by Tussaud's, I believe they paid £200 for them!

This makes it certain I have only a short time. So I have forced myself to take that infernal unopened box and placed it on the desk beside my writing pad. Then I cannot shrink from the task when I return in the morning . . .

Surely it will be easier in the daylight . . .

PROLOGUE

10:07 A.M., 14 OCTOBER 1898

I woke up early this morning and it was almost as if he stood there in the room. The feeling of fear and dread in me was so palpable.

A few feeble rays of early sunlight gleamed on the mantelpiece of the dressing room where I have slept since my wife became ill. My window was ajar and, as the curtains shifted slightly in a breeze, I kept telling myself there was nothing unusual. Yet I felt his presence so keenly that I almost expected him to be crouched on the sill behind them. It is strange to think that the reader of these words has no idea of who he is or what he has done. Of how many women have died in what vile circumstances. And of how I will be dead—yes, perhaps, if I am fortunate, long dead—before this is ever read. All I can tell you is that if Satan himself were behind those curtains, I do not believe I would have been more frightened.

Some weeks ago I received a parcel containing a picture from one of my stories. There was writing disguised in the picture and, though he had contrived a puzzle for me, it was effectively an announcement of his return. Last night another parcel came. This time the handwriting with its wild vowels and fanciful elongated consonants, was unmistakable. I can be absolutely sure now he is coming back. The man who destroyed so much of my young happiness and hope, and who stands for everything in the future that the Doctor fears and despises, has returned.

Of course in my heart I suppose I had known as soon as I deciphered the first puzzle, but I shrank from the knowledge. I thought he was dead; there could be no reason to think otherwise, but now I can be absolutely sure it was a deception. And his timing as always is lethal. There is a reason—to do with my personal life—why he might have chosen this time. Knowing the author of those parcels, I would be surprised by nothing, but I cannot allow myself to entertain such fears. They will only paralyse me.

As soon as I was certain of his return, my mind naturally turned to the Doctor. But the loss of his son affected him so badly that I have decided for the moment to deal with this on my own. The postmark on the second parcel was Dumfries in Scotland and, given my tormentor's propensity for games, I believe I may have a little time before he makes a firm move. And so I must leave word of my encounter with him. It is a strange unnerving story, set in many different places, which encompasses horrors I have always fervently wished to forget, horrors enough for several tales. Nothing about it was constant; lulls would be followed by a sudden descent into the blackest hell. Inevitably there were connections to my working life and I suppose it was no coincidence that I wrote the death of my own fictional detective just a few months after a black flag outside Newgate appeared to bring our ordeal to an end. Of course, I am aware that to describe all that took place is to break the Doctor's trust, for I swore confidentiality. But I do so now because I cannot be sure what will happen to me.

Therefore I got up, assured myself that my wife was untroubled—indeed she was still asleep—and came down to my study where I stared at the parcel before me. Then, like a diver not wishing to think before he plunges into an icy pool, I tore it open. Unlike the one before, there was fine tissue paper inside and I felt something within the paper.

At once I dreaded what I might find, for more than once he has sent human remains. But it was not like that. In many ways it was far worse.

Inside the parcel was a pale blue silk scarf.

I did not flinch or cry out. I suppose a week or so earlier I would have, but not now. Partly because I was prepared for anything, but I also had to pause to take in the enormity of it. I could recall the garment below me so clearly. Once again I was back on a beach long ago. And I heard a song.

> *And one could whistle*
> *And one could sing*
> *And one could play on the violin*
> *Such joy there was at my wedding*
> *On Christmas day in the morning*

But that was enough. I thrust the garment aside, telling myself that only my own application of the Doctor's principles could have any hope of defeating the man. I am not someone who resents progress. In many ways the fabric of our lives has seen improvement in my time. But the idea of a murder for no reason—the idea of a man killing

a series of women for nothing more than a minor thrill—
was, when the Doctor and I first came together, as incom-
prehensible as it seemed impossible. There had been bar-
barism and bloodlust in the mid-century, of course, and
plenty of it, just as there was in the last. But murder as a
casual and sophisticated game had not yet been invented
or even foreseen. *He* was one of the first to give us that,
perhaps he was the first, which is why his shadow seems
cast over the start of the next century.

And so it is that I put the parcel to one side and take
up the box I have long dreaded to open. The first item I
see is a map, though of a bizarre kind. Hand-drawn, it
marks in a curious way the streets and byways and medical buildings of Edinburgh. Some of the streets are tinged
with scarlet, others with black, some of the names are odd,
others conventional. It is in fact a diagram marking the
dark night-world of the city and the scene of several of
his crimes, starting in 1878.

Beside it there is a sketch of what seems to be a labyrinth—which indeed it was, though I reflected often
enough that I would far rather face a monster in there
than what I found. This drawing in fact follows the corridors and cupboards and staircases and roofspaces—yes
and the bedrooms—of a notorious Edinburgh establish-
ment, a building long since shut down, called Madame
Rose's.

It is unnerving to see these things again, for I know
where they lead. I have placed them beside the scarf,
which lies there mocking me as I go back to that time
when I was just a young and somewhat disillusioned student in my second year of medical school. How aimlessly
I walked the streets that winter. Until there came a night
I shall never forget, when I heard that lilting, other-
worldly music from a beggar's violin, and I am sure even
then I sensed him somewhere. Waiting . . .

PART ONE: HIS COMING

THE TUNE FROM ANOTHER WORLD

I always think of the beggar as the beginning. His name was Samuel and, with his ancient red shirt and sky-blue eyes, he stood there like some vision from heaven on the corner of one of the most colourful and depraved streets in the whole of Edinburgh. I never once heard him play a real tune, only a series of wild and rambling flights of musical fancy which sounded eerie enough in themselves but all the more so in that spot, only yards away from the town's more notorious brothels and drinking dens.

The night I first heard him, I stood there for a long time, drinking in his music. To me it sounded a hundred times more spiritual than all the empty catechisms of the Jesuit boarding school I had just left. And the playing healed some of my anguish, for it so happened that evening had been particularly miserable at home.

My mother was away delivering some mending. And for some reason I never fathomed, my small brother Innes, then still a very young child, climbed the stairs and ran along the red corridor which led to my father's study. For some years our house had been blighted by my father's condition. Now he was barely able even to speak, his mind utterly fogged by drink and near-insanity. Yet, unusually for him, he happened on this occasion to hear the infant playing and opened his door.

Both of them undoubtedly had a shock as they faced

each other. By this time my father, with his lank beard, unshaven pallor and stale clothes, was rarely sane or sober enough to venture downstairs. No doubt my mother was relieved that her four younger children, Innes and his three sisters (for the two older girls were seldom at home), saw him so rarely. I am sure at times he would hardly have recognised them.

Even so, beyond a little fright for both of them, the incident might well have come to nothing. Except that someone else now appeared. Our so-called lodger Dr. Waller, who was then in his mid-twenties and not so much older than myself, had come out of his room and witnessed this unlikely meeting. I say "so-called" lodger for really it was more as if we were *his* lodgers. For some time, Waller had paid the entire rent for the house as a favour to my mother and, though he was careful to be civilised and even fawning with her, I knew quite well in my heart he felt an unspoken power over all of us. Nor was he by any description a kind man. I will acknowledge that he was cultured, and when I was away I had on occasions corresponded with him about literature. But by this time I knew that his mask of sensibility concealed much that was arrogant and inhumane, including a deep distaste for children, which ensured that they generally kept out of his way.

I can still see the little tableau in my mind's eye framed in the dim light of the flickering corridor lamp. Innes was still, puzzled by these figures. My father was about to retire, the shadows playing over his whiskered head. But Waller stood upright beside them, a look of great irritation on his face. And then, quite suddenly, without the slightest provocation, he slapped Innes hard around the face and sent him, howling, away. After that, he gave my father a brutal shove that sent him back into his room and closed the door.

I am quite sure to this day Waller did not know he was observed, and the sight confirmed all my suspicions. I had always strongly suspected that my father's illness and our poverty suited the man admirably. It had allowed him to rule a roost of his own without all the tiresome effort of building one for himself. As he slammed my father's door, he had never looked to me so much like a sadistic jailer.

And then he saw me and we faced each other with poor Innes's sobs still ringing in my ears from below.

Given Waller's arrogance, and his position of authority, you would think perhaps that I, then an eighteen-year-old student, would often have come into conflict with him. This was the opposite of the truth. My mother had enormous faith in the man, and never tired of reminding me of the unpleasant fact that he had kept us from the workhouse. So for her sake he and I both generally kept an uneasy peace. The night I describe was one of the few occasions our hostility erupted into the open.

I walked towards him in fury at what I had observed and told him he had absolutely no right to strike Innes. "You are not even his father any more than you are—"

I could not go on for I knew at once that I had given him his opening. Waller was aware I had been about to challenge his position in our house, and he stared at me, his brown eyes gleaming. "Any more than what? Would you like to consult your mother? I think you will find she enjoys my company here in this house."

I wanted to strike him. He was, as I have said, only a few years my senior, yet he was not a physical man, and always dressed with the meticulous care of someone much older. Tonight, as ever, he was immaculately groomed and coiffured, not a whisker of his thick dark hair was out of place. I clenched my fists, longing to let fly with a punch that would have ruffled that fine appearance. But, as ever, the thought of my mother restrained me and I offered no answer.

"And where would you be? Where would that child be?" he continued. "Where would your father and mother be if I were not here?"

Still I would not reply.

"I will tell you, you would be in the workhouse. I wonder if you realise, Arthur, I am not exacting even a farthing for what I have done for you personally. I could, if I wished, insist it came out of any future earnings you make as a doctor—that is, if you make any at all." And with that he turned and walked away.

I am sure the exchange had only occurred because my mother was out of the house. Even Waller would never have dared to express his own sense of power and supremacy so crudely in her presence. Of course, I could have tried to tell her, but I knew from countless arguments on the subject she would not have listened. And the bitter truth was that, even if I could have persuaded her to see the dreadful hypocrisy of our arrangement, I would only have hurt her more deeply. What, after all, was the alternative?

So, as often before, I took to the streets. And it was this very night, with my emotions already stirred, that I first heard Samuel's music and stood there on the pavement, quite overwhelmed by it.

After a little I offered the player a coin I could ill afford, but he only wished me to buy him a cup of something warm. Naturally I thought he meant strong drink but it turned out he was an abstainer, or near enough, and we went to a little stall, not far away, where he had a mug of some hot cordial, made from blackberries. As I handed him his cup, I told him his music sounded like it came from another world.

The large genial stallholder laughed at this. "That's what I say, sir. Why can he not play an air like everyone else?"

He moved away as Samuel looked over the steaming mug at me with a twinkle in his faraway eyes. It was impossible to tell his age, twenty-three or sixty-three. "Another world? D'you believe in one, sir?"

The question was as unexpected as its speaker. I did believe in something, I knew that, but the discipline and eagerness for hell that I had seen at Stonyhurst, my Catholic boarding school, had clouded my vision.

"I do not know," I said simply. "Do you?"

He smiled. "Well, as for my music I was taught by a man who sailed wi' me. And aye, I believe in something. Something else. But I hope to bide hereabouts in this world a wee while longer. For I like to watch all that goes on. Some strange things there are too, sir, but the police willna hear o' them from me."

With that he downed the drink and was soon back to his post where he raised his violin and took up an even sadder and more poignant form of that strange music. I walked on, trying to avoid the eyes of the women in the doorways as I reflected on his last remark. There was no doubt that any beggar on that street would see some odd sights, but his mention of the police inevitably brought my mind around to a subject I had been avoiding and to a person I had not seen for many weeks.

Dr. Joseph Bell was the extraordinary teacher at the university, who had first asked me to be his medical clerk, and then in great confidence initiated me into his pioneering study of criminal investigation, or what he called his "method." I was of course intrigued and flattered, all the more so after he allowed me to accompany the police on a highly confidential case. But, although I was impressed, I had never from the beginning quite been able to accept the vast claims Bell made for his system of deduction. And so it was that one afternoon in February, shortly after he took me into his confidence, I had been bold enough to try and test the man's deductive powers.

Among the many claims Bell made for his precious method, one of the most outlandish was that a close study of any object could lay bare the character of its owner. I was highly dubious of this and had therefore offered him my father's watch as a trial. It had been recently cleaned so I felt absolutely confident that he could get nowhere with it. However, Dr. Bell proceeded to use every mark and feature of that watch—certain indentations, some pawnbroker's notches, the tiny scratches around the key— to expose in unbearable detail its owner's mental condition. It was utterly horrifying to me to hear the secret my family had struggled to conceal being analysed and reviewed in so casual a fashion. To his credit, the Doctor saw my anguish and tried his best to make me aware he had been indulging in pure deduction. But even so, for some time after that day, I did my best to avoid him and pleaded my studies as an excuse.

Now, with the fiddler's melancholy notes still in my ears, I thought of that incident with the watch once again. And I found that I missed my jousts with Bell even if, despite my painful lesson, I still had doubts about the man's "method." Perhaps he had won that particular contest, but was there not, even here, some plain old-fashioned luck? After all, in his attempt to divine human character from an inanimate object, I had fed his ego by handing over a damaged artefact. But supposing that cursed watch had belonged to some fussy old solicitor rather than an artist whose mind was giving way? If the thing had been in utterly pristine condition, what could

Dr. Bell have had to say then beyond some vague and useless observation? Much of my old spirit returned as I remembered how disconcerted the Doctor had looked at first when he realised it had been cleaned. Supposing it had not only been cleaned, but bore no marks whatsoever? Bell's expression might well have remained just as unhappy for the whole test.

As the music faded behind me I smiled to think of that, and before the walk was over I had made up my mind that I was ready to see him again. Not that I would abandon my scepticism. Perhaps now a part of me wanted to challenge his method because it had inflicted such pain. But surely such challenges were good for him and for me, just as long as I took more care?

And so the next morning I made my way along the dark stone corridors to Bell's strange vault-like room in the university. As you entered it, you passed through a kind of tunnel between huge shelves of various compounds and chemicals until you arrived at an enormous tank which ran halfway to the ceiling. Today that tank was dry, rather to my surprise, for I was used to seeing strange things in its watery depths. Beyond it a huge bookcase towered to my left and I came past it to find his empty desk.

"Well," said a familiar and sharp voice from somewhere below me.

I whirled round. At first I could see nothing at all in the shadows, but eventually I made out a shape lying down very flat between two low bookshelves. The space was so confined you could hardly see Bell's wiry body. But slowly I made out his features and saw he was staring at me. He was indeed quite horizontal, lying between two shelves that were so close together only the smallest volumes could possibly have fitted them, and yet Bell had somehow clambered in and managed to lie flat. He had a watch in one hand.

"Doctor?" I said in amazement.

He ignored me and looked at the watch. Then his legs moved and he wriggled out from under that tiny crevice and drew himself up to his full height, which was more than six foot. His expression was fierce. "Your business?" he said.

"But what are you doing?"

"I am establishing whether a man called André Valère was truly able to lie in a chimney space much smaller than a grave in order to conceal himself from the constabulary of Rouen in 1780."

"1780?"

"Nothing has been presented to me in months, but I do not wish to remain entirely inactive in the field. If I cannot obtain fresh material, I can at least occasionally exercise my powers with older cases, especially those unsolved. Perhaps you are not aware of the Rouen matter? Valère was a suspected strangler, but they could not place him near the scene. I think he was in a chimney crevice no bigger than this when the third murder was discovered. He seemed to vanish into thin air and, though there was speculation, they thought the space was too small. This bookcase is a few inches smaller and I could have stayed longer; he only needed twenty-three minutes. So I am convinced." He had taken up a brush and was removing some dust from his jacket lapels as his tone became more clipped, but his eyes never left me. "Now, your business, please, I have a lecture to give."

And he continued to stare at me with a somewhat pugnacious expression.

As I think back to this small reunion I sense again how energised and indefatigable the Doctor was in those days. Recalling his eager yet assertive gaze, I can see now that there was still almost an innocence in him for he had not as yet been fully tested. His most recent case at that time, involving a man called Canning, had proved a typical triumph, even if it had irritated the local constabulary. The Doctor was yet, in fact, to be seriously bloodied in any quest he had undertaken. That would come, and a good deal sooner than either of us might have wished.

"I merely came to tell you I could make myself available again for my duties."

He looked at me with a certain amusement. "Your letter said you were obliged to undertake intensive studies for another course. So in that at least you must now be accomplished?"

After the business with the watch I had written him a polite but vague letter, explaining that I had to take a leave of absence as his clerk to further my studies and his written reply did not press me though he must have guessed the real reason.

"I feel enough time has been devoted to them."

"Do you really, now? Well, you may assist me in my operating theatre today."

Of course it was the lowliest task he could have offered, and an hour later I was running around like a madman fetching instruments and dressings as he desperately tried to speed the progress of a woman patient having an emergency amputation. In those days patients survived in a fairly direct ratio to the speed with which their doctors worked, and I truly sensed the Doctor's frustration for I had to mop his brow over thirty times as he cut and cleaned. I had rarely seen him so determined, but he managed to get the woman off the table alive.

Later, as I performed the mundane chore of sorting through his surgery papers, he sat in his workroom making a few notes and offering very little in the way of conversation. Then he got up, without even glancing in

my direction, and disappeared through the locked door
leading to the extraordinary room where he kept relics and
other more private records of criminal cases. Clearly I was
not be admitted to this inner sanctum again for the moment.

It took me some time to finish my work and at last I
walked home, deliberately extending my journey until I
reached the street where the beggar Samuel played his
violin. The night was cold yet clear, and the stars above
made a perfect setting for the player, who seemed in a
kind of trance and did not notice me. But I paused some
minutes to listen and am glad that I did, for it was a sound
I was destined never to hear again in this world.